It's in Her Blood

S.S. Roswell

Printed in the United States of America

PRINT ISBN-13: 978-0692364086

ISBN-10: 0692364080

Edited by Lisa J Lickel

Cover design by Damonza

Visit www.ssroswell.com

For my family

Chapter 1

The smell of fresh coffee permeated the bedroom. Gail Finn placed the tray with the coffee on the bedside table next to Brian. "Are you awake, honey?"

He rolled his well-toned six-foot frame to the side of the bed where she was standing. She stroked his face with the back of her hand. Despite being a busy plastic surgeon, Brian Finn engaged in a lot more outdoor activities than Gail, but the difference in their skin tone indicated the opposite. Brian opened his eyes and pulled Gail into the bed. Just as he leaned over to kiss her, the doorbell rang.

"Who the hell rings someone's doorbell five thirty in the morning?" Brian asked. "I'll get it." He had on the only garment he slept in during the summer months, his underwear.

"You're a tad too sexy for the front door, so let *me* get it," Gail said as she made her way downstairs. The door was barely open before Brian's older sister, Celia, pushed past.

"Hey, Gail, where are the guys?" She handed

over a DVD case.

"What's this for?" Gail asked.

"Oh, I shot some great videos of Alex. The boy is a genius. I've been meaning to share these with you and Brian but kept forgetting. I've uploaded them online and burnt a copy for you."

A chill ran down Gail's spine.

When Alex started displaying the ability to memorize a few things in a short period of time, Brian thought it was a coincidence since it was not consistent. As Alex got older, his skills seem to have developed. Gail also had this gift. Although to her it was more like a curse. It was a link to her past. A past she wanted to stay buried.

"You did what?" Gail asked, trying to remain as calm as her body would allow her to.

"Haven't you been listening? I—"

"Are you out of your mind?"

Celia took a step back. "What do you mean?"

Gail could not read her sister-in-law's expression. Celia Wilson was in her late forties, and looked more than a decade younger, but her mouth and her eyelids were the only things on her face that moved.

"You can't take pictures or videos of Alex and post them on the Internet without our permission."

"It's no big deal. My friends share pictures and videos of their family with me online all the time."

"I don't care what your friends do. Some of your friends drink bourbon instead of coffee. The point is, you don't have the right to make that kind of unilateral decision regarding Alex."

"Alex is family, and I see no reason why I can't share some videos of him if I want to. Besides, any parent would be proud to show off how smart Alex is."

"Alex is *my* child, not yours. So that's not your decision to make."

The moment the words escaped her lips, Gail realized the damning impact they had on Celia. But Gail was more concerned about those videos of her son and what they may reveal.

"Look, I know you love Alex and you want to show him off, but this is not the way. I need you to get online and remove those videos now."

"I don't have the time to do that." Celia slumped in the chair and buried her face in her hands.

Gail dropped her ire as she realized her sister-in-law had bigger problems. She got down on her knees and touched Celia's shoulder. "I didn't mean to upset you this much. Just...please, promise you'll take them down as soon as you can."

Celia brushed Gail's hand from off her shoulder. "Fine!" she snorted.

Gail saw that something behind her caught Celia's attention. She looked up and noticed Brian staring at the both of them.

"Hey, sis. What brings you by so early?"

"I've an early flight and I wanted to see Alex before I leave."

"Where're you going?" he asked.

"Nathan and I are going to the Virgin Islands for a couple of weeks. It's a week earlier than we originally planned but I promised Alex I'd see him before I leave," she explained.

Gail glanced through the window at the taxi parked outside and then back at Celia. "So, where's this Nathan?"

"He's meeting me at the airport."

Brian was about to say something when Celia said, "I don't need anyone's permission or approval."

"I didn't say you do, but I thought we'd get a chance to at least meet the guy before you two run off in the sunset."

"I don't want to get into this with you right now. Is Alex awake?" Celia asked. "I really need to get going."

"He'll be down in a minute," Brian said.

Gail wandered over to the window that

looked out to the backyard. She could feel Brian's eyes on her. She knew it'd be hard to explain her reaction to him. She'd worked really hard at keeping her past in the past. He came and stood next to her.

"What the hell happened between you two?"

"She uploaded photos and videos of Alex to the Internet without our permission. I asked her to take them down."

Brian glanced back at Celia. Gail did too, and watched as she gently patted under her eyes to get rid of the tears without smearing her makeup that was more than enough for two faces. "Celia, why don't you run to Alex's room? He should be out of the bathroom by now," Brian said.

Celia hurried upstairs.

Brian folded his arms and turned his attention to Gail. "What's going on with you?"

Gail stared at him. "Me? Your sister is out of line."

"It's still not an excuse to be so mean to her."

"I'm not trying to be mean to her."

"I heard what you said to her about Alex being your child. You know the pain she's been through after losing her own son. Alex is the only person who seems to fill that hole in her heart. How could you be so cruel?"

"I've done everything I can to help foster the

relationship between Alex and Celia. She gets to spend time with him as much as she wants, even at her home. However, it's our job to determine what, if anything, about him is uploaded to the Internet."

"Celia loves Alex. She's not going to upload anything that would embarrass him or us."

"I know she loves him, but she needs to consult us before..." Gail paused mid-sentence as she heard Celia's footsteps. Celia came downstairs looking a little better than she did before she saw Alex.

"I'll be in touch," she said as she went through the front door.

Then came the deafening silence between Gail and Brian. Gail wished she had not gotten so worked up. Brian was right. She sounded mean and that's not like her. It's the opposite of who she was. No wonder Brian found her reaction strange, but that's because Brian knew nothing about her past, and the people from her past had no idea she's alive.

"I didn't mean to hurt her. I..." Gail raised her clasped hands to her lips and closed her eyes as if she were saying a prayer. "I'm sorry. I don't want pictures and videos of Alex to be all over the Internet without our approval." What she really meant was she did not want them there at all, since she knew she'd never approve.

The warm look in his eyes earlier that morning was replaced with suspicion and doubt. "I hear what you're saying, but for a moment, you're like a completely different person. I know you're trying to protect Alex, but people put pictures and videos of their kids on the Internet every day. It's nothing for you to get so upset about."

Aside from her hidden reason for not wanting information about her son flying all over the Internet, Gail felt she had a valid point about who makes decisions for Alex. However, she was not going to make the situation worse by hammering that point.

"Why don't you take a look at the DVD to see what's uploaded?" Brian said. "I'm sure it'll put your mind at ease."

Gail wanted to do nothing more than to pop in that DVD and have a look, but she wanted to view it alone. "Sure, in a little bit," she told him and changed the subject. "I'll get you some coffee before you have to leave."

"Right." Brian backed down. "I forgot...I have to run in early for a meeting."

She kept herself busy tidying up a house that was already in tip-top shape. Brian left for the office earlier than usual. But to Gail it felt like it took forever for him to leave. While Alex ate breakfast, Gail took the DVD upstairs. Her hands were shaking as she opened the DVD drive on the laptop. She put the disk in, slid the drive close and then took a deep breath. There were a lot of photographs to go through, but Gail was more interested in the videos and what may have been captured in them.

Gail watched as Celia and Alex played chess. Celia asked Alex to close his eyes. While his eyes were closed, she cleared the chessboard then asked him to open his eyes. Alex was able to replace each piece in their exact position.

Gail tried to move but her body would not respond. The only thing she could hear was her heartbeat. Drumming in her ear. She finally brushed away the hair that clung to her face with both hands. Gail knew this was not a harmless video...not by any stretch.

To everyone else, a few videos of Alex on the Internet seemed like nothing for Gail to get upset about, but her gut told her otherwise. She was desperate to have those videos pulled from the Internet.

A million thoughts raced through Gail's mind. The DVD continued playing, but her mind was hard at work, as she tried to piece together the implications of these videos on the web. She needed to have them removed as soon as possible. But how? She picked up the phone and dialed Celia's cell phone number. Gail wasn't sure how she would ask Celia to remove the videos without exacerbating the situation. "Come on, pick up!" The call went to voice mail. Now what?

Gail's former school counselor, Ms. Hemmingway, had told Gail that she may have eidetic memory. She said she was not quite sure it was eidetic memory since Gail's ability seemed to have surpassed what they would expect from someone with that capability. Ms. Hemmingway also said eidetic memory was very rare, and some researchers question if such ability really existed. If this capability was so rare, one can only imagine how fascinated people would be with Alex. How long would it take until someone from her past saw the videos of him and put the pieces together?

Sacramento Federal Prison

Nicholas Colson was serving twenty-five years-to-life for a string of charges including money laundering and conspiracy to commit murder. His attorney was working hard to get him a parole hearing, citing good behavior and his deteriorating health. Nicholas lay on his back on the bottom bunk bed. His eyes were wide open, but he wasn't registering anything that was in the space with him. His cellmate talked up a storm, but Nicholas remained engrossed with the possibility of finally being outside of these walls. He'd spent over a decade mourning the loss of his son that occurred during an FBI raid. The same raid that was ultimately responsible for his current abode.

He remembered it like it was yesterday. The lifeless body of his son Leon, lying among the rubble of what use to be his home. Nicholas was no stranger to pain. He'd been shot, stabbed, tortured and experienced the loss of people he loved dearly. The loss of his son trumped them all. Some of the evidence that was used against him in his trial was known only to a very few people outside his family. They'd all had tragic accidents since, including the young girl he'd taken in as part of his family who also died in the explosion.

Nicholas was not the kind of man who forgot about people who wronged him or hurt the people he loved. There were a lot of stones he wanted to turn over, questions that needed answers. For now, his main focus was to get out of prison and into a cancer treatment center.

Chapter 2

G ail entered the family room where her seven-year-old son Alex sat watching cartoons. He sprung out of the sofa and charged towards her as she opened her arms to embrace him. On any other day, Gail would have sent him to put his cereal bowl in the dishwasher. Instead, she held him for a while. As she closed her eyes, she felt a burning sensation as the tears were about to break free. She fought them back as best as she could before she released Alex. Gail strode to the sofa and picked up a cushion to hide her face until her eyes were dry.

In a playful gesture, Alex threw a sidekick at Gail. "Are we still going to practice today?"

Gail and Brian ensured Alex enrolled in at least one extra-curricular activity of his choice. The activities were to provide social interaction with other kids since Alex was homeschooled.

Playing along, Gail used her forearm to block his kick. "Absolutely."

She had a strange feeling in her stomach, like

something's wrong. It made her lose interest, at least for the moment, in an activity she normally enjoyed.

Gail managed to put on a happy face, but she could see Alex's eyes peering at her as if he was searching her face for answers. "Why don't we start now?" Gail asked.

"Really?" His questioning stare was replaced with excitement. "Awesome!" he said, grinning.

Gail was bombarded with fear, anxiety and nervousness and needed to stay busy in order to keep those feelings at bay as best as possible. What better way to stay busy than to help Alex prepare for his Taekwondo exam? "Go get the manual. I'll be ready by the time you get back." Alex took off in a sprint up the stairs, and then stopped.

"I don't need it, Mom. I already know the katas. I just want you to help me with my form."

"Oh! That's good. But I want to make sure we don't miss anything," she said. She didn't need the manual either, but always pretended she did.

"I'll be right back." Alex disappeared upstairs.

Gail glanced at the clock on the wall. Celia's plane should've taken off by now. She found herself trying to mentally calculate the time it would take Celia to get to her destination in the

Virgin Islands after landing. Everything seemed to be moving at snail's pace today.

Alex jumped off the stairs. "I'm ready," he said, while throwing practice kicks. He handed Gail the manual and then headed to the room next to Gail's studio that Brian had converted to a home gym.

Gail leafed through the book until she got to the moves he should be practicing. She turned to the next level up. These are katas that Alex had not studied. She walked into the room where he was eagerly waiting for her. "Take a look at these," Gail said as she handed him the manual.

"You're on the wrong page, Mom. We're not there yet."

"I know, I know, but I wanted you to have an idea of what you will be doing at the next level."

Alex let out a loud sigh. "Okay, fine!" He looked at them and in less than two minutes handed the manual back to her. "Can we practice now?"

"Sure. Let's see what you got."

Alex was more than happy to start demonstrating his moves. He knew the katas very well. She demonstrated each move and he followed. Before long, he was able to demonstrate with great form. She high-fived him.

"Pay attention." Gail demonstrated moves from the next level up. Alex watched her keenly as she flowed from one move to another.

"You missed one!"

"Are you sure?"

Alex got up and demonstrated the move she missed. His form was poor, but his memory was spot on. She'd tested him deliberately. Gail's aware of his abilities, but had never probed them before. What prompted Celia to record him?

She beckoned to Alex. "Let's get something to drink." They headed to the kitchen. She poured him a glass of orange juice and watched as he gulped it down in seconds.

"Aaaahhhh! That's good. TV, here I come!" he said in a different voice.

Gail chuckled as she recognized the character he attempted to mimic. As soon as Alex was completely engrossed with the television and no longer required her attention, Gail fixated on the videos that she needed Celia to delete.

The more she thought, the more worried she became. Gail knew she had hurt Celia deeply earlier that morning, and felt quite terrible about it.

Celia had gone through a dreadful ordeal. She'd been in a car accident fifteen years ago that claimed the life of her husband and five-year-old son, Chad. She'd never remarried. Gail and Brian encouraged her to adopt, but she would break down every time they tried to have a conversation about it. However, something changed on Alex's fifth birthday. Celia found comfort spending time with Alex and he adored her as well. Gail really wanted to smooth things out with her for more reasons than one.

Dr. Brian Finn had just completed a post-op consultation with a patient who had breast augmentation, when his cell phone rang. He checked the ID and was surprised to see the call was from Celia, who was supposed to be on an airplane.

"Hey, where're you?"

"Actually, I'm outside your office building. Do you have time for me?"

"Sure." A few minutes later he answered the knock on his door. "Come in." Brian hugged his sister. "Can I get you something to drink?"

"No thanks." Celia dropped into a chair in front of Brian's desk.

Brian sat in the chair next to her. "You're not

on the plane. Did you abandon the vacation idea?"

Celia put her elbow on the desk and rested her forehead in her hand. "Not exactly. It was more business than pleasure."

Brian could tell there was more than business eating away at her. "I thought you had an early flight."

Celia raised her head up to look at Brian. "I'd the time wrong. There's another flight leaving about two thirty."

Brian got up, walked over to the water dispenser, and filled a glass. "But you're not taking that flight either, I presume?" He already knew the answer to that question. She might be a little upset from her confrontation with Gail earlier that morning. But still, he felt there was something else. He knew when she had something she needed to get off her chest. "What's bothering you?" He asked, as he returned to his desk.

Celia sat back in the chair and stared at Brian as he finished his glass of water. "Listen, Brian." She paused. Celia got up a walked across the room to get herself some water. "How much do you really know about Gail?"

Brian pushed back his chair and folded his arms across his chest. "What? Where is all of this coming from? We've been married for nearly ten years. I know everything I need to know about her."

Celia walked back to the desk. "How about her family? Have you met any of them? Doesn't it strike you as odd that she never had anyone come to visit?"

Brian shoved his chair back and got up to face Celia. "Her parents are dead, and she was an only child. Alex and I are her family now. I know you're torn up over what happen this morning, but you're taking this way too far."

"I'm just trying to look out for you. I'm older and wiser," Celia said, as she slowly lowered herself into her chair.

"Well, you should've done it ten years ago."

"Ten years ago I didn't know what I know now."

"What do you know?" Brian glared at Celia as he awaited her response. After about ten seconds, he sighed and shook his head. "You're really something else."

"Well, for starters I know you don't love her."

"I'm not going to entertain this conversation."

"I want what's best for you and—"

"Enough! Was that your reason for stopping by?"

"I...I wanted to talk to you about Alex, and

the videos that I recorded of him."

"Did you take them down?"

"Not yet."

"Why not? Gail made it clear she wanted them removed from the Internet."

Celia hung her head, seemingly in shame. "I don't know what I was thinking. I've been under a lot of stress and I guess it has taken a toll on me. I can take the videos down now, if you lend me your laptop."

Brian watched as Celia logged on and removed the videos and photographs of Alex. There were numerous comments on her web page about the video. The majority of persons thought the video was tweaked. One comment in particular caught his eye, and he noticed that there were more commenters who indicated they had downloaded the video.

"I suggest you keep this to yourself. Gail doesn't need to know anyone downloaded the video," Celia said.

Brian did not believe there was anything to be concerned about and therefore agreed to keep the information from Gail.

Sacramento Federal Prison

Nicholas met with Alvin Craig, a second-generation defense attorney. His father's law firm had been representing the Colson family for years. Alvin took over after his father retired. With his guidance, Colson hoped he could convince the parole board to release him.

"You have a really good shot at this," Alvin told Nicholas. "But it's extremely important for you to stay cool."

Nicholas had blown his previous parole hearing because he had not been able to control his anger.

"Unlike the previous hearing, there will be no family members of the alleged victims present."

"I'll do whatever I need to."

"Well, that's good to hear."

Alvin cleared his throat and straightened his tie. "You will also need to admit what you've done."

"You want me to say I'm guilty?"

"Look, Mr. Colson, you have to trust me. If you want to get out of here, you have to play your cards right."

"I thought you said my age and my failing health were aces."

"Well, they can be, but you still have to convince the board that you are a changed man."

"By saying I'm guilty?"

"If you want to go home, yes."

Nicholas looked at Alvin long and hard. He'd known Alvin since he was a young boy. He was friends with his late son, Leon. Nicholas imagined that Leon would've made a fine defense attorney.

"If that's what it takes, then I guess I've no choice." Nicholas was about to get up.

"Oh, there's one more thing."

"What?" Nicholas asked. "You want me to say that I found God in prison and now I'm a born-again Christian?"

"That actually wouldn't be a bad idea, but that's not it."

"Well! Spit it out, will you?"

"I received a text message from one of my sources a few minutes before I came in here. He sent me a video."

"A video of me?"

"No. It was a video of a kid with a remarkable ability to remember things. Remind you of anyone?"

Nicholas recalled the young girl who was a

part of his family for a few years. She had an amazing ability to memorize information. Bank accounts, location coordinates, to name a few, but she'd died seventeen years ago. Hadn't she?

Chapter 3

Later that evening Gail opened the oven and the smell of roast beef saturated the entire downstairs. "Aaah, perfection," she uttered as she placed it on the table. For the moment, fixing Brian's favorite meal kept her mind from worrying thoughts. She was not always the best cook, but over time she'd learned how to prepare what her family liked. Gail stood back and admired her beautiful work of art laid out on the table. Her moment was disrupted by the home phone. It rang a number of times before Gail was able to pick it up.

"Hello?"

No answer.

"Hello?"

Still no answer. The person at the other end of the phone hung up. Gail heard the garage door opening. Brian was home. She hung up the phone and went to the door so she could greet him as he entered. "Hey, how was your day?" she asked.

"The same as always with one small twist,"

Brian said as he gave her a hug.

"A twist? Can't wait to hear about that."

"I bet you can't."

"Well?"

"Not now. I'll tell you after dinner," Brian mumbled as he headed upstairs.

"Alex, dinner in fifteen minutes," Gail said as she passed the family room.

Gail prepared the dinner table and looked forward to a lovely evening with her family, yet she couldn't wait for tomorrow so she could get in touch with Celia and sort everything out. Talk about a twist.

Brian was back from upstairs and ready to dive into dinner. "Where's Alex? Alex, your mom said it's time for dinner."

"She did, huh?" Gail asked in a whisper.

"Well, he seems to move faster when your name is attached to the command."

"That's not true," Gail retorted. Alex came charging into the dining room.

"I rest my case," Brian muttered.

They were barely seated at the table before Brian started eating. "I'm starving. I missed lunched today," he said apologetically.

The sound of something vibrating caught Gail's attention. Gail let her gaze wander to Brian's cell phone on the kitchen counter, then to Brian who continued eating as if he heard nothing. "Are you going to get that?"

"Get what?" Brian asked. "Oh, the phone. No phone call comes between me and my roast," he said. "If it's important, they'll leave a message."

Gail nodded in agreement. Besides, the only incoming call she would be interested in was a call from Celia and, based on her calculations, Celia had not yet reached her destination.

"So what'd you guys do today?" Brian asked. "Anything exciting?"

"I practiced for my Taekwondo exam," Alex replied with a grin. "Mom knows all the moves."

"I do *not*," Gail interjected.

"When's your exam?"

"I'm not sure," Alex replied while looking at Gail.

"In two weeks," Gail muttered.

"Yeah, two weeks, but Mom says I'm ready now."

"Really?"

"Yeah, Dad. She even started teaching me the more advanced moves."

"I didn't want him to get bored. I wanted to change things up a bit...you know, keep things interesting for him," Gail explained.

"It was awesome, Dad. Do you want me to show you what I learned today?"

"Sure, but not now. You might kick the roast off the table."

They all laughed.

"Will you come watch me take my test?"

"I'm not sure. I'll have to check my schedule. Your mom is going to record it, so if I'm not able to be there, I can still see you in action."

Gail got up and started clearing the table. The very mention of the word "recording" reminded her of another recording she wished hadn't happened.

"Aunt Celia said she'd be back in time to watch me. She *is* coming. Right?"

"Your Aunt Celia had some last minute changes, so she might not be able to make it," Brian replied.

Gail looked over at Brian. As he caught her stare he mimed twisting with his hands. "Celia missed her flight this morning," Brian said. "She might not leave until next week sometime."

Gail perked her ears. Celia was still here? I could talk to her and get this mess sorted out tonight, she thought.

"So, she's *not* coming?" Alex asked.

"Maybe not," Brian replied.

"Is Uncle Mike still coming?"

"Yes, I think so," Gail said.

"*Yes!*" Alex said as he threw a punch that almost knocked over a glass. "Oops."

"Are you finished eating?" Brian asked.

"Yes, Dad."

"Good, then you may be excused."

Gail continued to clear the table after Alex left the dining room. She knew Brian had his eyes on her. "Look, I'm really sorry for what I said to Celia this morning," she said. "And as soon as I'm done cleaning up, I'll apologize. I know how much she loves Alex, and that she means well. I don't want her to make certain decisions for him without our approval."

"I agree with you, but I've never seen anyone freak out about a video the way you did this morning."

"I didn't freak out about the video. If anything, I was more taken aback by Celia's actions."

Truth be told, this would not be such a nail biting incident if this was a video of Alex playing soccer, or riding his bike. In fact, there would be no incident at all, Gail thought.

"We've always included Celia as part of Alex's life. That's not going to change. However, it's important for her to understand that she cannot make unilateral decisions on his behalf. I know it comes off sounding mean when I say this, but it's the truth. We're his parents, and ultimately, we're the ones who should make those decisions."

Brian ambled to the kitchen counter, picked up his phone, and started looking through it.

"Well, you've made your point. I really think you could've been a bit more sensitive given the situation. I'll admit Celia can go out on a limb sometimes, but she does it out of love."

"I get that," Gail replied. "It still doesn't change the fact that she needs to respect our roles as parents. What I do, I do out of love too, and she can't possibly love my son more than me. The problem is Celia sometimes forget that Alex is not her child. I think sometimes she looks at him and she sees the son she lost. I can't imagine the pain she's suffered losing her son, but I'm not about to relinquish control of *my* child simply because I empathize with her."

"That's not what I'm saying."

"What exactly are you saying?"

Brian sighed. "Just let it go. You're blowing things way out of proportion. Quite frankly, I don't see what the big deal is. So what if Celia sees Alex as her child? Where's the harm? That's her nature. She always looked out for me even when I don't need her to. It's a part of who we are. You probably can't relate because you've no one you're really close to. You're trying to suggest that Celia has issues, but maybe you need to look in the mirror."

Gail studied Brian as the words sunk in,

trying to understand how they got to this point. "What do you mean by that?" she asked, though she wasn't sure she wanted an answer.

"That didn't come out right. I didn't mean you've no one, because obviously you have us. I meant like a brother or a sister, like the connection that Celia and I have. I really think that helped to mold us into who we're today, whether we like it or not. You lost your parents at a very young age, and you don't seem to have any other family."

He's right. This family is all she had and she wanted nothing to disturb it. Gail was numb. She studied the knife she was about to wash. If it pricked her, would she feel it?

Brian came up behind Gail and hugged her. "I'm sorry," he whispered. "I never meant to hurt you. You've always been overprotective of Alex and I shouldn't expect that to change. I guess it's what mothers do. All I'm saying is, you need to cut Celia some slack."

Whether he meant to hurt her or not, the end result was the same. Gail felt as if she'd been punched in the gut. She pulled away from Brian. He was still talking but she could not hear most of what he was saying. She expected Brian to be on her side, despite the fact that he's clueless as to her motivations for keeping her life as private as possible. This is the opposite of most people he knew, who post pictures of themselves and videos online on a daily basis. *Did he always think I was odd?*

"Are you even listening to me?"

"Sure."

"Sure, what?"

"Whatever you say."

"Whatever you say? What kind of response is that?"

"The last thing I want or need right now is an argument."

"I didn't realize we're arguing. I'm just trying to make sense of what ensued between you and Celia this morning. Gosh! You're so…wound up."

"I already explained myself to you this morning, and I was under the impression you understood."

"I've got to be honest with you. I'm not sure I understand. I've never seen you like this. It's almost as if you turned into someone else this morning."

The house phone rang, and Gail was happy for the distraction. She hurried to the phone and picked it up. "Hello?" No answer. "Hello?" Then Gail heard the dial tone. Before Gail hung up, she heard Brian's cell phone vibrating.

Brian answered. "Hello? One second." He looked over at Gail. "I'm going to take this upstairs." He started up the stairs then turned back to Gail, "I forgot to tell you, Celia took down the videos of Alex." He then continued upstairs.

As Gail listened to him climb the rest of the way, she wondered if that was Celia on the phone now. Maybe she was the one who called and hung up earlier. So, her sister-in-law was mad, but Gail was ready to mend fences.

Eager to smooth things over with Celia, Gail ran upstairs hoping to catch Brian before he hung up from the call. She reached the top of the stairs and could hear Brian whispering. He sounded upset. She paused as she heard Brian say, "Please don't call my home again."

That didn't sound like a conversation he'd be having with his sister. The door to the bedroom was closed. She opened the door and entered the bedroom. Brian was still on the phone, but not in the bedroom. He was actually in the bathroom. As soon as Gail tried to open the bathroom door, Brian said, "I've to go." He ended the call, flushed the toilet and turned on the faucet.

Brian unlocked the bathroom door and emerged looking disheveled. He was still wearing work clothes but everything seemed out of place, even his usually sleek blond hair appeared as if he'd grabbed patches of it.

Well, that was strange. Unhappy client? But why would he hide that?

"Everything okay?" She hoped that this would create a window of opportunity for him to tell her about the phone call. She didn't want to accuse him of anything. Besides, she'd have a hard time explaining how she was able to hear his conversation.

"Yeah, yeah." Brian ran his fingers through his hair to smooth it back in place. "I've to go out."

"What? Now?"

"Yes. I won't be long."

"Is there something you need to tell me?" Gail asked.

"No, is there something *you* need to tell *me*?" Brian retorted as he glowered at her.

Gail was taken aback, not only by Brian's question, but his attitude. Where was he going with this? "I thought you're talking to Celia, and since you seem rather upset after the phone call, it's natural for me to ask what's going on. Don't you think?"

"I guess so. I left something at the office and..." Brian took a deep breath. "I need to get it. I'll be home as soon as I can." Before Gail could respond, he was on his way downstairs.

What just happened? Her brain started to replay the incident from the moment she got to the top of the stairs. Had she really heard what she thought, or was it all in her head? She walked to the top of the stairs, looked down to the second flight of stairs, then looked in the direction of the bedroom. The master bedroom suite was to the right of the stairs. Gail slowly walked back to the bedroom. On entering the suite, there was a large sitting area which is separated from the bedroom area by a pair of decorative columns on each side. At the end of that space was the entrance to the bathroom. As Gail gazed at the length of the entire space, her eyes stopped at the door to the bathroom. She realized that no one could, or should've, been able to hear someone whispering behind two closed doors from that distance.

Mom always told me I was special, and that as I get older, I'd be even more special. "Well, I'm especially losing my mind right now," she whispered.

Gail shifted her thoughts to Alex. She could hear him talking to her.

"Alex!" She dashed out of the master bedroom, across the hall and into Alex's room. His door was open and he was on his computer.

"What..." She realized what was happening before she could complete the question. Alex had painted a picture of her on the computer. He'd copied a photograph of her that was in the family room. He'd been talking to the picture on the screen.

"Wow! That's beautiful," Gail said.

"Do you like it?" Alex asked.

"No, I love it. It looks exactly like me." Gail grinned and opened her arms. Alex wasted no time. He threw himself at her and she wrapped her arms around him. "I love you sooo much," she whispered.

"I love you too, Mom."

"Did you draw this from memory?"

"Yes, but I made your hair darker, like mine."

"I noticed that." Her natural hair color was dark brown, but to most people it looked black. Gail had colored her hair to a much lighter medium-red ginger color when she'd started her new life. Alex had never seen her with her natural color.

"This was a test run," Alex said as he closed the program.

"A test run for what?" Gail already figured out where the conversation was heading. She had a room downstairs she used as a studio.

Painting relaxed her, made her feel calm. Some people wrote in a journal; Gail painted. That was her release, or at least the more subdued form of release.

"I'm planning to paint the family portrait,

but on real canvas," he said with a wide grin.

"And?" Gail asked with a smirk, pretending to be clueless.

"And since you love me so much, I know you'll give me a spot in your studio to follow my dreams."

"Nice speech. Are you finished?"

"Yeah, that's all I got. I wasn't really prepared. Otherwise, I'm sure I'd come up with a better argument, but that should do. So, is that a yes?"

"It's a yes, *but*." Gail was about to lay down some ground rules about the use of the studio. She saw how excited he was and decided she would skip the rules for now. "It's your bath time."

"Ugh." Alex groaned.

Sometimes he opened his mouth and sounded like a twenty-year-old, then in a flash he was back to being seven again. "I tell you what, after your bath, you and I can set up an area in the studio for you."

"Awesome! I'm going to paint a masterpiece. I'm going to make lots of money, because people pay lots of money for paintings."

"Whoa, slow down, mister. You're getting way ahead of yourself. I thought you wanted to do this for fun."

"I do, but that doesn't mean I can't sell it.

Well, not the family portrait, I wouldn't sell that, but the other things I'll be painting. You do it for fun, and Aunt Celia said people pay a lot of money to buy your paintings. She said you could get a lot more if you wanted."

"Good point. Let's get the bath thing out of the way. Shall we?"

Bath time was quick because Alex so wanted to get his workstation set up in the studio.

Five minutes after they got downstairs, the doorbell rang.

Chapter 4

California

Alvin Craig had reached out to an investigator his father used for a number of jobs when he was alive. His father use to say, if this guy can't find it, it didn't exist. No one knew his name or where he lived. Money and information exchange usually took place by drops. He would arrange the time and place for the exchange. Following the directions he received, Alvin drove to the curb and parked his car. He turned off the ignition and sat there for a while. His phone rang.

"I'm here." He got out of the car, removed his briefcase from the backseat and walked towards the house. He could see a flicker of light from a cigarette as he got closer to the building.

"Can I help you?" the man asked as he continued puffing on his cigarette.

"I'm here about the property for lease. The agent asked me to meet him here to go over the documents. Is he here?"

"Let's go inside," the man said, as he headed

to the door. Before entering, he took one last puff of his cigarette, dropped it on the ground and stepped on it.

The house was empty except for a small breakfast table in the kitchen and a kettle on the counter. The little information that Alvin had about this man would put him about in his sixties. He might have been in his sixties, but he had the physique of a man his forties, a fit man in his forties.

"Do you have something for me?" Alvin asked. Because I'd hate to drive all this way for nothing."

"How much is it worth to you? Hmm?" The man sauntered to the counter and turned on the electric kettle. "You know what I think?" He opened the cupboard, removed two tea cups.

"I think the information I have is worth a whole lot more than you're offering."

"Well, I wouldn't know. I'm doing this on behalf of a client. I'll make you a promise, you share everything you have with me, and I mean everything, and I'll make sure you get what you deserve."

"What makes you so sure that your client will pay what I want? I haven't even told you what I want. But since we're on the subject, I want enough to retire. You see, I realize that this was no simple search, and I've learned a lot of things that made me realize how valuable this information is. Now, I am willing to spill it all...for the right price. Tea?"

"Excuse me?" Alvin asked as he gazed at the man with the kettle in his hand. "Oh, tea! No, no thank you. I'm more of a coffee person."

"So was I, until the doctor gave me a cock and bull story about how my smoking and heavy coffee drinking wasn't good for me. He told me to give it up. So I did."

Alvin clearly remembered seeing the man smoking not too long ago and although he did not wish to continue the laborious conversation, he wanted to remain polite in the hopes that he would get the information he needed. "You gave up smoking?" Alvin asked.

"No, coffee. I gave up coffee. But as soon as this stash of tea has run out I'm going right back to drinking my coffee."

"Oh, I see. Why would you want to do that?"

The man sat down and took a few sips from his tea cup. "Don't you read the news, mister? Cigarette and coffee are good for my liver. That's what the research said. You can't argue with research."

"No, you can't." Eager to move things along, Alvin sat on the opposite site of the table. He placed his briefcase on the table, opened it, took out a small bundle of money and shoved it towards the man. "That's ten thousand dollars. That's the balance of the original payment, but you can consider it a part payment of your new fee for the additional information."

The man placed his cup on the table, picked up the bundle of money and flipped the edges a few times.

"There's a lot more where that came from," Alvin said leaning in to the table. "So, do we have a deal?"

The man grinned, he reached into the same cupboard where he kept his tea, pulled out a large envelope and handed it to Alvin. "Everything you asked for is in there."

Alvin opened the envelope, took out the contents, which included some photographs and started examining the information. "You're sure this is everything?"

The man chuckled. "As a matter of fact, there is something else. Hence the fee increase. It seems your client is not the only one searching for this young woman and her boy. I think there's someone else who is interested in the same person. In fact, I'm quite sure of it."

Alvin threw the documents in his briefcase. "How can you be so sure? Do you even know who this person is? Or are you just making shit up as you go along?"

"I don't know *who*," the man said. "But

whoever it is, he's no small fry. I've been doing this a long time and when I see—"

The sound of breaking glass made Alvin hit the floor. As he hunkered down under the table, he saw the man nearby, face up, blood streaming from his body. He'd been shot twice, once to his head, the other in his chest. The man was dead. Shot through the window with a silencer. Alvin realized this was a professional hit. He was not the target, which was the only reason he was still alive.

Washington State

Gail slowly approached the front door on the balls of her feet. Her heart beat a little faster than usual, as she was not expecting anyone so late in the evening. She positioned her face next to the door so she could look through the keyhole. Gail was relieved to see Mike, who appeared as if he belonged on the cover of a fitness magazine.

Mike Matthews was an old friend of both Gail and Brian. A former army surgeon who'd spent some time in Iraq, Mike's not-so-recent divorce seemed to be proving more problematic than the war's toll.

"Hey, what's up?"

"May I come in?"

"Of course. Don't you have better ways to spend your vacation time?" He didn't respond. Gail closed the door. "Something wrong?"

"I was in the neighborhood and I thought I'd swing by. I hope you don't mind," he said, playfully.

Gail was five feet, six inches. Mike stood noticeably taller than her but not as tall as Brian. For all the years she'd known Mike, he'd never been able to look her in the eyes and lie to her.

They'd come to know each other so well, he'd confirmed her suspicion when Brian cheated on her six years ago. Mike had stuck by while they worked out their issues. Sadly, he hadn't been able to work out his own and the divorce hit him harder than his service in Iraq.

"Rubbish. It's a long drive to get out here, and you know it. So, what really brings you by?"

He held up his hands in surrender. "You got me. What if I told you I wanted to see you? I mean, to make sure you're okay. Would that be good enough for you?"

"It *would* be, if there wasn't more to it. So, what is it?"

"Where's Alex?" Mike asked.

"He's in the studio, painting."

"Painting?"

"Could we get back to the matter at hand?"

"Do you mind if we go over to the family room?"

Gail gestured for him to lead the way. They sat and Mike turned on the television.

"I don't want Alex to hear this, although I don't think there's anything to worry about." He moved closer to her and spoke in a whisper. "I called Brian tonight, and something was off. I honestly don't know what it is but, he sounded...I don't know, strange. I told him I was going to swing by his office and he asked me not to."

Gail remembered his phone call from earlier. He was quite shaken up by that phone call and he clearly wanted to keep whatever it was a secret. "He had a phone call earlier this evening. He took the call upstairs."

"Do you know who he was talking to, or even get a sense of what they were talking about?"

"Not really. All I can tell you is that he seemed really rattled after that phone call. It's obvious that something's wrong. He started to get defensive when I tried to ask him about it."

"How defensive? Did he hurt you?"

Gail sprung to her feet. "No! No, God, no. He wouldn't. Do you remember when he had that...mishap, as he called it that almost ruined our marriage?"

"Do I remember? I don't think he ever forgave me for what I did. He said I ratted him out."

"During that time, whenever I asked him about her or anything that pointed to him being anything other than a faithful husband, he'd get very defensive and actually started accusing me of having an affair. It's his way of turning the attention away from himself and let me be the focus."

Mike got up and faced her. "Unfortunately I was on the receiving end myself with my ex, so I know exactly what it feels like."

"Well, I got a version of that earlier this evening when I tried to get him to tell me what the phone call was about. Whatever it is, he wants it to remain a secret." The moment the word secret came out of her mouth, she realized she's a hypocrite. She was not exactly an open book herself but forgave her husband for his indiscretion in lieu of opening up about her past.

Mike walked up to her and put his hands on her shoulders. "It's going to be okay," he whispered. "I know Brian, and I know how much he loves you. He'd never do anything to hurt you."

A cheating husband was not exactly at the top of her worry list. She was more concerned about Brian and what kind of trouble he may be in. Although the state of this family would be in jeopardy if she found out he's in fact cheating, somehow she got the sense that there was more to it than that.

Mike pulled her close to him and wrapped his arms around her. She closed her eyes and for a brief moment allowed herself to be comforted by his familiar scent of vanilla and sandalwood mixed with leather, one she'd never grew tired of whiffing. She'd introduced him to this cologne many years ago, before he introduced her to Brian.

She remembered the day he opened that present. He picked her up and spun her around until they were both giddy. They fell to the ground. Gail landed on top of him. "I'll always wear this cologne," he'd told her.

More than twelve years and their respective marriages later, he still wore that cologne. She could feel his fingers gently stroking her scalp.

"I'm here for you, if you need me," he said. "I don't know what's going on with Brian but there's one thing I do know...you mean the world to him. From the first day he met you, he was hooked. I didn't have the heart to tell him that I was waiting for the right moment to transition from just friends."

She changed the subject. "I need to check on Alex." She gently released herself from the fold of his arms.

"Sure. Do you mind if I come along? I'd love to see him."

"Come on. You're his godfather, after all."

Gail turned to walk away, she felt his hand on hers in a firm but gentle grasp. She twirled around to face him.

"I'm sorry if I made you feel uncomfortable. I didn't mean to. With everything that happened, I couldn't help but wonder what my life would be like today if..." He took a deep breath. "I'm not making things any better, am I?"

"Not exactly, but I get it. You're hurting. It's normal for you to think back and wonder 'what if?' We're all guilty of it at some point or another. Not everyone is brave enough or bold enough to actually say it out loud. I value our friendship. Honestly, I can't imagine not having you in my life."

"So, you're not mad at me?"

"No, but I'm not going to play that 'what if' game with you. You and I have been through a lot together. We've supported each other through some really difficult times and I know I can always count on you. I couldn't ask for a better friend, but Brian is my husband and as much as I care about you, I—"

"You don't have to explain," Mike said. "Please don't think I'm trying to come between you and Brian. I'm trying to do the opposite, because I know he makes you happy. I'm not going to lie to you and say I don't have feelings for you, but I always have and that's never going to change. Nothing hurts me more than to see you hurting...well, maybe the only thing that could hurt me more is if I messed up our friendship and made you hate me. I'm babbling.

One more thing, could we keep this conversation between us?"

Gail was surprised by Mike's sudden attack of openness. "Do you have a terminal illness?"

Mike looked at her puzzled. "What?"

"I'm sorry, but this is unusual for you. You've had many years and numerous opportunities to tell me this. Why are you telling me all of this now?"

Mike kept looking at her for a moment, then he asked, "Do you remember Chris, that buddy of mine I told you about?"

"The one whose tanker blew up in Iraq?"

"Yeah. He died today. His mom called me this evening."

"Gosh, I'm so sorry."

"He had this girl he was really close to before he was shipped off to war. He never had the guts to tell that girl how he felt. The fear of rejection, I guess. After seeing so many of his friends shipped home in a casket, he swore that if he made it out alive, the moment he was home he'd take his chances and pour his heart out. The funny thing is, he *did* make it out alive, but he had neurological damage. He couldn't speak."

Gail could see the pain in his face. She searched for the right words to say but couldn't come up with anything that she thought would be of any comfort to him. She reached out and took his hand and gently pulled him towards her. He was always comforting her. Now it was her turn to comfort him. As he buried his face in her neck, she wrapped her arms around him. He was shaking. She placed one hand at the back of his neck and gently stroked it. There was a sense of calm and the shaking ceased.

She pulled back enough for her to see his face. "Why don't we go see what my little Picasso is up to?" she asked, hoping that a shift in focus would change the mood of the moment to something lighter. She held his hand and led him to the studio.

When Alex saw Mike, he dropped his paintbrush and sprung into his arms. "Uncle Mike! I'm painting a masterpiece. You wanna see?"

"Absolutely," Mike said as he flipped Alex over his shoulder and moved closer to what vaguely looked like the face of a woman.

Alex had made a royal mess of the studio and himself, as expected. Paint from his apron and hands was now all over Mike's clothes and light brown hair. It didn't seem to bother him one bit. He listened attentively as Alex explained the process of painting what he referred to as a masterpiece and, for the first time this evening, Mike had a genuine smile on his face. She watched and beamed as her little artist explained his painting to his very attentive and now equally messy guest.

Mike looked up and caught her stare. She could see his lips moving, but there was no sound. "Thank you," he mouthed as he turned his attention back to Alex.

Gail reflected on their earlier conversation. She realized it was time for her to be free from secrets. It was not fair for her to expect openness from her husband if she was not open about who she really was. She wasn't sure how to broach the subject with Brian. It was not going to be easy, especially since they'd been married for so long. Gail had thought she could leave her past where it belonged, in the past. However, her past was now a part of her son's future and her husband had every right to know.

As she pondered her strategy she heard the newscaster on the television said a name. "Colson." She thought her mind was playing a trick on her until once again she heard, "Nicholas Colson." She rushed to the family room where the television was still on and watched as the news was read.

"Former CIA agent Nicholas Colson will be granted another parole hearing. Sources say his attorneys are cautiously optimistic that Mr. Colson will be released early. This comes on the heels of new evidence which suggests that two of the investigating officers tampered with the evidence. Colson was charged and convicted for the murder of Christine Hemmingway. The prosecution argued that Colson killed Hemmingway to cover up their affair after Hemmingway threatened to reveal the affair to his wife."

"There was no affair!" Gail shouted at the television.

"How would *you* know?" Brian asked.

Gail spun around to see her husband standing behind her.

Chapter 5

Gail had been so caught up with the television that she completely tuned everything else out. She hadn't heard his car, as she usually did. She knew she needed to talk to Brian about her past, which would explain how she knew Nicholas Colson, but this was not the right time. There was too much tension already. She needed to get things leveled out before she unloaded that kind of information. Otherwise, there would be a greater risk for her marriage to hit rock bottom.

"You're back! Did you get what you went for?" Gail asked.

"Yes," Brian responded.

Gail used his own strategy on him. She quickly shifted the focus from her to him. Now he appeared uncomfortable. There was a moment of silence. Then Gail broke the ice.

"Mike is here."

Alex came running and laughing, with Mike not far behind him, making equally, if not more, noise than Alex.

"Yes, he is," Brian muttered under his breath.

"What are you guys doing?" Gail asked.

"We're playing a game. You wanna play, Dad?" Alex asked as he ran to his father for his usual hug.

"Not tonight, son," Brian said, as he looked at the mess on Alex's clothes. "What's all this?"

"Paint," Gail replied.

"Paint?" Brian asked.

"Yep, he was painting in the studio. Don't worry, it's water based."

"Come, come let me show you my painting, Dad," Alex said while tugging at his father's arm.

"In a minute, son," Brian said as his eyes met Mike's.

"Hey," Mike said to Brian.

"Hey, yourself. What're you doing here?" Brian asked.

"I, uh, I was in the neighborhood and I thought I'd stop by. I hope you don't mind?"

"No, not at all. At least, not tonight. I'm happy you were here with them." Brian walked up to Mike and extended his right hand. Gail could see Mike was just as puzzled as she was. They usually joked a lot with each other, but at that moment neither of them were laughing.

"You okay, man? You're starting to spook

me a little bit," Mike said as he shook Brian's extended hand.

"Yeah, I'm just tired."

"Rough night?" Mike asked.

"Something like that."

"Well, you know you can call me anytime, if you need...help."

Gail realized that Mike was trying to get Brian to open up about his evening but he was not taking the bait. Frankly, she didn't think it was the right time for him to do so with Alex in their midst.

"Hey, Alex, why don't we go upstairs so I can get you all cleaned and ready for bed?" Gail asked.

"But I'm not ready for bed," Alex retorted.

Before Gail could respond, Alex was pleading his case. "I don't need to go to bed early. It's not like there's school tomorrow. It's summer."

"All right, Mr. Smarty Pants, why don't we focus on getting you cleaned up first? We can discuss the bedtime afterwards."

"I'll take him," Brian said. "I'll get him cleaned up. If the paint on his and Mike's clothes are any indication of the state of that studio, then you'll have more than enough on your hands."

"Okay," Gail said.

Brian started off up the stairs. "Come on." He beckoned to Alex.

Alex ran to Mike and hugged him. "Bye, Uncle Mike. See you later."

"Later, Alex."

Alex ran past his father on the stairs shouting, "Race me, race me!" As soon as he got to the top of the stairs he announced, "I'm the winner!"

"I'm going to take off," Mike said to Gail.

"Thanks for coming over. You might want to clean off some of that paint before you go out in public. Otherwise people may try to hire you for their kids' birthday parties," Gail said, pointing to the paint all over his face.

"It's that bad, huh?"

"See for yourself." Gail said as she pointed him to the powder room.

When Mike emerged from the powder room they looked at each other and laughed. "I'll get you something to clean yourself up." She handed him a washrag and a face towel. "I'm going to start cleaning the studio. Let me know when you're done so I can let you out."

Gail headed into the studio to tackle the cleaning project. The moment alone gave her a chance to think about when she could schedule that talk with her husband. It had to be sooner than later. She knew that, but she wasn't sure how. Quite frankly, she still had a lot of blank spots she would like to be filled. Brian would have questions, lots of questions, but the problem for Gail was she didn't have the answers. She sat in the midst of the paper and paint on the floor. She heard someone approaching, but she was still deep in thought.

"Hey, I'm leaving now," Mike said. "What's wrong?" Just like she knew him, he could always tell when she was troubled.

"Nothing more than the usual. I'm good."

"You don't have to pretend with me," Mike said as he got down on the floor to be at eye level with her.

Gail chose to stare at the wall. Her husband was not the only person she needed to be open with. Mike had been her closest friend since they met in medical school. He was the only person she felt comfortable with, before Brian came along.

"Look at me! Please! Just, look at me," he said as he gently repositioned her head so that her eyes would face the direction he was sitting. "Talk to me."

"I need to talk to Brian first. All I can tell you right now is that there are things about me, about my past that..." She exhaled. "That I think I should've told him, and you, long ago. I tried telling him before but I wasn't sure what to tell him or how to explain things to him. I didn't...I still don't understand most of it."

"Then start with what you *do* know, and from there, you can figure out the rest of it together."

"Easier said than done, my friend."

"You're making it harder than it really is. Set aside some time for the two of you to be alone without any distractions. Maybe it's time you both be honest with each other."

"Yeah, let's hope we still have a marriage after we're done with all that honesty. They say 'the truth shall set you free.' Don't worry about wrecking your marriage as long as you've been 'set free,'" Gail said, half-jokingly.

"Well, there's that possibility. The question is, what would you prefer? Would you prefer to go on like this and see how far down the road you get before things crash? Or would you prefer to face it now, head on?"

Gail thought about what he said. He'd always been her voice of reasoning. At that moment she felt it would be much easier discussing it with him than her husband. "Is that what happened with you and your ex?" Gail asked.

Mike held his head down. "It was a little more complicated than that, but my marriage is over, so let's focus on you."

"Oh, come on, you and I are supposed to be best friends yet you shut me out when the subject is about *your* marriage. You've told me more than once that you're the reason she strayed, but you never shared the details with me."

"Fine!" Mike said. "I'll tell you what finally ruined it for me. I called her another name, another woman's name."

"That's it? There's got to be more to it than that."

"Well, it was while we were...you know."

"OH, OOOHHHH! You really screwed things up!"

"Thank you for pointing out the obvious."

"So, who...?" Before Gail could finish the question Mike stopped her in her tracks.

"Don't even bother asking, because I'm not going to answer. Although I *am* willing to make you a deal. You and I can revisit this conversation after you and Brian sort things out."

"At least answer this. Did you cheat on her with this woman?" Gail asked, wide-eyed.

Mike shook his head. "Technically, no."

"Technically, no? What does that mean? Either you did or you didn't. Which is it?"

"I wasn't unfaithful, okay? Nothing happened. By the way, can we change the subject? Better yet, why don't we get this place cleaned up so I can get out of here?"

"You can leave now. I'll clean up."

"I had a hand in this mess, so I'm not going to leave it all on you."

They barely said anything to each other for the duration of the cleanup. Mike left as soon as they were done.

Later that night, Brian reminded Gail he was scheduled to be off for two weeks.

"Why don't we take a family vacation?" Gail asked.

"Really?"

"Yeah. I think it'd be great for us to get away. Plus, you and I need to have a heart-to-heart talk. There are things that I need to—"

"How do you feel about going to the Virgin Islands?"

"I don't mind, but why there?"

"We're going to need some time alone. I'm not sure what's going on with you, but there's something I need to tell you as well."

"I see." She was ready to hear what he had to say to her.

"I could ask Celia to come along and babysit for a bit. I'm pretty sure she wouldn't pass up the opportunity to spend time with Alex. It would also give her a chance to catch up on whatever business she'd planned in the Virgin

Islands.

"Sounds like you have it all worked out."

"Is that a yes?"

"Sure."

"I'll call Celia."

After talking with Celia, Brian handed the phone to Gail. She was happy for the opportunity to talk to Celia and apologized for being so rough on her. She didn't change her stance on the videos, but believed she should've handled the matter with a bit more finesse. Celia was an important part of Alex's life and therefore very important to Gail. Celia will need to know about her past too, at least enough for her to protect Alex.

Brian made the flight arrangements. Alex was very excited when he heard about the trip to the Virgin Islands. He was even more excited when he heard his Aunt Celia would be coming along. Of course, he also wanted Mike to come along. That was a no go.

At the behest of Alex, Gail called Mike.

"Hey, what's up?"

"I wanted to let you know we're going to the Virgin Islands."

"That's sudden."

"I know, but it's perfect timing."

"Is Brian nearby?"

"He's not standing next to me, if that's what

you're asking."

"Does this have anything to do with the conversation we had this evening?"

"It does. I guess you could say I'm taking your advice."

"When are you leaving?"

"Tomorrow."

"I guess Alex and I will have to reschedule our meeting."

Apparently Alex had arranged another painting lesson with Mike. "I'm sure you two will work it out." She could hear Brian and Alex approaching the bedroom. "I've to go. I'll call you before I leave."

"Okay. Bye."

Gail was somewhat excited about the trip and at the same time apprehensive. Never mind what she had to tell Brian, it was more what Brian had to tell her that had her feeling a little bit on edge. They were both packing for the upcoming trip. She sent Alex to his room to select the toys he wanted to take if they fit in the backpack she gave him.

In the midst of packing, she froze. Gail wasn't sure she wanted to wait another day before hearing what Brian had to tell her. "Why don't you tell me now?" she asked.

Her question seem to have caught Brian off guard. "Sorry, what did you just say?" he asked.

"Why do we need to fly thousands of miles to hear what you have to tell me? Why don't you say what you have to say, now?"

"This was *your* idea. You're the one who suggested we do this. This isn't only about me. Don't you have your tales to tell, huh?"

Gail had a folded pair of jeans in her hand. Instead of putting it in the suitcase, she unfolded them, placed them on a hanger and returned them to the closet.

"I'm sorry," Brian said softly. "I know I have a lot to make up for and right now I am clearly not doing a good job of it, but please, let's follow this through. Don't be so quick to give up on us. *I'm* not giving up on us."

"I hope you feel the same way when all is said and done," Gail said.

Brian looked her in the eyes. "Just as long as I'm not going to lose you, I can handle anything. Anything but that. I've loved you from the moment I met you, and I love you even more today," he said softly.

In a moment of silence they reached out for each other. Their timing was like a well-choreographed dance that culminated in a warm tender embrace.

"I can't lose you," he whispered.

Gail loved him, but could she trust him?

She wanted to say "you won't," but the

words would not come out.

Chapter 6

They were all packed and ready to go.

"I want to swing by the office before I leave," Brian said.

"Go ahead. You can meet us at the airport."

After Brian left, Gail called Mike to let him know they were leaving. Mike wanted to take them to the airport but Gail insisted she and Alex would take a cab. Gail gave Celia a ring every now and then to make sure she would not arrive after the plane had taken off.

Gail and Alex got to the airport first. Celia showed up as promised. "I am here," Celia announced as she hugged Alex. "Where's that husband of yours?"

"He should be here any time now."

"Well, the next time you two are going to plan a romantic getaway, I'd appreciate a little more notice if I'm going to be dragged along to babysit."

Gail was about to respond when Celia said, "I'm just kidding. I'm happy to spend time with the most awesome little guy in the world."

"Are you talking about me?" Alex asked, barely looking up from the tablet he was playing on.

"You bet I am," Celia said.

Gail scanned the airport for Brian. They needed to check in. "Where *is* he?"

"And you were worried about me being late?"

Gail pulled her cell phone out of her handbag and called Brian. "No answer."

They both kept looking in different directions, examining every face in the distance, hoping one of them would be Brian. Then a phone rang. Gail quickly reached for her cell then she realized it was not her phone.

Celia answered the call. "It's Nathan," she said to Gail. Celia continued her phone conversation. "We're going to the Virgin Islands. Sorry, it was an impromptu trip but I'll be back in two weeks. San Francisco or LA?" she asked Gail.

"Huh?" Gail asked as she was on her own phone trying to reach Brian again.

"Are we connecting in San Francisco or LA?"

"Oh, LA," Gail said.

"LA," Celia told Nathan.

"Let's check in," Gail said while still looking around.

"I'll call you later." Celia ended her

conversation. "Did you get him?" Celia asked.

Gail shook her head.

"Did you call his office?"

"Yes, they said he left for the airport," Gail said as she let out a sigh.

"If he's not here in another fifteen minutes, he's not going to make that flight," Celia said.

"Where's Dad?" Alex asked as they joined the line to check in.

"Don't worry," Gail said. "He'll be here."

"When?"

"Soon, baby. Soon," she said.

After clearing security, they headed to the gate. Gail kept looking behind her still hoping to see Brian. Alex had his headphones on and for once she was thankful that he was engrossed in his game and therefore was not fully aware of the discussion between herself and Celia.

They should start boarding in the next few minutes. Gail realized Brian was not going to make the flight. It was obvious to Celia as well.

"Are we going without him?" Celia asked.

"No," Gail replied. She didn't think it made sense for her to go without him. The point of the trip was for them to be honest with each other so they could get past the building tension.

Gail slowly looked around. Then she had an uneasy feeling. She started hearing a lot of voices and conversations overlapping. For a moment, it felt like the place was spinning. She closed her eyes and tried to filter out the noise. Then she heard, "Colson." The voice was coming from the television not too far away. She zoned in on the sound from the television and learned that Nicholas Colson had been released. "Oh, my God!" She didn't bother listening to the rest of it.

"You go, and take Alex with you," she said to Celia.

"Wait, what? That doesn't make any sense. Why would you—"

"Please, Celia, I need to find Brian. I can't explain it but it'd be better if Alex is not with me right now. Hopefully, Brian got caught in traffic, and in that case, we'll catch another flight."

"You think he changed his mind about going?" Celia asked.

"Maybe, but I won't know until I find him." Gail couldn't share her suspicions with Celia. If Colson was out for revenge, then it was best if Alex was out of the country. She hugged Alex and told him she would find his dad and they would join him and Aunt Celia later. She and Celia didn't always see eye to eye, but knew without a doubt that Celia loved Alex like her own son. If she needed to trust anyone with him, it was her sister-in-law.

She waited for them to board then she called

Brian's phone again. This time it went straight to voicemail. She then called Mike.

"I can't find Brian."

"What do you mean, you can't find him?"

"He's not answering his phone."

"Maybe he changed his mind about the trip."

"I can't explain everything to you now, but could you meet me at my house?"

"Uh, sure. I'll give him a call."

"Let me know if you get him."

The moment Gail walked in the house she sensed something was wrong. "Brian!" She ran from room to room looking, yet not sure what she expected to find. Brian was not there.

She gazed around the family room. Nothing looked out of place. Suddenly she fixed her eyes on a portrait on the fireplace mantel. It was not aligned with the other portraits. Like someone picked it up but did not put it back the way she'd left it.

Maybe he was here...then she heard a vehicle outside.

She rushed out the door. "Brian! We were so...oh, Mike. Hi."

"Any luck?" he asked.

"No, but I think he came back to the house," she said as she went inside. Mike followed.

"What makes you say that?"

"Just a hunch." Gail was not ready to reveal

too much. Still looking around, she opened the back door to the garage. Brian's car was parked inside. "His car is here."

Mike came to the door. "Your hunch was spot on. He *did* come home. The question is, where did he go after? And with whom? Since he clearly didn't drive."

"We have to report it."

"Report what? He could be anywhere. For all we know he probably ran off with some woman! Sorry, I didn't mean that."

Gail did not respond. She went in and closed the back door. No woman wanted to hear that her husband had ran off with someone else, but in this case she would prefer that than the alternative. There was no way for Mike to understand why she believed Brian was in danger. Then she remembered Brian had his luggage when he left home. She went back into the garage and checked the trunk. His suitcase was still in the car.

"Well, we can rule out accident," Mike said as he inspected the car.

"I think we can rule out running off, too. His luggage is still in the trunk."

"I'm starting to get a bad feeling about this."

"There's something I need to tell you." This was not exactly how Gail envisioned telling Mike about her past. "I think Brian may have been kidnapped." She caught sight of Mike's questioning stare.

"Kidnapped? By whom? Is there a ransom note?"

"No. There's no note, no phone call. Nothing like that. Not yet, anyway. I can feel it in my gut and I think I know who's behind it."

Mike scratched his head and looked away, then turned back to her. "Okay, what is it you're not telling me?"

"Does the name Nicholas Colson mean anything to you?"

"Not really. Should it?"

"He's a retired CIA agent who was recently released from jail after serving time for murder. I have a history with him, and I think he may be using Brian to get to me."

"Come again?" Mike asked, looking totally confused.

"I'll tell you what you need to know, but right now I need to get the authorities involved so they can help me find my husband."

"He won't be considered missing until he's been gone forty-eight hours. The police are not going to put manpower on this so early in the game. It's not like you found blood or anything for them to suspect foul play."

"So, what do we do? Sit and twiddle our thumbs until we get to the forty-eight-hour mark? Colson could hurt him."

"If he's using Brian to get to you as you say, then he'll call. In the meantime, since Colson was trained by the CIA, we should scan the house to see if there're any bugs planted."

"Do you have the equipment for that?" Gail asked, knowing full well that he didn't.

"We're going to have to use the equipment we were born with. Eyes and ears. Start looking around." Mike led the way, looking into vases, behind paintings, photographs.

"So, how do you know this Colson guy?" Mike asked as he continued to look around.

"I lived with his family for a few years. After my mother died, he and his wife took me in."

"What happened to your dad?"

"He died in a car accident a few months before my mom. My mom got ill after his death and it all went downhill from there. She never recovered."

"How old were you?"

"I was thirteen when I went to live with the Colson's. He was nice to me. His wife on the other hand, well, let's just say I don't think she liked the idea of me being there."

"I still don't understand how you go from there to suspecting him of kidnapping your husband."

"I think he blamed me for his son's death.

His only child and the apple of his eye. He died in an explosion at the Colson's residence. I should've died too. I'm not sure how I survived. Maybe I was thrown out of a window somehow. Anyway, when I came to, I realize the Colsons thought we both died. So..."

"So you ran away and started a new life." He sighed and shook his head. "All this time, I blamed Brian for coercing you into giving up your career to stay home. It was your own doing, wasn't it?"

"Yes."

"I see. So, why would this Colson guy blame you for his son's death?

"The explosion that killed his son occurred during an FBI raid, but before the raid, an agent came to me. He wanted information about Colson. "

"Wait, he was involved in illegal stuff?"

"I don't know, I never saw any of it and I told the agent the same thing. Then he asked me about the school counselor, Ms. Hemmingway. Colson hired her to be my tutor."

"She was your private tutor?"

"More like homeschool teacher. I was not allowed to go to regular school. One day, she didn't come back. Colson told me she'd taken some time off to care for her sick mother and that she'd be gone for a while. I believed him until the FBI agent showed me a picture of her with a bullet hole in her head. The agent said he believed Colson had Ms. Hemmingway murdered and he needed my help to prove it."

"Why hire a private tutor for you and then kill her?"

"He said no one should know what I am capable of doing. Ms. Hemmingway was the counselor of my old school. She was already aware of my abilities. If I'd stayed in the regular school system, it'd only be a matter of time before other people would find out and he was adamant that no one should know."

"You've lost me. What exactly are you capable of?"

"Choose a book from the bookshelf."

Mike seemed a little hesitant but reluctantly complied. "Okay, I have a book. Now what?"

"Open the book to any page and make a note of the pages."

Mike did as he was told.

"Give me the book." Gail took the opened book and scanned through both pages in less than a minute. She handed the book back to Mike, then took a note pad and pen and started writing what was on the pages, word for word, with every punctuation mark exactly the same.

"No, no," Mike said, wagging his index finger. "This is your book. You probably read it a million times, so you may know a few pages by heart."

"Okay, Mike, choose something else. Anything."

Mike picked up several different books. "These are all your books."

"Could you memorize all the books on your bookshelf?"

Mike said nothing. He just stared at her.

"Okay, let's try something else." Gail's phone rang and she answered. "Hello? You guys are in LA? Great. Let me talk to Alex."

She retrieved the book Mike had in his hand and returned it to the bookshelf. "Hi, baby... Not yet, but Uncle Mike is here and he's going to help me find him," she said, as her eyes met Mike's.

"Sure." She handed Mike the phone. "Alex wants to talk to you. Would you mind taking the phone call upstairs?"

"Why?"

"I want to show you something."

"Huh?"

She put her index finger to her lips and pointed to the phone to remind him that Alex was at the other end.

Mike shook his head and headed up the stairs.

"Go into the master bathroom in our

bedroom. Lock both doors."

Mike looked at her and made a weird face.

"Please, just do it."

Mike headed upstairs and Gail waited patiently for him to return.

Gail was looking out the window when Mike came down and stood next to her. She repeated everything he said to Alex word for word.

Mike backed away from her, almost as if he was afraid of her. "What the? How did you—"

"I don't know," she said. "I don't know how or why. I just know that I can hear better than the average person."

"Can you hear from that distance all the time?"

"Only if I want to."

"Meaning what?"

"I have to be actively listening."

"What does that mean? You block certain sounds by default?"

"Something like that."

Mike took a few steps back and fell into the seat he bumped into. "That's not possible," he said, staring at her with his eyes looking wild.

"I can't explain it. 'Start with what I know.' Isn't that what you told me? That's what I'm doing. I'm telling you what I know. This is a hard pill for you to swallow, I know that and I completely understand if you don't want to help me."

She went to him. Kneeling, she took both his hands in hers. "I don't want to do this without you, but I will if I have to."

Mike stayed silent.

Gail got up and retrieved a ladder from the garage.

"What are you doing?" he asked.

"If I'm going to get Brian back, I'm going to have to fight. I can't fight these people with my bare hands and expect to win. Can I?"

She went up the stairs with the ladder. Mike followed her as she went through the master bedroom, master bathroom, and then finally into her closet. She opened up the ladder and placed it below an enclosed cut-out in the ceiling.

"You really think Colson killed Hemmingway to keep her from talking?"

"That's what I thought, until I heard that the motive was to cover up an affair. Something doesn't add up."

"Meaning what?"

"There was no affair, but whether they have the right motive is a moot point for me. It doesn't change the fact she's dead and Colson is capable of murder."

Gail climbed the ladder, pushed the piece of wood that was covering the opening out of the way to reveal an entrance to an attic space.

Mike followed her, and Gail turned on a lamp that was kept in the space. There wasn't much there except for a couple storage containers that all had combination locks. Gail watched as Mike gazed at the containers, then looked back at the small opening he crawled through. "I built the containers in here," she said.

"Oh, right!" Mike said with a nervous laugh.

"You know I collect guns, right?"

"Well, I know you had a thing for Glock since I taught you to shoot."

"I've collected a few more since then, and in keeping with being honest with you, I already knew how to shoot."

"You already knew how to shoot, before I spent all that time at the range 'teaching' you?"

"Yes, I had some training."

"Training? You make it sound as if you did more than just target practice at a range."

Gail kept quiet and gazed at the floor.

"Are we talking professional training?"

She nodded. "Before I met you."

Mike sighed. "Where....why?" He raked his fingers through his hair, then grasped the back of his neck with his hand.

"It's a long story and I promise I'll tell you everything, but not now."

"Okay, I'm all ears when you're ready."

"Thank you."

Gail entered the combination for one of the locks as Mike continued to scan the area. She opened the container and then removed the molded plastic covering that was on the top.

"You have the guns in your attic?" Mike asked. "Does Brian know about this collection?"

"He knows about it. He doesn't know how many I have."

"So, why the attic?"

Gail went on to opening the next container. "We wanted to keep them out of Alex's reach."

Mike said nothing. More than sixty seconds passed without a verbal exchange. "I'm sorry I didn't tell you this before, but honestly, I was afraid I'd lose your friendship."

"You—"

Gail's cell phone buzzed. "It's a private number," she said. They look at each other. Gail could see that Mike was thinking the same thing she was. She slowly picked up the phone and was about to answer it when Mike said, "Put it on speaker phone."

"Are you sure?"

"I'm sure."

Gail answered then put it on speaker.

"Hello, Gail. It's been a long time," the voice said.

Chapter 7

"Colson?"

Gail moved the phone to her lips. "Where's my husband, you son of a bitch!"

"Language, Gail. That language is very unbecoming for a lady. You were always such an eloquent speaker. What happened to you?"

"I'm not playing games with you, Colson, tell me what you want."

"Hmmmm. What do I want?" Colson asked. "Well, we can start with why did you betray me?"

"I didn't! I didn't betray you," Gail said. "Even if I did, Brian had nothing to do with this. Just let him go. You want me? I'll trade myself for him. Isn't that what you want?"

"To be honest with you, I haven't quite figured out what I want."

"Maybe we can let the police help you to figure it out." Mike said. "I'm sure they'd have no trouble throwing your ass back in jail."

"Stay out of it, lover boy. This does not

concern you," Colson snapped.

"Information," Gail cut in. "All that information I stored for you, back when I was a kid. It must be very valuable, and I'm not even talking about the numerous bank accounts."

"Oh, you've turned into quite a little negotiator, haven't you?" Colson said with a chuckle.

Gail was done bargaining. "Where is he?" she yelled. "If you hurt him, so help me God, I'll find you and I'll—"

"Whoa, whoa. I don't have him," Colson said.

"I don't believe him," Mike said.

"Who cares what *you* believe? I'm not talking to you. Gail, listen to me, I don't have him and I don't know where he is, but I think I know who's involved."

"Who'd want to kidnap Brian other than you? Wait, you know who took him?" Gail asked.

"Not exactly. Like I said, it's a hunch."

"A hunch?" Mike asked.

"You've anything better? Gail, you need to come and see me, but no police. I can't help you if they're involved. You can bring lover boy with you if it makes you feel better."

Gail was silent. She thought for a moment. "How do I find you?"

"Wait, you're buying this?" Mike asked.

She held her palm up to Mike to indicate that he should be quiet as she was listening to Colson's directions.

"Shouldn't you be writing this down?" Mike asked.

"She doesn't need to," Colson responded.

"Right," Mike said.

Gail ended the call.

"What now?" Mike asked.

"Now?" Gail let out a loud breath. "Now, we load these into the truck," she said pointing to the guns in the containers closest to her.

"Truck? As in *my* truck?"

"Is there another truck on the premises? Yes, your truck," Gail said as she started moving the guns from the attic to the closet.

Mike did the same. They loaded the guns and extra ammunition in a large duffle bag. Gail picked up two guns from the bag. She tucked the smaller Glock 42 in the waist of her jeans and the larger Glock 22 she placed in her handbag.

Mike picked up two Glock 17s. "It looks like you raided the Glock factory."

Ordinarily, that would have brought a chuckle from Gail but at this point, she couldn't even force a smile.

"Do you believe him?" Mike asked.

"Huh?" Gail was deep in thought.

"Colson. Do you believe he had absolutely nothing to do with Brian's disappearance?"

"I don't know, but I intend to find out."

"What makes you think he'll be any more truthful face-to-face than he was over the phone?"

"Oh, he will. He might need a little help though." She handed him a note on which she had scribbled "Sodium Pentothal." "I'm sure you've access to that."

Mike looked at the note. "Truth serum?"

"Will that be a problem?"

"No. No problem. I can get you what you need. I'm glad you're not taking him at his word."

They loaded the truck and were on their way. Mike stopped briefly at the hospital where he worked. Gail waited outside while Mike went in to get the drug. He was not long, but the wait felt like forever for Gail. When he returned, Gail was in the driver's seat. "Get in." She spun out of the parking garage, eager to get to Colson.

Once they hit the highway, neither of them did much talking. Mike turned on the radio and searched the channels for something to drown the silence. Like a stroke of luck, one of Gail's favorite songs was playing. She flashed a smile at him. Mike seemed pleased with himself. After that song ended, another of her favorites followed.

"That's not a radio station, is it?"

"Not exactly."

"Playing MP3. It's nice. Thank you."

Mike twisted in his seat several times then looked out the window. They were both quiet again.

Gail finally broke the ice. "When we get there, I need you to hang back. I'll go in first. If Colson is up to no good then he'll only have one of us." She glanced at Mike.

"How about I go first and you wait for my signal?" Mike asked.

"Not a chance," Gail said. "If he's out for blood he'll have you shot on sight. I can't have that."

Mike shook his head in disagreement. "You want me to hang back in the hopes that this man doesn't kill you? Are you crazy?"

"He won't."

"What makes you think he won't shoot you?"

"Oh, he may *shoot* me, but he won't *kill* me. I have a lot of information locked away in this brain of mine that is valuable to him. There's no way he will not try to retrieve at least some of that information before killing me."

"You know this for sure?"

"Call it a hunch."

"There seems to be a lot of that going around these days."

"A lot of what?"

"Hunches," Mike replied. "A lot of hunches. Let's hope this hunch doesn't get you killed."

"What do we have here?" Gail asked, as she repeatedly looked in the rearview mirror.

"What is it?" Mike asked as he turned around and looked through the back window.

"I think we're being followed."

"Are you sure?"

"Let's find out." Gail said as she pressed hard on the gas. The truck picked up speed and Gail switched lanes a number of times, weaving through the other vehicles. A black paneled van was also switching lanes back and forth and closing in on the truck.

"Yep. We're definitely being followed," Mike said.

Up ahead, there was a pileup of traffic. There was no way for her to get past that. Then suddenly Gail crossed from the extreme left of the highway to the extreme right, causing a lot of motorists to slam on their brakes to avoid a collision. She took the exit.

Gail and Mike breathed a sigh of relief, but it was short-lived. The black van was still hot on their trail. They eventually hit a single lane road with very little traffic. Gail had the truck going at full speed, braking every now and again for a corner. She overtook a truck in front of her and looked in the rearview mirror. The van glided right in front of the truck and was now closing in.

Mike pulled a gun out of his waistband.

"Keep it handy," Gail said. "If they shoot, we'll return fire."

"Their windshield might be bulletproof."

"Then aim for the tires," Gail said as she passed a truck going in the opposite direction. She heard the rumbling of more oncoming trucks. Gail eased off the gas slightly, just enough for the van to be right on her tail.

"Gail!"

The van bumped the back of the truck.

"Come on! Step on it!"

Gail sped up and put some distance between the truck and the van. "Mike, I need you to do exactly as I tell you." She did not hear a response. "You hear me, Mike?"

"Yes!"

"Okay, I want you to pull the lock on your door and wait for my signal. When I tell you, I want you to kick the door wide open and then lean over to my side. You got that?"

"Got it. I think."

Once again Gail eased off the gas just enough

for the van to close in on them. The two vehicles negotiated the corner bumper to bumper. Gail slammed the gas pedal.

"Now!"

Mike kicked his door open as Gail swerved the vehicle in the direction of the oncoming truck. The truck ripped off Mike's door and it flew right onto the front windshield of the van behind them. The van spun out of control, crashed into the truck and exploded. She stopped the vehicle long enough for them to see the van go up in flames.

Mike sat back in his seat. "Nice going. Do you think those guys were working for Colson?"

"Your guess would be as good as mine," Gail replied, as she hit the gas and sped off.

"Where the hell did they come from? Were they waiting for us? How'd they know we'd be on that route?" Mike was speaking to himself out loud.

His questions were valid, but Gail was now focused on the immediate future.

It was late evening, but this was Washington State, and late evening in the summer was like midday. "Let's wait until there's at least some dusk cover before we approach Colson's property."

"We need to ditch the truck," Mike said. "I feel bad saying this but, we'll have to steal a vehicle."

Gail nodded in agreement. She swung into a small town and looked around, spotting a plaza with cars in the parking lot. "How about that?" Gail stopped the truck and Mike got out.

"Coming?" he asked.

"No, you go ahead. Once you have it, follow me."

Gail waited with the truck still running. As soon as Mike drove up beside the truck, she took off. She turned onto a dirt road then drove the truck into the bushes. She got out, took her duffle bag out and put it into the car. Mike scooted over to the passenger side. Once again, they were on their way to Colson.

The sun was no longer in the sky. She slowed down as she got closer to their destination. Gail pulled off the road and parked in an inconspicuous area. They waited for a thicker sheet of darkness to fall before they continued their journey to Colson.

Gail turned on what looked like a private road. There were no other buildings except for the one at the end of the road.

"Are you sure we're at the right place?" Mike asked.

"Based on the directions he gave me. This must be it."

"That's not a residential building. At least it

doesn't look like one," Mike said. "That's a, that's a...what the hell is that?"

Gail parked the car behind some trees. Driving any closer to the gate would announce their arrival. They got out of the car and proceeded on foot toward the wall.

"Those trees might help us get over the top," Gail said. "With those shrubs giving us cover to get over the wall, it's like an invitation."

There were a few trees with very large trunks on the property. Gail signaled Mike and they crouched behind one of the trees. She looked at the building, trying to figure out the best point of entry. Although there was no movement, Gail was almost sure that Colson would not be there alone. There was no way of knowing which section of the building Colson was in.

"Stay here," she told Mike.

The grounds were adequately lit, but there were a number of shadowed areas. Gail used that to her advantage as she inched her way closer and closer. She got to the building. With her back against the wall, she moved closer to the window. She tried to pick up any sound coming from inside. She heard movement outside. Mike came running and ducking in her direction.

"Darn it!"

He leaned on the wall beside her. "You hear anything?"

"Yeah. You. I thought we agreed that you'd stay put."

"We didn't actually agree. You said it, but I didn't agree. You think I'm going to let you walk in there by yourself?"

"If we're going to do this together, you've to learn to trust me."

"I'm just trying to protect you."

"I told you, he's not going to kill me on sight, but that doesn't mean he won't kill *you*. How're you going to protect me if you're dead?"

"All right. What's our next move?"

Gail looked around the compound. Listened for indication of any talking inside. The place was suspiciously quiet.

Gail tucked her gun back in her waistband.

"You mind filling me in?" Mike asked.

"Change of plans," she said. "I think they're expecting us to do exactly what we're planning to do. Let's do the unexpected."

Chapter 8

Gail and Mike moved away from the wall of the building. Gail led the way down the driveway on the property until they reached what looked like the main entrance. Through the double glass door, she saw lights in an area that was set up like the front office of a clinic. The writing on the entrance door caught her attention. "Miranda's Cancer Treatment Center."

"A cancer treatment center? I'd never guess that. Talk about expecting the unexpected," Mike said.

"According to the news report, Colson has prostate cancer. I think they took that into consideration when they granted him parole. Seems like he conveniently found a treatment center tucked away in a little corner of nowhere," she said, looking around.

"I wonder why he chose to come here instead of someplace more established." Mike walked to the entrance and held the door open for Gail.

The door closed behind them. The layout was very much like a clinic. There was a receptionist area that faced both the entrance and the seating area to the right of the entrance. To the left was an elevator. There were a number of offices on both sides. A passageway on the right, Gail presumed, led to the stairway.

Gail heard movement. Before she could tell Mike, they were surrounded by six armed men. "I'm here to see Colson," she said.

"We've been expecting you," one of the men replied, as he waved his hand, signaling the men to search them. The men took Gail and Mike's weapons and the syringe in Gail's pocket which was handed over to the guy who seemed to be in charge.

"What is this?" he asked as he walked up to Gail. She stared at the seven-foot, three hundred pound figure who hovered over her.

She held her head back so she could look him in the eyes. "Medicine," she said with a smirk.

The man placed his right hand on Gail's throat. His hand was so large his fingers could almost touch at the back of her neck.

Mike head-butted the guy directly in front of him on his nose. The guy's head whipped back as he groaned in pain. He then landed his right knuckles in the eye of the man on his left. A third guy connected the barrel of his gun to the side of Mike's head, halting his efforts to save her.

Gail closed her eyes. She felt a surge of energy flow through her body.

"I'm going to ask you one more time," the big guy said, tightening his grip. "If you don't start talking, I'll start squeezing."

"I wouldn't do that if I were you," came a new voice approaching them.

Gail knew that voice. She opened her eyes. Colson stood in front of her. The man released Gail.

"Hello, Colson! How's cancer treating you? Very well, I hope?" Gail said. His once tanned skin was two shades lighter and his very dark hair was outnumbered by grays.

Colson held out his hand to the big guy who handed him the syringe. "So, what do we have here?" he asked. "Potassium Chloride?"

"You'd need to have a heart for that to work," Gail retorted.

"Some other poison?" Colson continued seemingly unaffected by Gail's comment. "No, you're not that type of person, and besides, how could I help you find your husband if I'm dead. Oh, wait! I get it. Truth serum. I have to say, I'm very impressed and must admit that it will come in quite handy for what I have in mind."

"Are you sure you're up for this?" Gail asked. "I mean, given your depleted medical state, the Grim Reaper could be right around the corner. Tick Tock!"

"Bring her," he said to the big guy as he stormed away. "And her sidekick, too."

They shoved Gail and Mike into an examination room. They tied Mike to a chair, then held a gun to his head.

"Now let's establish some ground rules before we proceed," Colson said to Gail. "Any funny move on your part will result in very painful consequences for your friend over there. Do we understand each other?"

Gail nodded.

"Good. Now we're getting somewhere. I have a few questions that I need some answers to and what better way for us to rekindle this relationship than with honesty?"

"Ask me anything, but are you sure you want these guys to hear everything I have to say?" she asked. "Not to mention the fact that I have some questions of my own. Starting with this place. Why do you have a treatment center named after my mother?"

The men working for Colson looked at each other, then at him. She could see they were shocked by the revelation.

"Mr. Burdock, would you be kind enough to

administer this serum for me," Colson asked as he handed the syringe to the big guy.

"With pleasure." Burdock rammed the needle into Gail's thigh then fixed his eyes on her. She did not even flinch as she looked straight back.

Mike, on the other hand, sounded like he was in pain just watching.

"Tough as a nail. I see motherhood hasn't softened you up," Colson said.

"I see prison didn't rehabilitate you," she replied.

"Get it over with," Colson yelled. Burdock pressed down on the syringe and injected every drop of the Sodium Pentothal.

"Are you crazy? That was enough for two people," Mike yelled.

Gail listened as Colson ordered the other guys to leave the room. The big guy, Burdock, strapped her to the examination bed, but not without her putting up a fight. Then she lay back, completely relaxed with her eyes half-open. Burdock held her face with one hand as her head flopped to one side.

"Not so tough now, are you?" he said. "What should we do with the other fella?"

"Let him stay," Colson said. "Thank you, you may leave now. Close the door behind you."

"I cannot tell you how much it hurts me to have to do this to you," he said as he pulled up a chair next to Gail.

He asked her a number of questions about the FBI agent she spoke with prior to the raid at his home. She told him exactly what she told the agent seventeen years ago. He also wanted to know if she'd told the agent about her abilities. Then he got to the most difficult part, the explosion that killed his son Leon. Once again, she told him everything she knew.

Discussing his son brought something he rarely displayed, if ever. Emotions; there were no tears, but he was visibly shaken.

During the struggle with Burdock, Gail had forced her arms against the straps so they seemed tighter than they really were. This allowed her to squeeze her hands free. She needed to loosen the straps on her legs. Gail made eye contact with Mike, then moved her eyes to Colson and back to Mike. He starting mumbling incoherent words which got the attention of Colson.

"Will you shut up?"

"Water. Can I have some water?" Mike asked.

Colson went over to him. "Water? What do you think this is? The Holiday Inn? Why don't you just ask for some orange juice while you're at it?"

It was enough distraction for Gail to release the straps from her legs. She shoved Colson onto the bed and pinned him with her right leg. "Scream and it'll be the last sound you make."

She reached down into the boot that was resting on him and pulled out a syringe.

"The serum was fake?" he asked, looking quite perplexed.

"Oh, it was real, all right. It just had no effect on me whatsoever," Gail said. "Now, what do you say we start this game over? I will ask some questions and you will answer them."

She stuck the syringe in his neck. "Truthfully," she said, as she pressed the plunger of the syringe and watched the serum level lower in the barrel.

"Don't!" Mike said. "Don't give him all of it. There's enough—"

"For two people. I know," Gail said. She pulled a knife out of her left boot and used it to cut Mike free. Mike wasted no time in grabbing a gun and turning the lock on the door. Gail turned her attention back to Colson.

"Your questions need to be specific. We only have a few minutes before the effects of the medication wears off so you better get started," Mike said as he moved closer to Gail.

"Where is Brian?"

"I don't know."

"Did you have him kidnapped?"

"No."

"Did you have him killed?"

"No."

"Do you know who kidnapped him?"

"No."

"Why are you here?"

"So the government thinks I'm being treated for cancer."

"Thinks? What does he mean?" Mike asked.

Gail continued her questioning. "Why do you want the government to think you have cancer?"

"Then they will leave me alone."

"This certainly begs another question, doesn't it?" Mike said.

"Do you have cancer?"

"No."

"Son of a bitch!" Mike blurted.

"Why did you come to Washington State?" Gail continued

"The treatment center is here."

"Who built this center?"

"I did."

"Why did you build this center?"

"In memory of someone very special to me."

"How are we doing on time? Do you think it's still working?" Gail asked Mike.

"Yeah," Mike said as he looked at his watch. "But you have to wrap it up soon. In fact, I think we should try to make a break for it now, while he's still under."

"I have a few more questions," Gail said as she once again turned to Colson. "Why are you trying to kill me?"

"I am not trying to kill you."

"Why are you coming after me?"

"To protect you."

Mike waved the gun. "By my watch you should have a little more time, but I think it must've worn off because now he's feeding you crap."

Gail held his chin, moved it side to side trying to assess if he was still sedated. She decided to squeeze in a few more questions. "Why would you want to protect me?"

"I promised your mother. I promised your mother I would do everything I could to protect you."

"Protect me from who? From what?"

Someone banged on the door. "Mr. Colson! Everything all right in there?" a man from the outside the door asked. Gail recognized Burdock, the big guy.

"I think the jig is up," Mike said as he grabbed another gun that had been left in the room.

"How are we on time?" Gail asked as she placed two fingers on Colson's wrist to check his pulse.

"He should be out by now, but I wouldn't worry about him. Instead, worry about getting out of here in one piece. Help me block the door. It will buy us a little time, enough to get through that window."

"What makes you think they don't have men outside?" Gail asked. She gently slapped Colson's face. "Come on! Snap out of it!"

Burdock kept banging on the door.

"Mr. Colson?"

"Just a minute," Colson said in a weak voice.

Burdock continued to bang on the door.

"Say it again," Gail told Colson.

"We're coming in!" Burdock yelled.

"Just a goddamn minute!" Colson roared.

"Sorry, sir," Burdock replied.

"And he's back," Mike said. "How are you feeling?"

"Just peachy!" Colson muttered sarcastically.

Gail helped Colson to his feet and walked him to the door, then placed his hand on the doorknob. Mike still had the gun aimed at Colson. Gail stepped back to Mike and gently lowered it.

"Stand down," Colson shouted. "We're coming out."

There was a flurry of guns rattling.

Colson opened the door and stepped out. "These two people are my guests and they should be treated as such. Anyone so much as causes her eyelash to hurt will suffer dire consequences."

"What about me? What will happen if they hurt me?" Mike asked.

"I'm sure I'll think of something," Colson said. "You're both welcome to stay the night. As a matter of fact, I insist." He turned and looked at Gail. "I had a room prepared for you."

"We can't stay. My husband is still missing and I need to—"

"You need to eat and rest. I told you I had a hunch about who might be involved. I have people following up on that. I can help you, Gail, if you let me."

Gail looked at Mike.

"He can stay, too, if that's what you're worried about." Colson brushed Gail's hair from her face. "I have so much to tell you."

"About my mother?" she asked.

"Yes, and about you. Don't you ever wonder how it is that you are able to do things better than the average person? Even heal without a scar? Although your reaction, or more precisely lack of reaction, to the sedative was a surprise."

Gail moved her face away from his hand and

headed towards the exit.

"Stay. It will give us some time to talk," Colson said.

She stopped. With no idea where else to look for Brian she was back at square one. Maybe she should stick around and find out what Colson knew.

Once again, Gail looked over at Mike. He shrugged his shoulders.

"All right, we'll stay," she said to Colson.

"Come, let's get something to eat. I'm starving," Colson said.

"You look it," Mike blurted out. "I mean you look really, really thin. Which begs the question, if you don't have cancer, why do you look so…emaciated?"

Gail was silent. She wondered the same thing.

"If you must know," Colson said, "I was taking a weight loss drug. I had to look the part. Fake test results alone would not cut it. I had to look like I was actually wasting away."

"I guess that explains it," Gail said.

"Now come." Colson ushered them to the elevator. They rode to the third floor of the building, which looked nothing like a clinic or a treatment center, but more like a hotel. Gail and Mike followed him into a dining area. The smell of food engulfed her.

"I didn't realize how hungry I was," Mike said, echoing her inward thought.

"Where's the bathroom?" Gail asked. "I'd like to freshen up a bit."

Before Colson could answer, she was already to the door. Mike followed.

"There are bathrooms in here, but if you prefer you could turn left, follow the corridor. The last room on the right is your room. It's unlocked. You may go in," Colson said.

As they walked in the direction Colson told them, Gail glanced behind her a few times to see if they were being watched.

She tested each door she passed.

"I'm not even going to ask," Mike said. He started checking doors on the opposite side. "They're all locked."

"For now," Gail said, as she headed into the room that was prepared for her. After cleaning herself up, Gail told Mike she would wait for him while he used the bathroom. She waited in the room for less than a minute before she stepped out to the hallway. Gail noticed another door off to the corner on the opposite side of her room. The door was different from the others. She glanced in the direction of the dining room then checked the lock. It opened. Gail went inside and looked around. There were no beds in this room. It was set up as an office. Mike was not too far behind.

"Gail," Mike whispered.

"In here," she said as she looked around the room. "Don't," she said, as he reached for the light switch.

Mike came in and closed the door behind him. "It's really dark in here. I can't see a damn thing."

"I can."

"You're kidding, right?"

Gail did not respond.

"Okay, what's in here?" he asked.

"It looks like an office, with a familiar face on the wall."

She turned on the flashlight on her phone and handed it to him. There were photographs of a woman on the wall.

"This must be his late wife," Mike said as he shone the light on one of the portraits.

"That's my mother."

"Why does Colson have portraits of your mother in here," Mike said as he moved the light from one portrait to the next. "Did you have a sister?" he asked.

"No, why?"

"Well, if this is your mother, then that must be you." Mike shined the light on a picture of her mother and her when she was very young. "What was—"

"Shh! Footsteps."

Chapter 9

Gail listened as the footsteps came closer and closer.

She took the phone from Mike and turned off the flashlight. "Under there!" she said, pointing to the huge desk in the room. Mike ducked behind the desk and tried to pull Gail to hide in the same spot. Gail yanked away and sat against the wall next to the door. She put the phone to her hears and started talking loud in a tearful voice.

"I'm sorry, baby, I promise I will find your daddy soon." The sound of the footsteps were at the door of her room across the hall.

Sniffle, sniffle, sniffle. "I miss him too," she said with amplified volume. The footsteps moved to the door of the room Gail and Mike were in. "I love you so much." She sniffled so loudly it hurt.

The door opened. Burdock turned on the light. "What are you doing in here?"

She looked up at him with tears in her eyes. "I needed some privacy to talk to my son."

Sniffle, sniffle. She clutched the phone to her stomach as if to prevent her son from hearing her conversation with Burdock.

"I'm sorry, ma'am. Please, finish your call. I'll tell Mr. Colson you'll be there shortly," he said. Just as he was about to close the door, he stuck his head back inside. "Where is your friend?"

"He's using the toilet. Something in that lasagna he had earlier didn't agree with his stomach."

Burdock made a face and left the room. Gail listened as his footsteps faded. She peered outside to make sure the coast was clear. "Let's go!" she whispered.

Mike got out from under the desk, and just before he passed her, he put his face really close to hers. "Oh, you're good. You're very good. Who knew you had such talent?" he said as he wiped away the tears from her cheeks.

"Just shut it!"

Gail and Mike joined Colson in his dining area. "Feeling better, Mr. Steele?" Colson asked Mike.

"You know my name?" Mike asked.

"I know who you are."

"Yes. Much better thank you," Mike said as he approached the table. He pulled out a chair for Gail to sit, then sat next to her. They looked at the food on the table, then at each other as if neither of them wanted to start eating first. The aroma of roasted garlic with a hint of coconut tickled Gail's nose.

"Well, don't be shy. Dig in!" Colson said. "The food is not exactly five-star, but it's palatable. It's hard to find people I trust who can also cook. I chose to go with people I trust, though they may not be the greatest chefs. Nevertheless, I had them fix the coconut shrimp you liked so much. I think it was also one of your mother's favorites."

She was touched he actually remembered after all those years. "I'll start with the coconut shrimp then," Gail said as she served herself. It looked the same, and smelled just as good as it did when she was a child.

"Hmm, not bad." But it was a little too salty for her liking. She cleared her throat and took a sip of juice.

"You never really were a good liar," Colson said.

"Oh really?" Mike asked with a sarcastic tone.

Gail stomped on his foot closest to her. Mike groaned.

"You all right, Mr. Steele?" Colson asked.

"Just my stomach acting up a bit, but I'll be fine."

Looking around the room, Gail asked, "When did you build this place? Because it looks like it's been here for a while."

Colson wiped his mouth with his napkin. "This place was built to care for your mother. Unfortunately she died before it was completed."

To Gail he looked as broken as he did the day her mother had died. She was surprised by Colson's sudden solemn mood.

Apparently, Mike was just as astonished. "So, you too were very close? You and Gail's mother?"

"Miranda and I were friends before we met our respective spouses."

"Kind of like me and Gail?" Mike asked.

Colson nodded.

"Why do you have a shrine of her?" Gail asked.

"What shrine?" Colson furrowed his brows.

"The little room at the end of the passage that—"

"It's not a shrine," Colson said with a raised voice. "The room I had prepared for you was the room she would have stayed in, if..." he lowered his voice. "That room was supposed to be her office. A place she could get some work done if she felt up to it."

"She was very ill. What could she possibly be

working on that is so important?" Gail asked.

"Your mother was not just a doctor. She was a researcher and she liked to stay busy."

"A doctor?" Mike asked as he glanced at Gail.

"Miranda was a fertility doctor," Colson answered, "and she was very helpful to my wife and me when we were trying to have a child. What's ironic was, she had a world of trouble when she wanted a child for herself."

"What kind of trouble?" Gail asked.

"I'm not quite sure, but I know the babies died soon after birth. After losing her first child to a rare blood disease, she worked tirelessly to find a cure for the disease that took her baby from her. Finally, after years of hard work, she had a cure but hoped that her second baby would not need it. She and your father once again procreated, and once again the baby had the same rare blood disorder. The baby was treated with the newly developed drug. Her hard work had paid off. The blood disorder was corrected. Then a few weeks later, the baby developed complications and died."

Colson told them Gail's father had not wanted Miranda to go through the pain of losing another baby, so he told her he no longer wanted a child. Miranda decided she would try one last time. However, this time the baby was created by in vitro fertilization. The drug she created was injected in the embryo before it was placed in her womb. That baby was her miracle child.

Gail froze as she hung on every word that came out of Colson's mouth. She didn't move a muscle in fear she might miss something. Mike placed his hand on hers and gently squeezed it. She tried to appear unaffected by what she just heard, but found herself looking away, instead of into his eyes.

The story session was not over. Colson told how the company that Miranda worked for never saw too much promise in this new drug since they had never seen or heard of anyone with such a blood anomaly. However, as the little girl grew, Miranda took her to the office from time to time. It didn't take long before a number of people at her office learned about the little girl's unique abilities.

"Her employer was suddenly interested in that new drug. They saw an opportunity to charge couples millions of dollars to create geniuses. Miranda had a falling out with her employer when she learned they were testing the drugs on the embryos of their regular clients without consent," Colson continued.

"What happened to all those other children? Did they all...you know, turn out like me?"

"Sadly, no. None of them survived. According to your mother they all died of cancer after a few years. At first they thought the drug had no effect since the children did not have any of their abilities magnified. Your mother threatened to expose them. They admitted they made a mistake and gave her their word that there would be no further testing."

"Did they? Stop testing?" Gail asked.

"I don't know. Your mother resigned and only had two weeks left in the company when your father died, and...you know the rest. What I do know is that your mother was scared to death for you. She asked me not to let anyone know what you can do, so that's why I hired Ms. Hemmingway as your teacher, since she already knew."

"Hemmingway, the woman who was killed?" Mike asked.

"Yes, but *I* didn't kill her."

Gail sat back in her chair and eyeballed Colson. He looked up and caught her stare. "I lied about her being on vacation, but that was only to protect you. I wanted you to have a normal life. Well, as normal as possible, but my main priority was to keep you safe."

"Safe from what? From whom?" She paused for a second. "Wait a minute, did my mother think her employer would want to hurt me?"

"All I can tell you is what I think. I think they are very clever in getting rid of people who they consider to be a threat. Case in point, they got rid of Hemmingway and set me up all in one swoop."

"Why would they want to frame you?" Mike asked. "Her mother, I could understand, but why you?"

"I was Gail's legal guardian, plus, after Miranda became ill, I was suspicious and I started looking into the company she worked for."

"And?" Gail asked.

"They disappeared. They shut down the operation and that was that."

"How does my husband fit into this equation?"

"I think it's a way to get to you. All these years, they probably thought you were dead, but that video of your son must have launched them into action."

"You know about the video?"

"What video?" Mike asked.

"Yes, and I was in prison with less resources. Imagine what *they* know."

"Will somebody *please* tell me what video?" Mike shouted.

Colson gestured to Gail for her to tell him.

"Alex can remember things too," she said.

"You mean, like you?"

"Yes, sort of."

Colson got up from the table. "This might have nothing to do with the company at all. It may be that your husband got caught up in something he shouldn't, or someone might be after information that you have locked away in that head of yours."

Gail recalled the discussion she had with Mike earlier about Colson keeping her alive until he got the information he needed. "Interesting theory," she said as she glanced over at Mike. "What information do I have that would be worth kidnapping someone to get it?"

"Well, the easiest one is money," Colson said. "And I'm not talking about the money you have in your regular bank accounts. You have offshore account numbers and passcodes with access to millions of dollars."

"How did I get all this information?"

"I gave those codes to you. That in itself is a huge motive. I suspect that may be the reason your husband was kidnapped. You give them the codes, you get your husband back. Something like that."

Mike edged closer the Gail. "Millions! That's a lot of money and definitely a lot of motive. Where did you get all this money? Real estate? Oil? Stock market? Or...?"

"I was never involved in drugs or anything illegal," Colson said. "I know that's what they told you about be, but it's not true."

Gail stood. "Good. Then why don't you tell me where all that money came from."

"Smart investment," Colson said. "I invested in a lot of things, including the stock market, but I was smart enough to get out before everything crashed."

"Where did you get the money to start investing, and please don't lie to me. My husband's life, and quite possibly mine, is at risk."

"Sit down," Colson told Gail. "I was a CIA black ops, meaning I did the work no one else wanted to do. After leaving the CIA, I worked a few private contracts. The pay was excellent but...things changed. I gave up that life. I started a new life, with new business ventures and invested wisely in stocks, real estate, etcetera, etcetera."

"There's more than money, isn't there? In my head?" she asked Colson.

"Yes. Yes there is, but I believe that the money is what the kidnappers are after."

"You really believe that?" she asked.

"I do. That's why I have arranged a meeting with someone to help us decipher what, or more specifically, how much the kidnappers might be after. The accounts, for the record, were not all mine. Some of them were your parents'."

"If they want money, how come they haven't contacted me?"

"Getting the money from you is a whole different process than having the money dropped off in a duffle bag," Colson told her. "They're not going to call until they figure out how to get the information they need from you."

Burdock came in and beckoned to Colson.

"I'll be right with you, Mr. Burdock." Colson turned to Gail and Mike. "Excuse me for a second." He left the room to speak with Burdock.

Mike gestured to Gail that she should try to listen in on the conversation. She could hear Burdock whispering to Colson as they headed to the elevator.

"We found the guy who snatched him."

She listened as Burdock told Colson the guy's last known location. "We have to get out of here," she whispered to Mike. As soon as she heard the elevator close, she headed out of the room.

"We're going now?" Mike asked, trying to keep up with her. "What did he say? Did they find him?"

She reached to the stairs. "They found the kidnapper. Act normal. If they ask, we're going to the car for something."

"Who is he?"

"I don't know. Daniel something. Try to grab a few guns," she said as they entered the first floor. There was no one around. They wasted no time to grab their guns and were out the door.

"Remind me again why we're sneaking out instead of letting Colson help us?" Mike asked.

"I want us to get there before them. Colson and I have different agendas. He may be more interested in protecting his money. I'm only interested in getting Brian back alive."

"I'll drive," Gail said as they got to the stolen car. She punched the address into the GPS.

"Let me drive," Mike said. "I know a shortcut that could get us to the address in under half hour."

Before long they were at the location, a dilapidated bungalow on a large lot.

"How are we going to do this?" Mike asked. "We can't just walk to the front door and ring the doorbell, if there *is* a doorbell."

"Ordinarily I would agree with you, but I'm fresh out of ideas and time is not exactly on our side. We need to get in there before Colson's guys get here."

Mike looked unsure. Gail got out of the car, walked across the street and then onto the property. There were no lights outside, but inside she could see a glimmer. She pulled out her gun and slowly approached the door. Just then, she heard Mike coming. She waited for him to get to the door. Gail was about to knock when she noticed the door was ajar. She pushed the door open and went inside.

A metallic scent hit Gail as soon as she entered the house. Trying to tread as lightly as she could on the creaky floor, she and Mike followed the light that led to a room in the back. A man, Gail presume to be Daniel, was sitting in a lounge chair that faced a window. The source of light was a lamp that was on a table to his right. They walked into the room, pointing their weapons at Daniel. The metallic smell Gail encountered as she entered the house was very strong in this room. She went to the left, Mike to his right. They expected Daniel to spring into action anytime.

As she rounded to the front, Gail noticed that Daniel's head hung so his chin rested on his chest. Her gaze wandered down. A massive amount of blood on the front of his shirt appeared to have drained from his neck and pooled on the chair between his legs.

Daniel was out of action for good.

Chapter 10

"Shit!" Mike blurted.

Gail raised her index finger to her lips. She signaled for them to check the other rooms. A quick search turned up nothing, and even Gail's superior hearing picked up only skittering mice.

They went back in the room where they'd found Daniel. They were searching the place when Gail heard a vehicle approaching. She paused.

"What is it?" Mike asked.

"Grab those phones and kill the light."

Gail eased the raggedy curtain back just enough for her to peer through the window. Two men exited an SUV and were headed towards the house.

She moved quickly to the door. "We need to go."

Mike bumped into the table the lamp was on, making it teeter. Gail hurriedly grabbed his arm and moved to the back door.

Trash cans were at the back of the house. Gail retrieved a bag from the recycle bin.

"Are you serious?" Mike whispered.

"Shh. They're in there, going from room to room." She cocked her head. "Now they're coming this way. Left, left." Gail and Mike exited the property and made their way to the car with the garbage bag.

"Where to?" Mike asked as he drove off.

"I don't know, but I'm not going back to Colson's place tonight."

"I didn't think you would. I know a place we could stay."

"Good. I'll work with that."

On their way, he swapped out the stolen car for another.

"You okay?" Mike asked.

Gail stared out the window, not looking at anything in particular. "I don't know. The kidnapper is dead. What does that mean for Brian?"

"He won't be of any use to them if they kill him. Don't worry, If Colson's theory is right, they need him alive. Who killed Daniel and why is up for debate. Maybe his own people killed him."

"Well, that's comforting," Gail said. "Brian is being held by people who slit the throat of one of their own. Gee, I feel better already."

"I know this is still not comforting news, but I think someone he knew killed him. If it was someone he was in league with, that could mean there's trouble in their camp."

"How do you know he knew his killer?'

"Let me ask you this. Do you think someone could have snuck up behind him in that room and slashed his throat before he had a chance to aim his gun or get out of that chair?"

"He would have heard them coming. The flooring is very old and very creaky."

"Exactly," Mike said. "It had to be someone he trusted. There were two beer bottles on the table next to him. Whoever was there had a drink with him before they retired him."

"Why would they want to kill him?"

"It could be any of a million reasons. Money, for example. Maybe he got greedy, or maybe they decided they don't need him anymore and for them he was just a loose end. Either way, it's one less bad guy to worry about."

"Given the circumstances, there is really no consolation in that."

"I know," Mike said as he parked the car in front of an inn. "I'm going to get us a room. You coming?"

"No, I want to give Celia a call and see how Alex is doing."

"Say hi to the little guy for me, will you?"

"Of course."

Mike set off to get them a room. Gail

completed her call with Celia, but still had the phone in her hand when Mike returned.

"Are you still on the call?"

"No, I'm done," Gail said. She got out of the car, opened the back door and grabbed the bag she pulled from Daniel's trash.

"I'll take that," he said as he took it from Gail. "I was kind of hoping you weren't finished with the call so I could say hi to Alex."

"You can talk to him tomorrow. Would it make you feel better to know he asked for you?"

Mike appeared pleased. "This way," he said, as he pointed in the direction of their room on the bottom floor.

"Apparently he's looking forward to a painting session with you. He's also looking forward to his mom and dad joining him on vacation."

Mike unlocked the door. As soon as they were inside he dropped the bag and pulled her to him. "We're going to find him," he whispered. She buried her face in his chest as he comforted her.

"I'm here," he said. "It's going to be okay."

She would have let him hold her forever if he wanted to, but she knew they had a lot of work to do.

They dumped the contents of the bag Gail grabbed from Daniel's house on the floor. Some of the papers were shredded. Gail was looking through them while Mike went through his phones.

"There was no electricity at that house," Gail said. "And I don't recall seeing a shredder there, but it was dark so I could've missed it."

"You wouldn't. You see better in the dark than most people and you're right, there was no electricity there."

"Which means this was shredded someplace else and dumped there. He had shredder troubles."

"What?" Mike asked as he scrolled through one of the discarded phones.

She held up a few pages of half-shredded paper. "The shredder jammed. This will make it a little easier for me to fit the pieces together." As she sorted, she came across a set that was not shredded. They appeared to be torn by hand. She started laying the pieces out on the floor in an attempt to recreate the destroyed documents. "Have you found anything useful on the phones?"

"I'm still going through the first phone. There're a lot of numbers and pictures on this phone. Hmm, I think he had a family. There's a picture of him with a woman and a little girl, maybe his wife and daughter," Mike said as he held the phone so Gail could see.

She looked at the photograph for a few seconds. "Yeah, and that's definitely not the house we just came from."

"Which means he probably didn't live at the house we found him. That was his meeting place."

"I guess it makes sense. He wouldn't want his colleagues showing up at his home." Still lining up the pieces of paper together, she said, "These look like print outs of photographs."

"Photographs of what?"

"I'll let you know when I find out. What about his other phone. What's on that? I'll bet you a dollar that's his work phone."

Mike laughed out loud. "Really? A dollar? What are we, in elementary school? Next time try to bet something that I'd actually like to win."

"Like what?"

"Nothing. You may be right about the phone. There're no stored numbers in the phone. There're incoming and outgoing calls between this phone and three numbers."

"When was the last call?"

"It was incoming, received about three hours ago. You might want to look at these numbers," Mike said as he handed her the phone.

She made a mental note of the numbers and handed the phone back to Mike. As he reached out to take the phone, they made eye contact. Mike held on to the phone. She could tell there was something he wanted to say.

"You want to tell me what's on your mind?" Gail asked.

"I keep thinking about what you did at Colson's place."

Gail released the phone. She was not sure what specifically he was talking about but since she'd asked, she had no choice but to listen. For a moment she wondered if he was referring to her fake cry.

"You know, when you baited Burdock and Colson so you could stick it to Colson. That was smart, but a hell of a gamble. Don't take this the wrong way, but please don't do that again. I almost ruptured a blood vessel worrying about you. Promise me you won't put yourself in that kind of danger again?"

That was not what she expected but it made her happy, if there was such a thing in their situation. "Okay." She looked at him and smiled. It was more than just a smile; it was her way of telling him "thank you for caring about me." Despite all hell breaking loose in her life, the one constant rock was Mike. He was always there, always caring. She realized that feeling a person got when someone not just said, but showed, how much he cared. It never grew old.

"That's a yes. Right?" he asked as he sat next to her on the floor.

She nodded.

"Good. Because you know I would die if anything happened to you." He kissed her forehead. "You can talk to me, remember that. Colson unloaded a lot on you earlier. You don't have to talk about it if you don't want to, and I understand if you don't. But if you do... What I'm trying to say is, you can talk to me."

"I know," she said. "I'm still processing it. Learning that I'm the product of an experiment is a little hard to swallow." How would this information change her marriage? Would Brian feel the same way about her, and about their son, once he learned the truth?

Still aligning the pieces of paper, she paused. "Why go through all of that? There were other options. She worked in a fertility clinic, for Christ's sake. I'm sure there were donor embryos she could have gotten that did not have whatever disease it is she thought she cured me of."

"I guess she wanted her own child. You know, one that bore her DNA. I don't think there's anything wrong with wanting that, or doing all that you can to get it."

Gail understood that feeling oh so well. The miracle of feeling that little baby growing inside her. Would she have done the same thing? "No, nothing wrong with that. Except in her case what she used to save one child, killed many others. What about those other mothers who lost their babies because of a drug she developed to save her own? She could have adopted."

As a mother Gail understood the miracle of giving birth, but she also understood that the real work of a mother begins after the baby is born. She didn't need to give birth to be a mother. She couldn't help but wonder if her mother felt pressured by society's expectations. "I wouldn't have loved Alex any less if he wasn't my biological child," she said.

"You're right, but hurting people wasn't her intension. I'm sure you know that and that's simply the pain talking. As for you being the product of an experiment — when I look at you I see perfection, so she must've done something right."

Gail frowned at him.

"What? You're perfection in my eyes and I'm sure your mother felt the same way."

"'Perfection in my eyes?'" Gail shook her head and chuckled. "You must be really tired, because you're starting to talk rubbish. Perfection in my eyes," she repeated mockingly.

Mike reached inside her handbag for her tablet. He used her cell phone to create a hotspot so he could connect to the Internet with the tablet and avoid being tracked on the hotel WiFi. "Well, if nothing else, it made you laugh, so that's good."

"It certainly did." Her mother had worked a lot, sometimes really long hours, but somehow Gail had never felt neglected. She'd known she was loved. "She was a hugger, like you. She hugged me every opportunity she got. I think I may have passed that on to Alex," she said. "What are we doing about those numbers?"

"I'm running a reverse lookup as we speak, but I don't expect to find anything. They have a separate phone for work. There's no way these numbers are going to be listed. We need help."

Gail knew exactly what he was saying but she wasn't sure she trusted Colson yet.

"Why don't you take over the paper work and I'll take the tablet," she said as she rose to her feet. While she was no specialist at hacking, she was not the typical tech user, either. She'd grown up with a father who was a tech guru. She was prepared to ask Colson for help if she had to. Only *if* she had to. She typed away on the tablet, then paused, as she recalled they had stolen two cars in one day. The downtown of the city was only a block from where they were staying. "We should rent a car tomorrow and leave this car someplace other than here."

Mike agreed. He continued talking, but she did not look up from the screen. It was almost as if she tuned out of the conversation, until she heard Mike say "Brian!"

She thought for sure she was hearing things, but then she looked down at the scraps of paper he'd been assembling on the floor. It was definitely Brian. As it turned out, there were many pictures of her husband taken in different places... from his office to the tennis court.

A few of the pictures were more disturbing to Gail because they seemed to capture him with a woman who she did not recognize. There were more than one shot of him with that woman. Mike snapped some pictures of what they pieced together.

"Do you recognize her?" she asked.

"No, I don't recall seeing her before."

"Who is she? Is he really missing or just don't want to be found?"

"Don't do this," Mike said and squeezed her hands. "Let's focus on finding him and then you can trash out whatever issues the two of you have. I won't tell you that you don't have any reason to feel the way you do. I'd be lying if I did, but the person identified as his kidnapper is dead. That means infidelity is the least of your worries right now."

Gail had no intensions of giving up on

finding Brian; if not for her sake, then for Alex. "Right. He's Alex's father, and Alex needs a father." She blinked away the anger and fear, and returned to her tablet and resumed working. Thinking about her sinking marriage could come later. The phone numbers from the kidnapper's work phone were listed to a security company. So far she was not able to tell the names that were assigned to each number. While she researched the company, Mike decided he would run out and get them something to drink. She was happy to be by herself for a few minutes.

She stared at the shots of her husband and the mystery woman. There were other papers to piece together. It would not surprise her if it was more of the same. There was no doubt in her mind that those pictures told a story. A story that quite possibly included the phone call her husband took in the bathroom. The one that left him rattled and defensive. Could it be that his disappearance had nothing to do with her past after all?

Maybe he was being blackmailed, but by whom? Then again, no one kidnapped the person he was blackmailing. She felt a little out of it. Not tired, but could certainly do with a pick-me-up. She got up and went to the bathroom and splashed some cold water on her face. That was exactly what she needed. As she dried her face she heard the door open. Mike was back.

Wait, the Mike she knew would call her name the moment he walked in the room and did not see her. She knew right away the person who entered the room was not Mike.

She looked around the bathroom for anything she could use as a weapon. There was nothing. When she peeked around the corner, a man pointed a gun and fired a shot at her. She pulled back and got on the floor. Her heart began to race. It was beating so loud she could hear nothing else. Then…calm. She was calm. Her handbag was on the bed. She heard the intruder close the door. She leaped from inside the bathroom right onto the bed, grabbing the gun from the bag as she flipped over. The man took aim. She kicked the gun out of his hand and fired several shots at him. He fired back from a second gun. Gail spun at the punch to her left shoulder, and when the door opened again she dropped and aimed.

Chapter 11

"How'd you find me?" she asked Colson. Although Gail still did not trust Colson, she was thankful he showed up after her encounter with the man who tried to kill her.

"I had Burdock place a small tracking device on your jacket collar earlier, while you were at the center."

The attacker was on the floor in a pool of blood. Gail checked his pulse; he was dead.

Colson had his men search the dead man for anything they could find that would give them some idea of who he was, and maybe who he was working for. "You should put some pressure on that," he said to Gail.

Gail had been shot in the left shoulder. "Where's Mike?" she asked as she headed towards the door.

"He's fine," Colson said. He tried to prevent Gail from leaving the room. "Don't go out there yet. Sit. Mike is going to be fine."

"You just told me he was fine. How does he

go from fine to 'going to be fine'? So he's not fine now? Is he hurt?"

Colson gently coaxed her to sit on the bed. "It appears he was knocked out by the fella on the floor. Unfortunately my guy did not fare as well. He's dead."

"Your guy? You had one of your guys watching me?"

"Yes. He followed you and Mike from the center. I believe this man here followed the three of you from the house of the dead kidnapper."

"I guess it's fair to say he was most likely responsible for putting the kidnapper in the state we found him. He must've kept a reasonable distance between us because we didn't notice we were being followed."

"I suspect he took out my guy, then waited outside in the car because he didn't know what room you were in."

"When Mike went out—"

"He knocked him out and came after you."

"Gail!" Mike called as he came running through the door. "Thank goodness you guys were here," he said to Colson.

Gail and Colson looked at each other as they realized Mike didn't know what happened.

He came to hug her and did a double take when he noticed the blood on her clothes. Without saying another word, Mike got up and went to the bathroom. He came back with a clean towel to apply pressure to the wound. "Let me see," he said as he gently eased off her jacket. He went white when he saw the wound. Gail knew the bullet had gone straight through. She looked down anyway and saw she was no longer bleeding. Most of the wound was replaced by new skin.

"That's impossible!" Mike breathed out.

"Don't worry, Mr. Steele, she's tougher than you think," Colson said as he patted Mike on the shoulder.

Mike turned to Colson. "You knew?"

Colson nodded.

"How did you find us, anyway?"

Gail used her hand to turn his face away from Colson and back to her. "I'll explain it to you later, okay?" She knew they both did not trust Colson, but she needed him. She had no doubt Colson had access to the software she needed to find the names behind these numbers. "How's your head?" she asked pointing to the swelling on his forehead.

"It's fine," Mike responded. "You did that?" he asked, referring to the dead guy lying on the floor.

She nodded.

"You have to get her out of here fast," Mike said. "Once the police get here, I'll tell them I killed him in self-defense." He picked up the gun from off the bed, wiped it down and then positioned his fingers as if he was going to pull the trigger.

"How noble of you," Colson said. "But that won't be necessary. We already have a volunteer and he won't be able to stand trial." Colson's men were already at work creating a set-up for the police to find two dead guys in the room. They would make it appear the two had fatally shot each other.

Gail got up and went inside the bathroom to clean some of the blood off her. She heard Mike and Colson talking.

"How long have you been in love with her?" Colson asked Mike.

"What?"

"Please, Mr. Steele."

"Mike. Call me Mike."

"Mike, I'm old, not blind. Quite frankly, a blind man on a galloping horse could see how much you—"

Mike cleared his throat as Gail emerged from the bathroom.

"Are we ready to go?" she asked, pretending she had not heard a word of their conversation.

Mike came up to her to check on her shoulder.

"It's fine," she told him. Still, he wanted to

see for himself. He unbuttoned her blouse just enough to reveal her shoulder.

"It's gone!" Mike gasped.

"I told you. It's fine."

Mike ran his fingers gently across the area of her shoulder that had been wounded. "What do you feel?" he asked.

"I feel you touching me. Just kidding. No, there's no pain."

Burdock came into the room to let them know they were ready to leave. Two of Colson's guys stayed behind to stage the scene. As they walked to the vehicle Mike asked about the car he and Gail had stolen. Colson told them he'd arranged to have it left in the same vicinity from which they snatched it. "I certainly can't have the police coming to my property for a stolen vehicle now, can I?" Colson said to Mike.

"Thanks, Mr. Colson."

"Nick. You can call me Nick."

Gail scoffed at the exchange between the two men. "Well, you two seem to be mighty chummy all of a sudden."

"I guess you could say Mike and I have a lot in common. Isn't that right, Mike?"

"I guess you could say that."

They got into the vehicle. Gail sat between Colson and Mike. "I'd like to swing by my house to pick up a few things," Gail said.

Mike looked at Colson.

"I don't think that's such a good idea," Mike said. "Someone just tried to kill you and who knows if they don't have someone watching your house."

It made sense to her. What was she thinking? A change of clothes would be nice, though.

"I guess your theory is a little off," she said to Colson. "If they wanted money or information or both from me as you suggested, it'd make sense they would want me alive. Don't you think? Now I'm even more confused than ever before. Did you find out anything about the guy who got his throat slashed?"

Colson straightened his jacket and cleared his throat. "Are you implying that my people are hacking into government—"

"Don't bullshit me! Cause I really don't have time for it. I don't really care how you find the information. I want to know if you have something. Now, do you have information on the kidnapper or not?"

"Easy, Gail," Mike said.

"Don't worry, Mike, she's more dangerous when she's quiet," Colson said with a smirk. "Yes, I did find out that the recently deceased kidnapper was an ex-mercenary. Most likely the one you met at the inn probably has a similar resume."

It was no longer just a mission to find her husband, she also had to elude professional killers who'd been sent after her. Colson told Mike earlier that Gail was tougher than he thought and he was right.

Gail first learned to fight by watching tons of videos on the Internet and practicing. She persuaded her mother to enroll her in a kickboxing class. That was short-lived as the parents of the other kids complained about injuries their children sustained while sparring with Gail. After completing high school early, Gail told Colson she wanted to join the marines. He signed her up to train in a boot camp. She aced the training. Colson asked her if she was interested in joining the CIA instead and that she could decide after the additional training he'd arranged for her. Gail was ready to say yes, but Colson changed his mind. He never said why.

She rested her head on the back of the seat and looked over at Colson to her right. His cheeks were sunken. His face was like skin over bone. Time had really taken a toll on him, or maybe that's exactly what he wanted everyone to believe.

Still, she thought Mike was right. Colson had been good to her so far and she hoped that didn't change. If it did, she might have to kill him. But could she? He meant a lot more to her than she cared to admit. She'd bonded with him after her parents died, like a daughter to a father.

Colson caught her staring at him. "There's a better view to your left," he said.

"Why didn't you let me sign up with the CIA?" she asked, still staring at him.

"What?"

"You told me I'd make a great agent. Remember?"

"Yes."

"You convinced me to do the training, then out of nowhere you decided not to let me join. What happened?"

"I changed my mind."

"That's obvious, but why? Why did you change your mind all of a sudden? You didn't think I would make a good agent after all?"

"I thought then that you would be an excellent agent, but I also thought, what better way to protect you than to have you learn to protect yourself? I still think you would make a great agent."

"You haven't said why you changed your mind."

She felt Mike's hand on hers. She looked down and realized he had interlaced the fingers on his right hand with the fingers of her left hand. Mike had learned more about her in one night than he knew about her in over a decade of friendship. He had his eyes closed.

"Let him rest," Colson said. "He took a nasty bump on the head. I'm a little curious, why is it you two never got together? I mean before the fella you married came along?"

"You're changing the subject. You're never going to give me a straight answer, are you? And don't tell me you're not sure my mother would approve. I don't buy that excuse."

"The best I can do right now is to tell you the decision was purely selfish. Let's just say there was some new information and it swayed my decision."

His phone rang. "Yes?"

"We found him," the voice said on the phone.

"We're almost there," Colson replied. "We'll talk then." Colson ended the call.

"They found Brian?" Gail asked.

"Sadly, no," Colson replied. "They found my attorney. I've been trying to set up a meeting with him for the longest time."

Gail let out a sigh of disappointment as they entered an underground parking lot. Colson had a separate entrance to the treatment center. He could go in and out without having too much activity at the front. Gail also realized the building had a basement.

Mike finally woke up. Her left hand was thankful to be free.

Gail and Mike were escorted to the third-floor. Mike had been given the room next to hers…both rooms were separated by a door. They were both provided with a change of clothes. Gail got a well-needed shower and then went to Mike's room to check on him.

"How are you feeling?" she asked.

"I still have a nasty headache."

"Why don't you get some rest? I'm going to follow up on those phone numbers. We can leave the adjoining door open if you want."

"Nice try. Sure, we can leave the adjoining door open, but you're not leaving me here. I'm coming with you." He slipped the T-shirt over his head. "Ready when you are."

"Fine." She returned to her room, pulled her hair back into a ponytail and was about to leave. Mike held her arm with a firm grip. She looked down at his hand on hers, then slowly looked up at him. He released his grip. "I'm sorry."

She didn't leave because she could sense that he had more to say. For a few seconds he said nothing. He simply stared at her as if he was searching for the right words. "You can talk to me, and not only about Brian."

"You weren't sleeping?"

He shook his head.

"If you knew everything about me, we probably wouldn't be friends."

"That's where you're wrong," he said. "After you." He held the door open for her.

They headed towards the elevator that would take them to the basement. This elevator was concealed, so it was no wonder they never noticed it earlier when they were there. On the way down Mike said, "I lied about the woman in the photograph."

"The woman in the photograph with Brian?"

"Yes. I don't know what I was thinking. I guess I thought I was protecting you."

"Who is she?"

"I don't know her name. I only know that she works in his office."

"I've never seen her before."

"She's new."

Gail exited the elevator without saying anything else. They both went over to where Colson was looking at snapshots of someone on the computer. "Who's this?" Mike asked.

"That's Alvin Craig. My attorney, or more precisely, my former attorney. His father used to be my attorney before he passed away. This boy almost grew up in my hands," Colson said.

"Is that why you're stalking him?" Mike asked.

"No. Alvin knew things about Gail that he shouldn't. He showed me a video of her son and he was able to create a link between that kid and Gail because of his...should I say...his abilities. Now, how did he know this? I asked myself that question a million times. I certainly never told him. I never told his father either."

Gail looked on as Colson clicked through the pictures of Alvin in different shots and with different people. "So you think Alvin might be involved with Brian's kidnapping somehow?"

"That's what I thought, and I thought the motive was money, but I have to admit that the attempt on your life tonight kind of debunks that theory. However, it still does not change the fact that Alvin has information he shouldn't. I want to know who his source is. Even if he had nothing to do with the kidnapping, he's still up to no good."

Gail pulled up a chair next to Colson as he flipped through the photographs. "So what exactly are we looking for here?" she asked.

"I'll know when I see it," Colson said.

"Photographs aren't enough," she said. "You should bug his office and his home...and don't tell me you can't. Wait! Go back. Mike," she said pointing to the photograph on the screen.

"Oh, shit!"

"You two know her?" Colson asked.

Mike showed Colson the photographs of the same woman with Brian. "So, who is she?" Colson asked.

"I don't know. Mike said she's a recent employee of my husband. From these photographs, there seems to be more than an employer-employee relationship between the two of them."

"You don't know that for sure," Colson said. "She's probably a plant. Her job was to make you believe there was a relationship between herself and Brian. Seduce him, have questionable photographs taken of the two of them together, then blackmail him, or better still, pretend to blackmail him. Then they could lead him to wherever they want all because he's willing to do anything to keep it from his wife. It's a tactic I've seen before."

"We need to find out who she is and where she is." Gail leaned in closer to look at the screen. "This woman knows where my husband is." She got up from the chair. "I'm going out. I need a vehicle."

"I don't think you should go back out there tonight," Mike said. "Besides, you could be a lot more productive sitting in front of a computer than breaking and entering, which is what I get the feeling you're itching to do."

Mike knew her a little too well. Gail wanted

to break in to Brian's office. She thought there might be something in the mystery woman's file that could help them find her. But if Gail stayed, she could see if these photographs yielded anything useful. She'd figure out how to get into Brian's office later.

"Fair enough." She once again took a seat in front of the screen. "Are there any photographs of Alvin and any of the two dead guys?"

"Nothing yet. Although I am curious about *that* guy," Colson said, pointing to the screen.

"That guy," Gail mumbled. "Can you zoom in on him? Or do you have a better shot of him?"

Colson moved the mouse over to her. "Here, why don't you take over?" She zoomed in on the man in the photograph with Alvin. He looked exactly like someone Gail knew. Someone from her past.

Chapter 12

Could the man in the photograph be who she thought it was? She was tired. Maybe her eyes were playing tricks on her. Gail kept searching for a better shot of this man. Finally, she found it.

"I know him. That's Johnathan Clarke."

"Who?" Mike asked.

She looked at Colson. "That's the FBI agent who questioned me about you. He's older now but that's definitely him. He showed me pictures of Ms. Hemmingway's body and—"

"Made you believe that I killed her, and that I would do the same to you. You know better now," Colson said. "I've never seen him before, and his name does not ring a bell. What's he doing, meeting with Alvin?"

As she flipped through some more of the photographs, they were able to connect all three players together. The mystery woman, Alvin, and the FBI agent.

Gail scooted over to use the computer at the next work station. "We have nothing yet that links these three to the two dead guys, but they're definitely involved."

"What are you looking for?" Mike asked.

"I'm going to check to see if Alvin owns any property in Washington State. Especially anything that's located in a remote area."

"A place to hold a hostage," Mike said. "Since we're going to be up all night, I better get some coffee."

Colson pointed to an area in the far corner.

"You want some?"

"None for me," Colson said.

"Gail?" Mike said.

"Yeah, I'll take one. Thanks."

Mike went off to make the coffee. She forgot to tell him how she wanted it, but then it didn't matter.

"I like him," Colson said. Gail glanced at Colson then back to the computer screen to continue her search.

"He's a good guy, you know," Colson continued.

"Uh huh."

"He really cares about you."

She stopped what she was doing and turned to Colson. "Of course he cares about me and I care about him. We're friends. Friends typically care about each other."

"Do you really believe that? He cares about

you, just as a friend?"

"Yes. Where are you going with this anyway? You do realize you're talking to a married woman with a child, who is desperately trying to find her husband. Do you know something I don't, because I feel like you're trying to fix me up."

"I'm only sharing my observation, and let's just say, I know what it feels like to be in his shoes. He learned a whole lot of unusual things about you in a very short time, and not once did that look in his eyes dim. Will your husband be as accepting of you once he learns the truth? Or will he use it as an excuse to be unfaithful? That's assuming he wants to stay married to you."

"You're really a buzz kill for an old man." But Gail thought Colson was right. Mike was very accepting and his support for her had never wavered, though it was easier to be accepting and supportive when a person was on the outside. It was a whole different ballgame when someone you vowed to spend the rest of your life with turned out to be a different person. It wasn't a fair comparison. "You're supposed to be helping me, not trying to stifle my enthusiasm."

"I just want you to be realistic about what the future holds. I want you to find your husband. I do. And I will do everything I possibly can to help you find him, but once he's safe, you should start thinking about your own happiness. I know from personal experience that sometimes people stay married for the wrong reason."

"Did you?" Gail asked.

"Did I what?"

"Stay married for the wrong reason?"

"That was a lifetime ago, and besides, we're not talking about me, we're talking about you. I'm not telling you to make a decision today. All I'm saying is, don't look past what's right in front of you."

"Don't let Mike fool you. He was a lady's man in medical school. Sure, he cares about me, but there's nothing more to it. I think he's still hurting from his divorce and may appear vulnerable, but he's not in love with me if that's what you think."

"Did he cheat on his wife?"

"Technically, no."

"That say's a lot about the man. Don't you think?" Colson asked.

Unfortunately, she could not say the same thing about her husband. Hiding her past from him certainly made her more forgiving than she most likely would have been if things were different. Now everything would be in the open.

There would be no more secrets. It wouldn't be easy, but they could make it work. She had to believe that.

Mike was on his way back with the coffee. Gail turned her attention to the screen and tried to look busy.

"Here." He handed Gail the coffee. "I hope you like it," he said as she took a sip.

"It's good. Thank you." It wasn't just good, it was fantastic. It was like she'd made it herself. For a moment she allowed her mind to drift as the smell of the coffee reminded her of her early mornings with her husband. She was jolted back to the present by a question from Colson.

"So, how did you know how much creamer and what not to put in it?"

Both Gail and Mike responded simultaneously. "I just eyeball it."

They looked at each other and laughed.

"How interesting," Colson said with a sly grin.

"Yeah," Mike said. "That's how we made coffee back in the days and it always seemed to come out right."

Colson started to lead the conversation in a different direction. "Oh! So you had his coffee before?" he asked Gail.

Gail did not respond because she got the feeling he wasn't really talking about coffee.

Mike, on the other hand, apparently totally oblivious to what was going on in that twisted mind of Colson, furnished him with an answer. "Oh, yeah, many times."

The old fart snickered. Gail had to excuse herself. "Where's the bathroom on this floor?" She took off in the direction that Colson pointed.

After composing herself, she returned and resumed her search. Not long after, Colson said he was going to call it a night and told the guys who worked with him to do the same. "I'll walk you to your room in a little while," he said to Gail.

The last thing Gail wanted to do was sleep, although she was tired of sitting in that chair. There was so much to get done and she wanted it done yesterday. Mike left for a few minutes, then returned with a laptop. "One of the tech guy said this has everything you need, and it's firewall-protected, so you can work from your room."

Colson hung around, then walked Mike and Gail to their rooms. He kept lingering as if he did not want to leave. He sat in a reclining chair in Gail's room. "I thought you were tired," she said to him.

"I am." He threw his head back and focused on the ceiling. "Do me a favor, don't sneak out tonight."

"Sneak out? I'm not seventeen. Besides, we already agreed that I'll work from here tonight."

He sat up straight and looked at Gail. "I have not forgotten, but what you do now and what you choose to do after everyone else is asleep, may be a different thing…again, speaking from experience."

Gail snickered but her little laugh quickly disappeared when she saw how deeply troubled he was. His eyes were a little glossy and his hands were shaking a bit. "Mike!" she called.

"Are you feeling okay?" she asked Colson. "When was the last time you ate?" She touched his skin on his neck and his forehead trying to assess if he had a fever.

Mike came over. "What's going on? Is he okay?"

"I'm fine," Colson said.

"Then why do you look like you're about to pass out?" she asked. "You're shaking. I've never seen you like this before. Except…" Gail remembered that look. He had that same look when her mother died. "Are you ill? And for heaven's sake, please don't lie to me. I can't take anymore lies or secrets."

"Do you remember Leon?" he asked. "My son?"

"Of course I do." Gail's heart melted. He still mourned his only child.

"My wife and I tried for a very long time to have a baby. The best doctors money could buy, but none of them were successful. Your mother was really good at what she did, but it was not good enough. Eventually, we decided to adopt this beautiful little boy. My son."

Gail knew him and she also knew how much Colson loved him. The mere thought of losing her own son would be enough to drive her out of her mind.

Mike got up. "Maybe I should leave you two to catch up."

"No. I want you to stay. Sit over there," Colson said as he pointed to a space next to Gail. Mike sat beside Gail on the bed.

That was not exactly how Gail planned on spending her night, but she owed the man a lot and the least she could do is sit and listen to him.

"I loved your mother. I loved her for most of my life."

Gail cleared her throat and looked at Mike. Now where was this going? It better not be a cock and bull story of lost love that was all going to come back around to Mike and his supposed love for her. Mike looked a little uneasy.

"Do you want something to drink?" he asked Colson. "I could get you something from the dining area."

"Yes, that would be nice. Thanks."

Mike left the room.

Nice going, Gail thought. He weaseled his way out and left her to listen to Colson all by herself. Although she was still concerned about him, she really didn't want to hear about what happened between him and her mother. Or did she?

Mike returned with a drink and gave it to Colson.

Gail watched the interaction between the two men and could not help but think back to when Mike and Colson first spoke. They had been constantly at each other's throats and now there'd been a shift.

Colson waited until Mike was seated before he continued down memory lane. "We were close. Your mother and I. Sort of like you and Mike."

"Oy!" Gail groaned. Mike elbowed her.

Colson was not in the playful mood he was in earlier. He was very somber. "Before your mother died, I could tell there was something bothering her. Something she wanted to tell me. She tried, but then she would say, 'Tomorrow. I'll tell you tomorrow.' It was very hard for me to watch her die and not able to help her. This place was intended for her. I was planning on having it fully staffed for her. For years, after she passed away, I wondered what it was that she wanted to tell me. Then I found out. I wanted to tell you this a long time. Now I think I understand why it was so hard for her to say it."

Gail was now curious. "Hard for her to say what, exactly?"

"You know I never told your mother how much I loved her."

Gail was getting tired of this part of the story. "Okay. But what is it that you want to reveal to me?"

"Sure, she knew I cared about her," he continued as he made eye contact with Mike.

Gail rolled her eyes and let out a loud breath as if to say enough already.

"I've always loved you like a daughter. You know that. Don't you?"

She moved to the edge of the bed so she could rest her hand on Colson's. "Of course I do."

He placed his other hand on top of hers so his hands were sandwiching one of hers.

"I want to be a part of your life," he told her. "Promise me you won't shut me out, no matter what I tell you tonight."

Gail looked at Mike, not sure what Mike would think. He placed his hand on her right shoulder and gave it a gentle squeeze.

"I promise," she said.

Colson pulled out a piece of paper from his inner jacket pocket and gave it to her.

"What's this?"

"When I was signing you up for the CIA, they ran a blood profile for you. You're looking at the result."

Gail gaped at the results Colson gave her. "This can't be right!"

Chapter 13

Gail stared at the piece of paper for over a minute without saying a word. Mike leaned in to look at the paper in her hand.

"This is a DNA test result," he said.

"One that shows there's a high probability Colson is my father." She shuddered. "Is this real? You know what, it doesn't matter because the match is not strong enough for the results to be conclusive." Gail crumpled the paper and threw it across the room.

"It was difficult not to tell you all those years."

"Then why tell me now? You couldn't have picked a worse time. With all that's happening with Brian, and you chose to unload this garbage on me now?"

"You wanted to know why I didn't sign you up for the CIA. Well, now you know. When I found out you were my daughter, I...I got a little over-protective."

"Actually what I want to know is, why you

chose to tell me this now?"

Mike remained quiet. Then he got up to leave. Colson asked him to stay.

"Am I being selfish by telling you this now? Maybe. I sure don't want to die without ever telling you the truth," Colson said.

"What truth? That you and my mother had an affair?"

"I loved your mother, but we never crossed that line. Never."

"Oh, yeah? Then how did your little spermatozoa crossed over her egg's border. Huh?"

The second the question came out of her mouth she realized her mistake. She'd been conceived through in vitro fertilization. They didn't really need to cross that line. "So how is it you didn't know if you donated sperm?"

"I didn't, but my wife and I used the clinic where your mother worked when we were trying. Your father gave up trying so she was afraid to ask him. I guess she used mine that was in storage. Look, I admit I don't have all the answers, but one thing is clear. The people who are after you know more about you than they should."

"What do you mean? Like what?" Mike asked.

"Think about it," Colson said. "If it was

really about a ransom for her husband, they would have contacted her by now. If they wanted information why would they need to send people after her with those kinds of skills? No, someone knew that I would be looking out for you and if they knew that, it means they will try to use whatever information they have to mess with your mind. Then you will be an easy kill."

"In case you haven't noticed, I can take care of myself."

"But for how long? And this is not just about you. These people will destroy everything and everyone you hold dear. Whoever is after you is hiring trained killers, some of them already dead, according to the government's database. If you try to go this alone, you will die, and after they kill you they will go after your son. You have to let me help you. I know my timing seems off but I need you to trust me. I thought it would help if I showed you that, as your father, there is no way I could hurt you."

"Who are these people who are after me, aside from your attorney?"

"It's hard to say for sure, but it's possible these are the same people who were behind the company your mother worked for."

"How does your attorney fit into this?" Mike asked.

"I'm not sure yet. I'll let the both of you know as soon as I get anything." He turned to Gail. "Don't try to do this by yourself. The easiest way for them to get to you is if you isolate yourself from me. No, I can't kick ass like I use to, but I have eyes and ears to guide you. I know this is a lot to take in, but please don't go out there tonight."

Mike looked at her as if he too didn't trust that she wasn't going to sneak out.

"Like I said, I'm working from here tonight," Gail replied.

"Thank you," Colson said, sounding somewhat relieved. "If you two will excuse me, I think I'll go get some sleep now."

"Thanks to you, *I* won't," Gail said.

"In that case, I have some documents that I haven't had a chance to go through. While I was a guest of the government, I had my associates continued the research. I'm sure the two of you would do a great job going through that information together." He got up and exited the room.

Gail and Mike followed him to one of the locked rooms Gail tried to get into earlier. They eyed each other as Colson pulled the key out of an inner pocket and unlocked the door. He retrieved a file from a safe he had in the office.

"You can go through this first," he said to

Mike as he handed him the file.

Gail was still unsettled from the paternity discussion with Colson. She wanted to avoid eye contact with him so she was looking everywhere else but at him. Mike seemed to have sensed the uneasiness and attempted to change gears. He started browsing through the documents.

"This looks like records of clinical trials. Where did you get this?" he asked Colson.

"Miranda gave it to me. She said there was evidence in it that could take the company down, but the company no longer existed. I really didn't understand what was on it and I didn't trust anyone enough to share it."

Mike kept reading. "Well, you can't take down a company that doesn't exist. From what I'm seeing, the drug was causing unusual cell proliferation."

"English, please!" Colson said.

"It caused cancer, and from what's on these files, they knew it was causing cancer, and still continued to administer it."

"You've got to be kidding." Gail leaned in to take a closer look at the data herself. "It's bad enough that they continued to test this drug but why would they knowingly inject a drug that they knew would not yield the desired effect, but instead cause cancer? Did you find any information on this company at all?" she asked

Colson.

Colson handed her a file. "This is what my guys were able to find. I haven't gone through it but from what they told me, the company your mother worked for was a front."

"A front for what?" Gail asked as she started looking through the documents. "I get the feeling they wanted these kids to be inflicted with cancer. She leafed through pages of documents. "What is this? Zsulrick Inc.?" She showed the document to Mike. "Why does that name sound familiar?"

"It's a drug company, with branches all over the world. So you think the research company was a front for a big drug company?" Mike asked.

"I'm not a betting man, Mike, but if I were I would put money on it. They wanted to test new drugs on embryos. What better way to cover up this testing than through their own fertility clinic?" Colson said.

"I wonder what other type of drugs they tested in that clinic. Did you find anything that indicated that they conducted any clinical trial on adults?" she asked Mike.

"Nothing in your mother's files, but that doesn't mean it didn't happen. Why? What are you thinking?"

"My mother died of cancer. Now I have to

wonder if she was infected by accident or was she given a death sentence. Strange, the same drug that apparently saved me is lethal to everyone else. By the way, when this is all over, we're going to do this test again just to prove you're wrong," Gail said to Colson.

Colson kissed her on the forehead then handed her the key to the door. "Lock up when you're done." He patted Mike on the shoulder and left.

She caught Mike staring at her. "What?"

"Nothing," Mike said. "Do you mind if we work from your room?"

"Whatever."

"What did I do?"

"Nothing. I'm sorry. I feel...I don't know what I feel."

"I'm not sure what to tell you," Mike said. "Except you're the same Gail yesterday as you are today, give or take a gunshot wound to the shoulder. Sorry, I digress. My father died in the war before I was born and all I have are pictures. If tomorrow I find out that some other guy is really my father, would that change how or what you think of me?"

"That's a stupid question!"

"Exactly, so shake it off and let's go."

They locked up and headed back to Gail's room. They agreed to resume the search for properties in the Washington State area that may have been owned by Alvin Craig. Gail was looking through the database when she glanced up at Mike and noticed he had a smirk.

"Something funny?" she asked.

"Not really," he said still smiling. "It just hit me...your father likes me."

"Oh, just shut it!"

"All joking aside," Mike said, "do you realize how happy Alex is going to be when he finds out he has a grandfather who's not in a cemetery?"

That was not a conversation Gail wanted to have at that time. She changed the subject. "Alvin Craig doesn't have any property here. Not under his name, anyway," she said.

"You should search for property owned by the law firm," Mike said. "Oh, and clients. Check for properties owned by their clients."

"All right. I'm on it." Gail placed a pillow against the head of the bed. "Ah, that's better," she said as she rested her back against the pillow. "I don't get it. How do you kidnap a grown man without drawing a lot of attention? In the middle of the day, no less?"

"They knew he had a weakness. Brian found it difficult to resist...you know. That doesn't mean he doesn't love you. I know he does, but he, ah...he had a tendency to cross the line."

"Mike, if you're trying to—"

"No. I'm not trying to do anything but to help you figure out how this could have gone down. So please, hear me out. According to Colson, these people used this kind of trickery before. Remember that phone call Brian got? That was probably when they were threatening him. Once they had something he doesn't want you to know about, he's like a puppet on a string. I'm sorry to say this, but he was an easy target."

"What do you want me to say?"

"You don't have to say anything. I don't want you to blame yourself for what happened. If Brian was a different man, they never would have gotten to him, not in that way."

"Right."

"Not every man is like him. Despite what most women think...Just saying...for the record."

"Alvin's law firm doesn't own any property here but they have a lease for an office in Redmond," Gail said as she stretched her neck.

"That's certainly not suitable to hold a hostage so...maybe you should get some rest. We can continue this in the morning."

Gail got up. "I'm going to get a drink. You want one?"

Mike got up too. "I'll be right behind you."

"Why is that?" Gail asked. "Why is it you'll be right behind me?"

"Because I'm feeling a little parched and I would like to stretch my legs in the process. Is that a problem?"

Gail rolled her eyes and left the room, Mike following. They got to the dining area and she grabbed two drinks from the refrigerator and handed one to him. She headed straight back to the room. Not long after she got up again.

"What is it?" Mike asked.

"I'm going to the bathroom. What is with you?"

Mike got up. "I didn't want to say this in front of Colson but I agree with him. If I take my eyes off you for more than two minutes you would be out the door."

Gail shook her head. "You should get some sleep." She came back from the bathroom thinking Mike was off to get some rest. Instead of going to his room, Mike found a spot next to her on the bed. He placed his pillow against the bedhead and leaned back, just as she had. Eventually, tiredness started to win him over.

"Did you find the list of clients?" he asked as he scooted down so that the back of his head was resting on the pillow.

"Yeah. The firm has quite a long list. I'm going to work through the individuals first, then the companies after."

"Are you picking names at random?"

"No, I'm going to sort the list then work in alphabetical order. So what else did you find in those papers Colson gave you?"

"Your mother had a note I'm still trying to figure out. She made the notations over a period of time."

"What notations?" Gail asked.

"I don't know if I can even call it that but the note said 'something changed.' I guess she ran some kind of test and something changed, but she didn't say what it was. Do you recall if she took blood from you, say on a monthly basis, in the months before she died?"

"Yes, she said she wanted to run some routine tests to make sure my hemoglobin and all that was in order."

"Well, I didn't see any lab results. Not saying they weren't done, but they're not in her file. Besides, if she was referring to your hemoglobin, she would have recorded the number. She was talking about something else."

"I guess we'll never know," Gail said.

"When this is all over, humor me and get some tests done. A complete blood workup."

She looked over at him.

"I want to make sure you're okay," he said as he stretch both arms above his head and yawned. "Where are we on that search?"

"We?" She smiled. "We are on the letter B."

"Good. I'll try to stay awake but if I fall asleep and you find something, wake me up. Okay?"

"Sure, or maybe I could read it to you like we did in medical school."

"I always thought you were amazing for doing what you did. I remember I'd be so tired. I needed to close my eyes and you'd read aloud…your descriptions were pretty good too. It was like studying for the both of us. Today I realize you already knew all that stuff. You didn't need to be burning the midnight oil beating the books." He glanced at Gail. "You did that for me?"

"Go to sleep."

"Every girl I dated or tried to date would break up with me because they swore you and I were sleeping together. Although technically we did *sleep* together, but that was it."

Gail could feel his eyes on her but she kept her eyes glued to the monitor.

"Then Brian entered the picture," he continued. "And the rest is history, as they say. For the life of me I can never figure out why nothing ever happened between us. Would you've gone out with me? If I'd asked you back then?"

"You? Are you kidding? I wouldn't have felt safe with you."

"Is that why you married him? Because you felt safe with him?"

"Brian was not like you."

"You got that right! Because I would've never cheated on you. I'm sorry. That was out of line."

"It's okay," she said, but it wasn't really okay. No woman expected her husband to cheat on her. Especially when he seemed so loving and acted as if his world revolved around her. Maybe that was what Brian wanted her to believe, or maybe, she saw what she wanted to see.

Then she looked at Mike, who'd dated several girls during any one semester. Who would've thought he was capable of a monogamous relationship? He closed his eyes and just when she thought he was sleeping, he opened them again.

"Did I snore?" he asked.

"You mean back then? No. Do you snore now? Because I don't want the noise in my ears."

"I don't know. You can tell me in the morning. Don't stop talking to me, though. I want to know what you're doing and if you're talking, it means you're still in the room."

"All right, I'm wrapping up the Bs then I'll start on Cs."

She started feeling tired and wanted to call it a night but she kept on looking. The more she searched for Brian, the more desperate she became to find him. It was painful for her to have to deal with his infidelity so openly. She wondered if it was worth risking her life to try to find him. They were worlds apart now more than they'd ever been. She knew in her heart it was over. Still, the father of her child was out there somewhere and she needed to find him, if not for her, then for her son.

She was almost finished with the list of surnames that started with a C. She was on Colson. He had properties in Washington State. That was no surprise since she was currently staying in one of them. This place didn't show up as a property owned by Colson, but there were three properties in the state registered to him. He had a house in Bellevue...a possibility. A parcel of land. From the look of it online it seemed undeveloped. Then she saw it. The one that really jumped out at her. It was a fifteen-acre property in Colville with two cabins on it.

Chapter 14

Mike was fast asleep beside her. It was a few minutes after four in the morning. She heard every breath he took. Well, at least he still didn't snore.

She shook him. "Mike, I think I have something."

He rolled over on to his side and threw an arm over her. He was still sleeping. She gently removed his arm. "Mike, are you awake?" She put her face close to his to check if he was still sleeping. "Mike?" He did not respond. He was obviously out of it.

So, Gail had promised she would not go out last night, but she'd said nothing about not going out this morning. She gently inched her way closer and closer to the edge of the bed, being careful not to disturb him. As soon as she got off the bed she heard him.

"Going somewhere?" Mike was wide awake and staring at her.

"I thought you were sleeping," she said.

Mike laughed. "I'm sure you did." He rolled

over on to his back and placed both hands behind his head. "You still didn't answer my question. Oh, wait, don't tell me. You're just going to the bathroom."

"I don't have time for your antics. If you've been awake all along then you know I've found something." She showed him the address and description of the properties owned by Colson. "The property is a long way from where we are. It would take hours of driving before we get there."

"So what are you thinking?" Mike asked.

"We could leave now. Give ourselves a head start without the traffic. We can leave a note for Colson so he knows where we're heading." She zoomed in on an area of the map. There's a municipal airport in Colville, so option two would be we wait and hope Colson has access to a plane that can drop us here," she said, pointing to the airport on the map.

"I vote for the latter," Mike said. "In the meantime, I suggest you take some well needed rest."

"I can't sleep."

"You don't have to sleep if you don't want to. Just lie down and close your eyes," he said as he fixed her pillow. "Come on."

She reluctantly climbed back into bed.

"That wasn't so hard, was it? Now close your

eyes." He turned off the lights.

She closed her eyes but her mind was still in overdrive. His heartbeat was like a drum pounding in her ears. She heard the water drops from the leaky faucet in the bathroom. She was hearing everything.

She got up and turned the light back on. "I can't."

Mike held on to her as she was getting off the bed. "Hey, what's wrong?"

"I need to do something," she said. "I can't just lie there. I need to stay busy. Maybe we should wake up Colson. The earlier we start the better."

"Yes, but not *this* early. He's going to need a pilot to fly the plane and personally I want that person very rested. There's no telling what we're going to be up against when we get there. All the more reason you need to rest."

"I'm trying but I'm hearing every sound that's within my range and it's really disturbing."

"Can you block it out?" Mike asked.

"Yes. Usually I block things out by default and focus on what I want to hear, but when I'm stressed out I have to work at it."

Mike got up and sat on the side of the bed. "Put your feet here." He patted his lap.

"What?" she asked

"Oh, for crying out loud!" He lifted her legs and placed them on his lap. "Now, close your eyes."

She did. He started massaging her feet and soon all the sounds that bothered her disappeared.

"Wake up, sleepy head." Mike was sitting on the bed next to her, rustling her hair. "I brought you some coffee." He waited for her to sit up then he handed her the mug.

"What time is it?" she asked.

"It's a little after six and don't worry, I got Colson up to speed. He's kicking things into gear as we speak." He watched her sip her coffee. "Do you want some breakfast?"

"No, I'm good. Thanks. Is he coming along?"

"I don't think so. I think he has a meeting or is expecting a visitor, I'm not really sure, but it sounded like he has other plans."

"He doesn't own this property," she said.

"And?"

"So, he said he bought it and started construction while my mother was alive. I got the impression he owned it."

"Maybe he did, but it does make sense that it's not in his name. Think about it, he's supposed to be in a treatment center. Not on his own property. He probably had the title transferred to another name or an organization as a cover."

"That makes sense. I just wish he'd told us about these cabins."

"Hey, don't do this."

"Don't do what?"

"You're trying to find reasons not to trust him. I know being betrayed by someone you trust can't be easy and I can't tell you how or what to think, but don't lump everyone else in that same bundle."

"I'm not lumping anyone into anything. I have questions and I ask them. I don't have trust issues, if that's what you're trying to say. I trust you, don't I?"

"It's amazing the way your body heals itself, but emotionally I know you hurt just as long as the rest of us, maybe even more."

"What's your point?" she asked.

"My point is, I know you, and more important, you know me. You never have to pretend with me." He turned her face towards him. "Ever."

"Okay, enough with the touchy feely stuff. At the rate of how things are going I'm inclined to ask if you're my mother's reincarnation," she said as she got out of the bed and headed to the bathroom.

"I'll be in the dining area," Mike said.

"I'll be there shortly."

Gail entered the dining room and headed toward Colson, who was having breakfast.

"I hope you got a little rest," he said.

She looked around for Mike but didn't see him. "You should get something to eat. It's going to be a long day for all of us."

Gail sat at the table. There was more than enough food but she had no interest in any of it. The only thing she was interested in having was another cup of coffee and maybe a...

Before she completed the thought, Mike brought her another cup of coffee and a sandwich. He set them down on the table in front of her then sat next to her.

"Thank you," she said with a smile, trying to act normal and not the least bit impressed with his choice. The last thing she wanted was for him to know he basically read her mind...ahead of time. She would not hear the end of it.

She turned her attention to Colson. "Why didn't you tell us about this property?" Gail asked as she leaned forward and glared at him.

Colson was about to put some food in his mouth when the question rang out. He looked at

Gail's piercing gaze. He returned the fork to the plate.

"It never occurred to me."

"It never occurred to you?" She felt a hand on the small of her back. She suspected that Mike is trying to tell her to take it down a notch.

"Remember, we're on the same team," Mike mumbled under his breath.

"Gail, I bought that property years ago. I was planning to build cabins for camping and vacation rental. I didn't remember the property already had two cabins on it. I tried selling it before I was incarcerated and turned it over to a property management company."

Gail sat back and relaxed in her chair. "I'm sorry I came at you like that. This whole thing has me on edge. I really want it to be over."

"No, I understand completely," he said. "We all want this to be over. The sooner the better, then we can all get on with our lives. Which will most likely involve some changes, hopefully for the better. Mike, who made that sandwich?" Colson asked. "I will have to commend the chef because it seems to be the only thing she enjoyed, other than the coffee, of course."

"Actually, I made it," Mike said.

Colson cleared his throat. "I see!"

Gail watched as the two men looked at each other and grinned.

"Did you find anything on that woman in the photograph with Brian?" she asked.

"The guys are still following up, but she started working as the receptionist at your husband's clinic less than two weeks ago."

"Less than two weeks? Did they know each other before she started working there?"

"No. At least I don't think so," Colson said. "The receptionist role is filled through an employment agency. The previous receptionist quit abruptly. This girl was the replacement."

Two weeks, she thought. He only knew this woman for two weeks and he chose to destroy their marriage for her. But the reality was Gail would not have felt any better if she'd worked there for two years. It stung like hell no matter which way she looked at it.

"You okay?" Mike asked.

"I'm good," she said. She looked at Mike and realized how right he was about her ability to hang on to painful memories. The pain from the gunshot she received in her shoulder was long gone. Not even a tiny hint of tenderness. But the more she found out about how Brian spent his free time, the more it dawned on her she would bear this pain for a very long time. She kept telling herself none of that mattered anymore because her marriage was no more. She wanted to find him...make sure he was safe, then she wanted the opportunity to look him in the eye and tell him they were done.

Mike put his arm around her shoulder and gave her a gentle squeeze. "You're going to be fine," he said.

Colson's phone rang. "Yes? We're on our way down. There's some more information on the mystery woman," he said.

"We're right behind you," Mike said.

Colson left the dining area. Gail waited until he was out of sight. "Did he say who he was meeting with today?"

"If he did, I didn't hear. Does it matter?"

"Just curious, that's all. Let's go." She got up and walked to the door.

By the time they got to the basement, Colson was already examining the file he received on the woman in the photograph.

"Here's what we know so far," Colson said. "Her name is Jeanine Grayson, a twenty-eight year-old call girl, who also went by the name Nina Ray, and Jean Gray. Her clients were usually high-level executives. Sometimes she was paid to travel with them as their companion. However, at some point she transitioned from being a paid companion to being a party to kidnapping and possibly murder."

"You think she had something to do with the

guy who got his throat slashed?" Mike asked.

"We don't know yet, but the original receptionist she replaced has not been seen since," Colson said.

"Has she been reported missing?" Gail asked.

"She has no family here, and as far as her landlord is concerned she was taking some time to travel. She called her supervisor the morning she quit and told her the same story. Her rent is paid up for a few months. There's nothing to report," Colson said.

"Clever. By the time anyone suspects she's missing, their mission is already accomplished. I take it you know where her apartment is?" Gail asked Colson.

"We do."

"Have you been able to get a pair of eyes in her apartment?"

"No, not unless the owner of that pair of eyes wants to be arrested for breaking and entering. And no, I'm not giving you the address." He walked away before Gail could respond.

"Mike! I'm going to need your help over here," he said.

The moment Mike left, Gail rifled through the papers Colson left on the desk. Clearly the address for the apartment was not in there, otherwise he wouldn't have left them. But she was hoping there was a name that she could track down. She looked at Jeanine's profile. High profile clients? Was Alvin a client? Was that how she became part of this scheme? If that was the case it meant there must be money involved, and lots of it. Who was paying her?

"Is there a way to find out who her clients were, at least for the last few months?" she asked when Colson returned.

"Not unless you get your hands on her little black book, if she even had one. Jeanine was not your typical call girl. She was more like a companion for hire. Unless we were tracking her activities from earlier, it's hard to say what we will be able to find. But it's definitely worth a shot."

"Maybe you can have your guy see what he can find."

"Yes, about that," Colson said. "We could cover a whole lot more ground if *you* worked on it. I have some leads I have them following up on and of course, if it turns out that this property is not were your husband is being held, we'll need to know where to look next. That means you need to identify all the possible locations by continuing your research."

"I agree, but we have to leave in a couple of minutes and I can't be in two places at the same time," Gail said.

"Correct. Now, if you'll excuse me for a minute," Colson said as he walked over to the other side of the room.

"What the hell does that mean?" Mike kept quiet the whole time. She looked at him and she could tell he was not telling her something. "Out with it!" she said.

"No, no, no. You're not dragging me into this," Mike said as he backed away from her. "Although I'm sure he has your best interest at heart."

"Oh, so you *do* know what it is?"

Mike still did not budge.

"Fine," she said as she took her gun out and checked the clip. "Did you reload this for me?" Mike didn't answer. "Okay what now?"

"He doesn't want you to go."

"Since when do you care what he wants?"

"If what he wants is to keep you out of harm's way, then it's the same thing that I want. We're not dealing with a bunch of ordinary guys, we're dealing with trained killers and you have a bull's-eye on your forehead. You should stay here. You could get a lot done."

She scoffed at him. "I trusted you. I can't believe you're ganging up on me with Colson. Do you really think that I can sit here and tap away on a computer knowing that Brian may be in one of those cabins?"

"Gail, he said he's assembling a group of guys to go in and check this place out. We don't know what to expect out there. If Brian is there, their job is to rescue him. You don't have to worry, I'm going to be there."

"Good. When do we leave?" She tucked the gun in her waistband, picked up another and checked the clip.

"Gail, you're not listening."

"You're right, I'm not listening, but I am hearing you just fine. Now you hear this. I'm going whether he likes it or not. Go tell that to your new best friend over there," she said as she glanced over at Colson.

Colson was talking to a group of guys all dressed in black. One of them beckoned to Mike. Gail shoved a dagger in each of her boots, tucked another gun in her waistband, picked up her bag and headed over to the group of guys. Colson stepped right in front of her. "I think it's best you sit this one out," he said.

"I think it's best you move your bony ass out of my way."

Chapter 15

The small plane was only able to fit four people, including the pilot. Gail being onboard meant they had to leave one of the guys behind. Mike and Marco Bellamont, a former marine, rounded out the small team. They landed at a municipal airport in Colville. A black SUV was already waiting to take them to their location. Gail and Mike sat in the backseat while Marco sat up front with the driver.

Marco held up a cigarette. "Do you mind?"

"I'd rather you didn't," Gail said.

"Not a problem, ma'am." Marco popped gum in his mouth and struck up a conversation with the driver. They obviously knew each other and chatted for most of the ride.

Gail looked out the window but she saw nothing. Yes her eyes were open but all she could see was the life she had with Brian. Everything else was just a big blur. There were flashes of good and bad experiences, but sadly she thought the bad days were outnumbering the good. Finding him would make her very happy. She would know that he was safe, but she also knew it was not going to be easy to let go of her marriage.

"When you spoke to Colson, did you get the impression there would be more guys here?" she asked Mike.

"Yes, I was expecting another team and another vehicle," Mike said. "Hey, Marco, where's the rest of the team?"

"En route, sir."

Mike was not as playful as he'd always been. "When we get there, I want you to stay close to me." He was as serious as she'd ever seen him.

"Okay." She reached into her pocket and pulled out a phone.

"Is that a new phone?" Mike asked.

"Yes, Colson gave it to me. He wants me to check in with him at each stage. He got rid of the old phone before we left for fear I'm being tracked."

She called Colson's number and handed Mike the phone.

"Give him an update for me, will you?"

Colson had saved the number in his phone and told her he'd take the call from this number anytime. He wanted her to be able to reach him with the press of one button. It was kind of strange for her, but she realized he was actually worried about her. Mike updated Colson and handed the phone back to her. As she reached out he held on to her left hand and looked it over.

"You're not wearing your wedding ring."

Gail did not respond. She simply returned the phone to her pocket.

"Does that mean what I think it means?" he asked.

"I don't know. What do you think it means?"

The driver took a phone call. "Yes, we're on our way," he said. "We're about five minutes away from Buena Vista road." He ended the call. The driver gave them an update based on his conversation with the other team.

"We're almost there." Marco said. "Instead of meeting up with us, the other team will approach the property from the north. We'll park out of sight and then proceed on foot. Both teams will converge on the property from opposite directions."

"Sounds good," Mike said. He looked at Gail. "You okay?"

It was funny he should ask because she was about to ask him the same thing. He looked a little tenser than she expected him to be. "As good as I can be in a situation like this. How about you?" Gail asked.

"Honestly, I would've felt much better if you stayed back like we asked. It would've made this operation a lot easier for me if I didn't have to worry about you," Mike replied.

"You don't have to worry about me. I can take care of myself. Or haven't you noticed?"

Gail was dressed in full black. Her calf-high boots carried daggers. She had a gun strapped to her right thigh, two in her waistband. She crossed her arms across her chest. "Do I look like a damsel in distress to you?"

But behind all that tough display, she was just as worried about him. He did not need to be here. This was her problem, her fight. It would kill her if anything happened to him.

Mike barely pulled off a smile. It was a weak one but she was happy to see it. "I know the Mike I know is in there somewhere," she said.

"The Mike you know would be eager to know what's next. After we find Brian, then what? But he's on a break. This Mike is focused on finding Brian and keeping you alive."

"Sounds like the Mike I need," she said.

"Well, that's new," Mike said looking somewhat revived. "You need me?"

"I didn't actually say that," Gail said. She was about to launch into a long-winded explanation and realized it was probably not the best time. He was an integral part of her life. Though she would not necessarily say she needed him, not out loud, anyway. She glanced at him and there it was, that smile.

He touched her finger that was absent her wedding band. "Whatever you decide to do is your decision. Focus on what's right for you. Everything else will fall into place. I'll support you either way."

"That's the thing," she said. "It's not only about what I want. It's about what's best for my son."

"Is that why you stayed with him?" he asked in a low voice.

She had asked herself that question many times. Had she stayed because she thought it was best for Alex, or because she thought Brian loved her? Or had she thought he'd made a mistake but he loved her and would never go down that road again? Or maybe it was a little bit of both? "You think I made a mistake by staying?"

"No, not at all. I think you made the right choice then, all things considered, but I know you've had your suspicions. I guess what I'm curious about is if you would have stayed with him all these years if it were just the two of you."

"When you don't trust someone, every little thing looks suspicious to you, but that doesn't make that person guilty. You of all people should know that. Besides, we got past it, at least I thought we did. I'm sure your ex-wife was pretty suspicious of you a lot of times you said you were working late, or your pager went off because of an emergency. Who knows, maybe she thought you were spending most of your time with that girl whose name you won't tell me."

"It was not like that," Mike said. "There were no secretly planned rendezvous and I never lied to Erica about where I was going to be."

"You still haven't told me who she is. You don't have to tell me her whole history, just a name."

He shook his head. "I'll tell you after this madness is over," he said. "Although I'm curious to know if you would now consider your marital status 'separated.'"

"After this madness is over, you can ask me that question again." The discussion served as a well-needed distraction to the both of them, but now they were on a section of May Road with forest on both sides. Gail knew it was time to switch thoughts.

The property was densely populated with mostly Western Hemlock trees. The cabins were not visible from where they were since most of that area was covered by forest. The team of four traveled in a northeasterly direction which would take them to the cabins.

Finally, from within the forest Gail saw a cleared area. It was daytime, so they had no shadows to hide in. "There are a few smaller trees near the cabin closest to us," she pointed out to Mike. The second cabin was on the farther side of the cleared area.

"We'll sweep the first cabin, the larger one," Marco said. The other cabin would be handled by the team that came in from the north. The driver had dialogue with someone from the other team to confirm that they were in place and ready to go.

They moved closer to the cabin, taking cover behind the trees in the yard. Marco and the driver proceeded while Mike and Gail covered them and vice versa. Marco and the driver reached the cabin first. Marco took a quick look through one of the windows. "There's a woman inside," he whispered.

Mike could not hear him so Gail repeated what she heard.

"She's lying on the floor. I can't see her face, but she may be dead or hurt. We're going in," Marco said.

Gail and Mike were moving closer to the cabin as Marco and the driver approached the front door. Marco attempted to open the door.

The cabin exploded.

The next woozy thought Gail had was that

Mike was on top of her. He must have jumped on her to shield her with his body. The echo in her ears had faded, but Mike's body felt unusually heavy, like dead weight. Her worry meter went off the charts, and suddenly, she felt nothing. Except an excruciating pain in her heart.

"Mike!" she called. He did not respond. She was facedown and could not see him but he was not moving. She pushed up just enough for him to roll off her. "Oh, God! No."

Mike was bleeding from his nose. "Mike, can you hear me?" He had a pulse, but he was not breathing.

She pulled out her cell phone and hit the redial button to Colson so he could send help. "Stay with me, Mike." She pinched his nose, opened his mouth and blew. "Come on, breathe!" She blew again and again. "Come on, Mike, I can't lose you." She blew again. "Please, Mike. I need you. Please!"

Tears rolled down her cheeks as she placed her mouth on his. She blew with everything she had.

He took a breath. "Mike! Oh, thank you, God! Mike!"

She wiped the blood away from his nose with her hands and turned him on his side. Gail suspected he'd hit his head when he threw himself on top of her. She was covered with dirt and sweat but took her top off and placed it under his head. She knew help was on the way, but she had no idea how long it would take for them to get to her.

"I'm going to get you out of here," she said, speaking louder than usual. "Can you hear me, Mike?" She placed her hand in his. "If you can hear me, even just a little bit, squeeze my hand."

He squeezed her hand ever so slightly. "That's good. You're doing great. Keep breathing. I'll be right back."

She scanned the area for any movement. Nothing. No sign of the other team anywhere. There was no way anyone in the cabin survived that blast. She prayed Brian hadn't been in it. Gail checked Marco and the driver and confirmed what she already thought. They were both dead.

She moved closer to the other cabin. Still no sign of anyone. Then she heard something right next to her. She heard it again. She looked at the tree she was standing next to. There were bullet holes in it. Someone was shooting at her from the cabin. She fired several shots at the window where she thought the shots might be coming from. Then she ducked behind the tree. More shots were flying in her direction. There was more than one shooter.

Mike was still on the ground where she'd left him. If she ran they would come after her, and Mike would be as good as dead. With a gun in each hand, she stood up. She closed her eyes and took a deep breath to calm herself. She was ready.

She dashed from behind the tree, firing at the window and the front door. She kept running towards the door with one gun aimed at the door and the other at the window. As she got to the door, she twisted and threw herself on the floor so she slid inside on her back. She took out two guys, fired at the third guy but her guns were empty. She threw her gun at him while she reached for a dagger in her boot. She wasted no time releasing it. He dropped to his knees as he clutched his throat.

Gail quickly grabbed a gun from the floor and checked it for bullets. She checked the entire cabin room by room to see if Brian was there. She had questions and she needed answers. She was hoping she would find one more of these guys alive, but the last one was wearing her dagger in his throat.

Gail got back to the tree where she'd left Mike. He was sitting up, leaning against it. "What happened?" he asked in a raspy voice.

"The cabin blew up and some guys were shooting at us... I would have to say this was a trap. These guys were a few steps ahead of us."

"Where's the other team?" Mike asked.

"For all I know the other team could be the ones shooting at us. Or maybe these guys wiped out the other team and took their place. I swept the other cabin and there's no one else in it besides the three guys who were firing at us." She stooped down in front of him to check his nose. He touched the blood on her chest.

"What happened here?" he asked.

"It's not mine," she said. "Besides, I'm more concerned about you." She tilted his head back slightly so she could look into his nostrils, then repositioned his head to face her. "I almost lost you today," she said.

"You can't lose me," he said. "But evidently you lost your shirt." She chuckled and put her top back on.

"I take it you didn't find Brian," he said.

She indicated no. "How's your head?

"Hurts like hell, but the pain is not getting worse, so don't worry."

"How's your vision?"

"I'm starting to enjoy you fussing over me."

She cupped his face with both hands and scrutinized him. He had undeniably the most beautiful blue eyes she'd ever seen.

"How are things looking, doctor?" he asked jokingly.

"It's good to see you haven't lost your sense of humor, but you need to take it easy. You're not out of the woods yet."

"When I was out, did you cry?" he asked.

"What?"

"Something wrong with the question?"

"There's nothing wrong with the question but our first priority is to get you checked out as soon as possible and pray that everything is okay. I believe you're going to be fine."

"And what if I'm not? Better yet, what if I didn't make it today?

"Look, you took a really nasty bump on the head. Maybe we should have this discussion when you're in better shape."

He did not respond. "Mike!" Gail realized he'd lost consciousness again. Her heart sank as she feared the worst.

Chapter 16

Hours later, Gail eagerly awaited the results of Mike's brain scan. She watched as people went back and forth. Everything seemed surreal.

Mike and Gail had been transported to a small hospital in North Marysville, via an air ambulance courtesy of Colson. The hospital was small but well equipped. She noticed a waiting area to her right as she was escorted by a nurse beyond a double door. Gail entered a passage way with rooms on both sides. She was asked to wait in one of the rooms, which looked more like a private lounge than a waiting area. Gail was restless and kept pacing the floor. It seemed like forever, then finally a tall lanky man with spectacles entered the room.

"Hi, I'm Dr. Tolido," he said as he peered at her through his spectacles. "You must be Gail."

How had he known her name? But she was more concerned about Mike at this point.

"I am. How's Mike?"

"He has swelling in his brain as a result of a

head injury, which is increasing the pressure in his skull. We're doing everything we can to reduce that pressure."

"Where is he? What have you given him?"

"We're treating him with Mannitol. A diuretic. We need to monitor him to see if he's improving with that treatment."

"I need to see him."

"He's not conscious, he—"

"I *need* to *see* him."

The doctor's face turned pale. She had blood all over her and a gun in her waistband. She realized she must have scared him. "I'm sorry," she said. "I really do need to see him."

"Okay. Come with me." As he opened the door to leave, Burdock presented himself. He asked the doctor to wait outside while he had a chat with Gail.

"Ma'am, Mr. Colson has instructed me to take you back to the center. Please come with me."

"I'm not leaving Mike," she said as she headed towards the door. Burdock closed the door and stood in front of it.

"I have strict orders to take you back with me. I don't want to have to use force," Burdock told her.

She walked up to him. "You touch me, and *you* will need to stay here. Now *move!*"

Burdock raised both brows and moved himself out of her path. As she was leaving she turned to Burdock and told him, "You tell Colson I'm not leaving Mike." She followed Dr. Tolido to Mike's room.

"Oh, Mike!" She went to his bedside. "Hey, Mike, it's Gail. I don't know if you can hear me, but I'm here. You're in good hands." She was encouraged by the fact that he was still breathing on his own and did not need to be connected to a ventilator. "You're going to be okay." She reached out her hand to touch him, then stopped herself when she saw that her hand still had blood and dirt on it. She held up both her palms and looked at them. What had she become?

"If you want to clean up, I can show you where you can..." Dr. Tolido stopped talking as Gail looked at him. He just pointed.

"I'd like that," she said. Hopefully she wouldn't look as scary after she had cleaned up. She wouldn't want the first thing Mike saw after he woke up to be a dirty, bloody face.

She cleaned up and put on a scrub top Dr. Tolido offered her.

"So you can cover that," he said pointing to her gun.

"Thank you."

"There's a cafeteria in the building if you

would like to get something to eat, or maybe something to drink."

Still cognizant of the fact that there were people trying to kill her and it was quite possible Mike was now a target, she pushed back the hunger pains. "If you don't mind, I'm going to check in on Mike again."

"It's going to take fifteen to thirty minutes for the medication to take effect. I don't know how successful this treatment will be for him, but he'll have a better chance if he remained undisturbed. I'm sorry."

"No, don't be. I understand." She headed back to the waiting area. "I'll wait in here. Let me know when he's awake." To Gail's surprise, Dr. Tolido came into the waiting area with her. "What are you doing? Don't you have other patients?"

"I was instructed to make you and Mr. Steele my number one priority. The hospital is owned by a foundation so members of that foundation get what you would call special treatment."

She didn't have to ask who that member was. It was all beginning to make sense. He knew her name and although he looked a little uncomfortable around her, he still hadn't called the police. She could live with that.

"Right." The minutes felt like hours and the doctor looked like he was going nowhere soon.

"So, you're a neurologist?" She figured some small talk would help her pass the time.

"Yes," he said. He went on to tell her quite a bit about himself, most of which she tuned out along with the other overlapping sounds. She was so worried about Mike, it affected her ability to listen selectively. Her olfactory nerve was also in overdrive, and Gail felt as if she was smelling everything, which coalesced into the scent of a skunk dipped in air freshener. It took her a few minutes to sort things through.

"I also specialize in genetic medicine."

That got her full attention, then his pager went off. He politely excused himself.

Gail frowned so hard she could feel the skin on her face stretching as it moved to create a crease between her brows. Colson had some explaining to do. Just when she was beginning to trust him, she found out he was hiding something else.

The wait was torture. She paced the floor outside Mike's room for what seemed like forever. Finally, the doctor emerged. "He's awake, I—"

"Thank you, doctor. You can fill me in on all that other stuff after." Gail pushed past him and went in to see for herself.

She slowly walked up to Mike's bedside. His eyes were open but she was not sure what to expect. "Hey, you," she said to him.

"Hi, are you my nurse?" he asked.

She held his hand. "It's me, Gail."

"I know it's you, silly," he said. She was overcome with joy. She hugged him.

"Too tight! Too tight!" he screeched.

"Sorry." She pulled back but still held his hand.

"How are you?" he asked.

"Hey, let me worry about you for a change." She kissed his hand. She felt tears rolling down her cheeks.

"Don't cry," he said. He was still trying to comfort her even though he was the one lying on a hospital bed. He wiped her cheek with his thumb then gently pulled her to him. "It's going to be okay," he whispered. Those blue eyes of his were pulling her in, the more she looked at them, the stronger the pull. Now her face was so close to his, she could feel the warmth of his breath.

"Mr. Steele, you have another visitor," Dr. Tolido said as he entered the room. "I'm sorry. Am I interrupting something?"

"Yes!" Mike snapped.

Gail attempted to smooth things out. "No, not at all."

Colson marched in and greeted them. "I've made arrangements to have Mike moved to the cancer center. Dr. Tolido will be staying with us for a while. He'll make sure Mike is well taken care of. He will also serve as your physician, Gail."

My what? Gail thought. *Did I tell anyone I needed a physician?*

Colson sat next to Mike, and Gail saw the strangest thing. Mike was actually happy to see him. Maybe she really had trust issues.

"Gail, Gail!"

"Huh?"

"May I speak with you for a minute?" Dr. Tolido asked.

"Go ahead," she said. "I'm listening."

"I meant in private."

They stepped outside the room and closed the door.

"I'm not quite sure how to say this, but I'm just going to give it a go. Mike is not back to normal, not yet anyway. At this point, there may be some sort of behavior change."

"Meaning what?"

"Meaning he may do or say things he normally wouldn't, if he were himself. I wanted you to be aware."

"Thank you. Is that it?"

"Yes, for now," he said. "If Mr. Colson asks, I'm going to grab some things from my apartment I'll be back in a few minutes."

"You live near the compound?" Gail asked.

"Yes."

Interesting. He's going to pack up and move in, just like that. Why? Because Colson asked him to? Didn't he have people in his life who would wonder where he was? "Are you married, Dr. Tolido?"

He shook his head.

"Do you have a girlfriend?"

Still shaking his head he added a smile.

"Boyfriend?"

The smile disappeared and he started coughing vigorously. Apparently he'd choke on his saliva.

"I wanted to know if you had anyone to explain your whereabouts to."

He cleared his throat. "I'm currently unattached at the moment," he said. "If you'll excuse me, I better get going."

Colson stepped out of the room just in time to see the somewhat awkward exchange between Gail and Dr. Tolido.

"Please don't give him a hard time," Colson said. "He's a smart young man and we need his expertise."

"And what expertise is that? His medical genetics expertise?" Gail asked.

"I was going to discuss it with you, but there were so many things happening. I need him to run some tests on you. A regular doctor might not know what to look for, but he has special training, and more important, I trust him. Since he's caring for Mike I thought it would make things easier if he came with us."

"Hmm, trust, the word of the day. How do you know you can trust him? Or maybe I should ask why? Why do you trust him? What is he to you?" she asked.

"Let me worry about him. You have another doctor to worry about," Colson said as he opened the door to Mike's room and held it for her to go in.

"I'm fine with him caring for Mike. I don't care to have him run any tests on me," she said as she passed him.

Mike's face lit up when she walked in. "Hi, I'm back," she said, equally happy to see him.

"I can see that," Mike said as he tried to move into a sitting position.

"I don't think that's a good idea. Not yet anyway." She walked over and stood next to his bed.

He held her hand. "Today was probably the worst day of my life, but it's the best day I've had in a very long time."

"You almost died. Of course it was a bad day."

"That's not the worst part," he said. "The

worst part was knowing that you were in danger and I couldn't help you."

"But you saved me. Remember?" She touched his face. "You saved me, and I'll never forget that."

"I think it's the other way around," he said. "Do you want to know what made this day so fantastic?"

"I don't think fantastic is a word I'd use to describe this day, but I'll bite. What made this day so fantastic for you?"

He put his hand next to her face and she gazed into his eyes. "This is what made it fantastic."

"I don't understand."

"That look in your eyes. I know you won't say it, but it means something, and seeing that made it all worthwhile."

New York

Alvin planned on working out of the New York office, but could not stay focused. He decided to head back to his hotel. Alvin tried reaching Jeanine but she didn't take his call. He was not too keen about calling Johnathan since he suspected Johnathan had something to do with the private investigator who'd been executed in front of him. Things were not going as smoothly as he'd hoped. At this point he was feeling like he'd bitten off more than he could chew. His role was simple, but never did he imagined the plan would unravel the way it had. He was looking for a way out.

Alvin picked up the phone and dialed a number.

"Mr. Mohler's office, may I help you?" a female voice said.

"Yes, may I speak with Mr. Mohler please?

"May I say who is calling?"

"Alvin Craig."

"One moment, Mr. Craig."

The call was placed on hold. Then after a brief wait the person at the other end of the line returned. "I'm sorry, Mr. Craig. Mr. Mohler is not available to take your call at this time. Do you wish to leave a message?"

"No. Actually, yes," Alvin said. "Please ask him to call me as soon as possible."

"May I have your number, Mr. Craig?"

"He has my number."

"Will do, Mr. Craig."

The call ended. Alvin got himself a drink from the minibar while he patiently waited to hear from Mohler.

Chapter 17

Gail watched as Dr. Tolido prepared his new work space. The lab at the center was already furnished with all the equipment he needed to conduct blood and DNA analysis. To Gail the place now looked more like a crime lab than a treatment center. Before leaving the hospital, Dr. Tolido ran another scan on Mike just to verify what he already knew. The treatment was working.

Mike was on bed rest, so he was confined to his room, or rather, Gail's room. She didn't mind, not until she realized the good doctor had moved into a room not too far and kept popping in to check on Mike. At that point she decided it was better for her to work from the basement and leave Dr. Tolido to watch Mike.

Colson got off the phone and beckoned to her to come over. "How are you holding up?" he asked.

"I'm not really worried about me right now," she said.

"Well, I am," Colson said. "They're searching

the wreckage from the blast, I'll let you know what they find."

"What about the woman who was in the cabin? Any idea who she was?"

"Not yet, but Dr. Tolido will help us figure that out. We should have the samples within the hour."

"Interesting," Gail said. "Always thinking ahead, aren't you?"

"It doesn't hurt. Which brings me to another matter," Colson said. "I'd like you to cooperate with Dr. Tolido and not make his time here a living hell."

"You lost me. How and why would I make his life a living hell? I barely speak to the guy."

"That's my point. You're going to need to interact with him a little more and you can start by letting him take some blood from you."

Gail had no problem with Tolido. She just did not want to be viewed as something to be studied. "I don't know what kind of agreement you have with Tolido, but leave me out of it," she said as she walked away.

"Gail!"

She stopped, then slowly turned around.

"This is for your own good. Listen to me, something that is a part of your DNA makes people ill. Do you understand what I'm saying? We need to be proactive. If there's something there, maybe we can head it off before it becomes a problem."

"It's been a part of my DNA for thirty-two years. I see no reason why it can't wait at least until after we find Brian."

"Because I want you to be proactive, get ahead of it," Colson said again. "Even if you don't care about yourself, think about your son. Right now God only knows what has become of his father." He came up to her. "This won't impact the search for Brian, I promise. Just a little cooperation, that's all I'm asking for."

"Fine, as long as you understand what my priorities are."

"Great, maybe we can get started after you convince Mr. Steele to get back into bed," Tolido said as he approached Gail and Colson.

Gail groaned and rolled her eyes. Dr. Tolido seemed like a nice guy and he was easy on the eyes, but Gail had a lot going on in her head and was in no mood to talk to anyone, with one exception, and he was walking in her direction. At that moment, having gone through all that she had, she was reminded that there was always something to be thankful for.

"Hey, any updates?" Mike asked.

"Aren't you supposed to be in bed? No updates yet."

"What about the woman who was in the

cabin?" he asked.

"We're waiting on some samples. Colson is going to have Tolido check her DNA. What I would like to know is, what is he going to compare it to?"

"Maybe they have access to a database common people don't have. They'll most likely compare the results for a match. Don't worry about how they get it done, just let them do their thing. The old guy has more connections than you realize," Mike said, as they moved away from where Tolido was chatting with Colson.

Mike sat in one of the chairs.

"Maybe you should go back to bed," Gail told him.

"I'm fine. How are you holding up?"

"I'm holding up just fine," she said. But did she really believe that? She was wrestling with the possibility that Brian might be in that rubble at the cabin. Almost as frightening was recognizing that she'd killed a total of four people since the search for her husband began. It'd been self-defense, but it was more than taking a life. She'd learned something about herself that would change the relationships she had.

She looked at Mike who was always worried about her. Good thing he hadn't actually seen her kill anyone, otherwise he would see her in a different light. "You should lie down, doctor's orders."

"Why don't you grab what you need and work from upstairs?" Mike asked.

Gail gave him a look.

"What? I can't stay up there by myself."

"I didn't leave you by yourself."

"Oh, him, no. Not the same thing. I'd much rather have your company. Although I'm getting the feeling he likes your company too."

"Why would you think that?"

"Because you are all he talked about since you left the room."

"He's probably a little excited about the 'work' he'll be doing here. Running some tests on me will be part of that. Maybe he's excited even about the prospects of finding out that I'm some kind of freak."

That brought a chuckle out of Mike. She thought about it, and his idea was a good excuse to get away from Tolido, at least for now. She waved her phone to Colson and told him he should call her as soon as he got something. Tolido came running.

"Could we start now? I'll make it quick," Tolido pleaded.

Gail looked at Mike and then back at Tolido.

"Mike can come with us if he wants to. There's an extra bed he could lie on."

"That works for me," Mike said.

"I thought you were only going to take some blood. Was there more?"

"Well, I want to conduct an assessment to better understand how your body functions."

"Great," Gail mumbled under her breath. It was bad enough she had to do that in the middle of everything, but to have Mike there would be a little nerve-racking for her. "I don't think that bed in there will be comfortable for you. Maybe you should get some proper rest in your own bed, and I'll catch up with you after we're done."

"I'll be fine," Mike said. "Unless you don't want me there."

"No, don't be silly," she said, as they made their way to Tolido's lab.

"You can sit here," Tolido said pointing to a chair.

Dr. Tolido took a sample of Gail's blood. The images she saw appeared a little fuzzy and she started feeling nauseous.

"What's wrong?' Mike asked.

"Mr. Steele, I would suggest you lie on that bed over there and let me take care of my patient," Tolido said.

"Lie down," she said. "I'm good."

Tolido labeled the test tubes with the blood and put them away.

"I'm going to run a full body scan," Tolido said. "You will need to change into this for me." He handed Gail a gown. "You can change over there," he said as he pointed to an area that was surrounded by a screen. She got up, but she saw multiples of everything and the room felt like it was spinning. She closed her eyes.

"Gail! Gail!"

She heard Mike calling her name but it sounded as if he was far away. She got it together and opened her eyes. Mike was on his feet. "Hey, how are you feeling?" he asked.

"Never better," she replied as she headed over to the changing area. She changed into the gown and made her way to Tolido who was standing at the scanner.

Tolido instructed her to lie on the scanner table. "This will only take a few minutes and then you're free to go."

Gail climbed onto the table and lay on her back.

"The images will give me an idea of what's going on inside your body now. I'm also going to be conducting DNA testing which will tell me what your vulnerabilities are in terms of diseases, and confirm if Colson is your biological father."

Gail could not wait for it to be over.

"You look like you're doing well so far," he

said as he glanced over his shoulder at Mike. "Although I have to admit, you looked like you were about to pass out a minute ago. Anything you want to tell me?"

"I was feeling a little nauseous," she said.

"Nausea. Is that all?"

"And a little dizzy, but I'm feeling much better now."

"Sure you are," Tolido said with a sarcastic tone. "I'll examine the scans of the gastrointestinal system first to see if I can identify what might be causing the nausea."

Mike was sitting up and appeared to be taking a keen interest in the conversation between Gail and Tolido. Gail couldn't wait to get up, but Tolido seemed to have encountered a problem. He kept repeating the scan of her abdominal area. "Don't move," he said. I'll be right back. He was off to another room before she could respond.

Mike came and stood next to the table she was lying on. "How are you feeling?" he asked.

"Better. Much better."

"Is the nausea gone completely?"

"Not completely but it's getting better."

"Do you think you might be pregnant?"

"No, I'm not pregnant."

"Are you sure?"

"I'm sure." She made a sound and exhaled.

"I didn't mean to upset you. I guess I want to know if there's a strong possibility that you are...you know, then you would need to make some changes."

"I know I'm not pregnant, but out of curiosity, what changes are you referring to?" Gail asked.

"Well, for starters, I don't think you should go out to find Brian. You'd need to leave that to me and whomever else Colson can find to make up a team. Second, you'd need to stop drinking coffee. Third...I don't actually have a third one right now, but I'll let you know when it comes to me."

"You won't need it." She shifted position several times. "Where's Tolido? I'm going to get bedsores by the time he returns."

Mike snickered. "Technically, it would be table sores, since you're lying on a table and not a bed."

"All right, I've had enough," Gail said. Before she got up, Tolido rushed back into the room.

"Mike, I need you for a second."

"What? Why?" Gail asked as she sat up. Mike held his position.

"Please don't get up. Just...give me a minute to figure something out. Mike, now, please," Tolido pleaded.

Mike took a few steps in the direction of the room that Tolido was in.

"Oh, no, no, no. If you two are going to discuss my results, you're going to do it in my presence."

"Fair enough." Tolido retrieved a scan result and held it up for Mike to see. "What does that look like to you?" he asked Mike as he pointed at something on the result. Mike examined it. He seemed to have lost his tongue.

Gail tried to read his expression, but was not sure what to make of it.

"That's not possible," he said as he looked at Gail, then back at the scan. "If this is what I think it is...no, it can't be. It's not possible."

"You know what it is?" Tolido asked.

"Well, I know what it looks like but like I said, that's not possible."

"What's not possible?" Gail asked. Mike attempted to pull up her gown.

"Hey!" Gail shouted.

"Sorry, very sorry. Tolido, May I have another gown to cover her lower half? I want to check her abdomen."

"If one of you don't tell me what's going on, you won't be seeing my anything, because I'll be leaving."

"You have what looks to me like gunshot pellets inside your body. Wait, did you get shot this morning?"

"I don't remember getting shot," she said.

"You had blood all over you when you came out. Are you sure you weren't shot? Do you remember being in pain"? Mike asked.

The only time she recalled being in pain was when she thought she'd lost him. This was not going to be easy, she thought. How could she explain to him that the entire event was like an out-of-body experience? First she visualized it, then she knew what she needed to do and it was like she watched herself execute the plan. She didn't have time to feel. It was ironic that someone so good at remembering things could not recall getting shot. What would Mike think of her if he knew she was able to switch into a mode where she was like a killing machine?

"So many things happened so fast, but I don't remember getting shot," Gail said in a very low voice. She was experiencing that queasy feeling again.

Tolido looked confused. "How is it possible for you to get shot and not know it? That doesn't make any sense," he said, sounding somewhat frustrated.

"Back off!" Mike said to Tolido. "If she said she doesn't remember, then she doesn't remember. End of story. We need to find out if these are really pellets inside her and then figure out how to deal with them."

"Right," Tolido said. "I apologize for my outburst, but could you please explain to me where the point of entry is because she does not have a wound or a scar."

"Oh!" Mike said. "We thought you knew."

"Knew what?" Tolido asked, wide-eyed.

"She can heal in a matter of minutes."

"Get out of here! Are you serious?"

Mike nodded.

"Oh, my word. May I?" he asked as he touched her belly. He move his hand across her skin in the location of the pellets. "No wound," he said as he continued to move his hand. Then he moved a little too far below her belly button. Mike held on to his hand.

"I think that's enough," Mike said.

"Apologies."

Mike placed a hand on her forehead. "What's happening?" he asked her.

"I think I'm going to throw up," she said as she rolled to her side and pushed herself up to a sitting position.

"Get her something to throw up in," Mike told Tolido.

Tolido made it just in time with the container for Gail to vomit into.

Gail watched as Tolido and Mike examined her vomitus.

"These are definitely gunshot pellets," Mike said.

Chapter 18

After running a few more scans, Tolido told Gail he thought her body moved most of the pellets to her stomach which explained her nausea. However, there were a few pellets still inside her. He said the pellets looked smaller with each subsequent scan.

Colson called Gail to let her know the DNA sample from the blast had arrived. Tolido left to collect the samples he needed to work on.

Mike stayed back with Gail as she got dressed. "Feeling better?" he asked.

"I'm actually feeling pretty good since I barfed," she said. "Good" was a bit of an understatement. She had a surge of energy, like she'd gulped down a pint of energy drink. Although she felt great physically, she could not help but notice that Mike appeared a lot less jovial. "How about you? Are *you* feeling okay?"

"Yep," he said as he nodded and smiled, but it was not enough to hide the ambivalence that enthralled him.

She yanked his shirt. "What's on your mind?"

"Nothing. We should go see what those guys are up to," Mike said as he left the room.

They joined Colson for an update. Gail noticed that Mike kept some distance between them as if he was trying to avoid her. Suddenly she was no longer the picture of perfection he'd said she was. Maybe her freakish bodily functions was too much for anyone to accept, even for him. Gail thought maybe he realized he didn't know who she was, nor what she was. She couldn't blame him for pulling away. Any thought she had on sharing her unusual experience during times of danger with him was immediately banished.

Colson whispered to Gail. "Maybe you should take a break and allow your body to heal."

Clearly, Tolido filled him in about the pellets inside her. "No, I'm good," Gail said, trying not to make eye contact with Mike. He seemed uncomfortable and she didn't want to make things any more unbearable for him. "How long is this going to take?" she asked Colson.

"Hard to say. Once Tolido completes the DNA profiles, we'll run a comparison against the government's database to see if we find a match."

"Profiles? Are we trying to identify more than one person?" Gail asked.

"Yes. There was another unidentified body buried in the rubble."

"Male of female?"

"We don't know that, either," Colson said.

Gail was almost afraid to ask why. "Why don't we know? Was it not that obvious to the person who collected the sample?"

Colson spoke slowly as if he was carefully choosing his words. "It's very possible the sample was from a woman, but since there was no body I can't say for sure. It was taken from an unaccounted-for body part."

Gail needed some air. "Maybe I'll go get some rest after all. Call me when you have something." She headed upstairs to her room. She stayed only long enough to close the door that separated her room from Mike's. While most of the buzzing continued in the basement, Gail exited the building through the main door, taking one of the vehicles parked at the front. She knew Jeanine Grayson, the woman in the photograph, was in the system. If the sample they had was hers then they would have no problem finding a match.

Keri, the missing receptionist, might not be in the system. Therefore, they will need a sample of her DNA for comparison. Earlier, Gail took the opportunity to take a peek at Keri's address in the file. She planned to grab a few strands of hair from Keri's hair brush at her apartment. She needed to do the same for Brian, although in her heart she did not believe the body part they found belonged to him. "He's alive," she said. "He has to be."

Gail drove into the compound where the receptionist lived. There was a sign at the gate that said, "Condo for Lease." It was the perfect opportunity to get into the building without raising suspicion. She parked her car and sat there while she took a look around. There was a couple who picked up a brochure and then went inside the building. Gail assumed they were there to view the available condo. She tried to cover as much of her face as she could by wearing large-frame dark glasses and pulling a cap over her forehead.

After retrieving a brochure about the condo, she headed inside. Gail opted to use the stairs instead of the elevator that was half full. Based on her apartment number, Keri's unit should have been on the second floor. Gail opened the door to the second floor. It was quiet, except for one man who looked like he was heading to the pool.

As soon as she found the unit, she got tools out of her backpack, including a pair of latex gloves. The lock proved easy to pick, and once Gail closed the door behind her, she glanced around the apartment. How could a receptionist afford this place on her salary? A two-bedroom condo in a prime location with an onsite gym and a swimming pool, according to the brochure. The place had a weird smell, but other than that, everything looked in order.

Gail went into the main bathroom and opened the medicine cabinet. There was more than enough blond hair in the brush, but Gail wanted to make sure she got hairs with the follicle intact. The smell was much stronger in the bathroom. Gail noticed the green toilet bowl cleaner was still in the toilet.

That must have been what she was smelling, that strong bleach scent. She checked the closet and there were some men's clothes in it but the closet didn't have a lot of empty hangers.

The living and dining area was a rectangular space defined by furniture placement. At the far end of the space was a kitchen which was separated from the dining area by a breakfast bar. The living room was at the front of the space and included a computer desk. The monitor was off, but the CPU's light was on. Gail turned on the monitor and fortunately, there was no password on the screen saver. She opened Keri's e-mail program. There were a lot of unread e-mails dating back to the day she quit her job. As Gail skipped through the pages, she noticed there were e-mails from her husband and that the subject line did not seem work related. She opened one of them. Her heart just about stopped.

It was one thing to suspect her husband was cheating, but a different thing when she had proof in his own words. If ever she thought those photographs of him and the other woman, Jeanine the new receptionist who'd replaced Keri, were manipulated, that thought no longer existed.

She got up and went back to the medicine cabinet and looked around again. Gail didn't find what she was looking for until she checked the top drawer of the bathroom vanity. There it was, a pregnancy test. Keri was pregnant with Brian's child and he'd wanted her to have an abortion. No wonder the girl quit so abruptly. Brian never even skipped a beat, he swapped out one receptionist for the other.

How could Gail have been married to this man for so long?

She heard the doorknob to the apartment rattling. Someone was trying to open the door. She looked around quickly for a window to go through, but then someone shouted.

"Not that one, the one at the other end!"

The jiggling of the door knob stopped, and the sound of footsteps finally faded. Gail breathed a sigh of relief. She was about to leave, but she couldn't. The curiosity of wanting to know more about the woman; well, one of the women her husband had been canoodling with, was overpowering.

The first thing on her mind were the men's clothes in the closet. She checked those. They didn't seem like Brian's size, at least not his length. Brian was six feet two inches. The pants in the closet were for someone shorter. It meant Keri was seeing someone else. She looked around for photographs that might give her an idea. She decided to check Keri's computer for digital photos.

The e-mail program was still open and Gail decided to torture herself by reading more of them from her husband. As she was looking at older e-mails, Gail noticed that there were frequent correspondence between Keri and another man. Gail read a few of the e-mails from the other guy, Nathan Clare. It seemed Keri wasn't sure whose baby she was carrying, so she'd told both men she was pregnant with his child.

Gail muttered under her breath. She wanted to find Brian and then they could go their separate ways. She thought of Alex, and how it would affect him if she broke up the family. She felt guilty for harboring thoughts of a life without her husband. Gail swore to herself she was done feeling guilty for wanting more. Because although it was possible that Brian was not the father of Keri's baby, the mere fact that the possibility existed meant he'd never really changed.

A call came in on her cell phone. Gail looked at it for a few seconds then hit the ignore button. She was not in the mood to talk to anyone. She figured Keri had good reason to want to leave and was most likely alive and well somewhere contemplating her next move. Gail was curious about the other man. Why? It was her nature. She checked the computer for digital photographs. None of the photographs she found yielded anything valuable. Gail checked the recycle bin on Keri's computer which had a ton of files in it. She opened a few documents, one of which got her attention. It was a letterhead for a security company called Protector Max.

The phones from the guy who had his throat

slashed and the guy who shot her at the inn had been registered to Protector Max. Things no longer seemed as clear-cut as it did a minute ago. She kept looking at more files, hoping she would find something that gave her an idea of where Brian could be. Something about the files made her stop. The letterhead was created the day Keri did not show up for work. The files were deleted a few days ago, when Keri was supposedly away on vacation.

Gail's cell phone rang again. She thought it was best to answer than have Colson looking for her. "Ah, hello?" she said trying to sound tired.

"Hey," Mike said.

"What are you doing with this phone?"

"Colson said I should call you and let you know that the woman in the rubble was Jeanine."

"What about the other sample, do they know the gender? Have they found a match?"

"Not yet, they're still working on it. Are you in your room?"

"Ah..." She didn't want him to know she was not there, but she didn't want to lie, either.

"Can I come up? I want to talk to you."

"I can't do a face-to-face now, maybe later. Or if you want, you could simply tell me over the phone," she said as she continued her search on the computer.

"I'm not sure how to say this, but I feel like you're trying to avoid me."

Gail heard him, but she was only half listening. Most of her attention was on the files she was looking through.

"I always felt like we could tell each other anything. Through the years, I think you come to know every little embarrassing thing about me, things that I would not share with anyone else."

That resonated with her, because she had one more embarrassing saga unfolding right in front of her. She clearly did not want Colson and the rest of the world to know the entire story. She wasn't even sure she wanted Mike to know. She felt ashamed, and wonder if she should bother to continue looking for Brian. Maybe it was best to assume that he ran off with someone and save herself the heartache and stress.

"I have one more thing to add to my list of shameful acts. Are you still there?" Mike asked.

"I'm listening," she said. And this time she really was.

"This morning when you were feeling sick. I prayed you weren't pregnant. I prayed that whatever it was that was making you ill to be anything else but a baby. I thought if you were pregnant, you'd be more inclined to give Brian another chance. Then when I looked at your results and saw that what was inside you could've killed you. I realized how selfish I was. I was thinking too much about what I wanted, not what you wanted, and I'm sorry."

Gail was moved by what Mike just told her. She wasn't sure if it was because she felt vulnerable or because she really believed he was such a fantastic man who she was happy to have in her life. She felt like God had created some sort of balance in her life. On one hand, she was hurting like hell from the actions of her husband, and on the other hand, she had Mike who was the most caring man she had ever met.

She wasn't sure what to say but wanted him to know she was listening. "I thought you wanted to stay away because you were troubled by what you saw. And for the record, I wouldn't blame you."

"I was worried for you, yes, but it doesn't change how I see you. Nothing will," he said.

"Don't be too sure about that," she said. Gail knew it was going to take a lot for him to see her the same way after she told him how her mind functioned, but she didn't want lies to start accumulating between them. They'd been honest with each other so far, and she wanted to keep it that way. "What I have to tell you may be scarier than what you saw earlier," she said.

"Does that mean I'm forgiven? I'm coming

up," he said.

"Don't."

"I won't stay long I just want to see you."

"I'm not in there. I'm out."

"Out. As in out on the road?" he asked.

"Technically I'm not *on* the road. I'm in a condo," she said.

"Stop stalling and tell me where you are."

"I'm at the receptionist's apartment. Promise not to say anything to Colson. I'll tell him myself when I get there."

"I guess there's no point in me asking you why you went there. Did you find anything useful?"

"I found more than I bargained for."

"Yeah? Like what?"

"Well, I got a sample of her hair for the guys to compare the female DNA to, but we know that's Jeanine."

"Okay, but it sounds like there's more."

There was, but it was hard for her to actually say the words out loud. She blurted, "Brian was having an affair with her."

"Well, we kind of suspected that based on the photographs."

"Keri. Brian was having an affair with Keri." She let out a loud breath at the end of that sentence as if she'd just completed a physically strenuous task.

"I hate to ask this, but are you sure?"

"Very sure."

"I'm really sorry."

"Don't be. You're not the reason my marriage is over," she said. At least ten seconds elapsed before Mike responded.

"Say that again."

"I said, don't be."

"No. Just the last four words. I want you to repeat the last four words," he said.

"What? My marriage is over? Is that what you want me to repeat?"

"Yes. But not as a question. I want to hear it as a statement."

She heard a strange sound.

"I know I promise to be less selfish, but I really want to know if you truly believe it."

She heard the noise again.

"Gail!"

"Sshhh. I heard something," Gail said. The sound was coming from the kitchen. She had a clear view of the kitchen, but she didn't see anything unusual. Still she pulled a dagger out of her boot and slowly walked into the kitchen. She looked around, trying to figure out what the sound was and where it came from. Then she realized the sound was from the icemaker in the refrigerator.

"It's the refrigerator," she said. "It looks

like...let me check something. Hang on."

The refrigerator had a double door with the icemaker on the left door. A smear next to the icemaker caught her attention.

She touched the spot. It streaked along the edge of the freezer. She reached to open the door. Nothing could have prepared her for what was inside.

Gail screeched and dropped the phone.

Chapter 19

"Gail? Gail? What is it?" Mike asked.

"A head. There's a head in the freezer," she whispered. "It's in a bag. Blond hair."

"Gail, listen to me, get out of there. Get out of there now!" Mike said.

"I'm leaving." She grabbed her backpack, and turned the monitor off.

"If you were planning on going to your house, please don't," Mike said. "Come straight here. Got it?"

"Got it." She exited the apartment, making sure to turn the lock on the door. There was no one in the hallway, but as she got close to the door that led to the stairs, she heard someone. Whoever it was entered Keri's apartment or the apartment next to hers. Gail was not sure because she did not turn around. She ran as fast as she could down the stairs, but was careful to stop and walk at a normal pace once she got out.

Not too long ago she wondered if she should continue looking for Brian. Now she had no choice. She had to find him. She could not go on with her life not knowing what happened to him especially now that so many people connected to him have turned up dead.

Gail made sure she was not followed before she headed back to the center.

"Hey, come here," Mike said. He held her next to him in a comforting embrace. He walked her to her room and told her he would take the hair sample to Colson. "Could you see…?"

"It's not him, I think it's Keri," she said. The head in the bag looked like Keri's. She could not understand how it was that she could kill four men without a second thought, but the decapitated head of her husband's lover caused such emotional distress. There was no doubt she was saddened by the discovery, but she was happy that it was not Brian's head in that bag.

Gail decided to take a shower after Mike left. She was stressed and always found the feeling of the water on her face to be somewhat therapeutic. As she closed her eyes and the water ran down her face, she saw flashes of the head in the bag, again and again. It was like her brain kept replaying a thirty second clip of her discovery of the head in the freezer. She got out of the shower sooner than she wanted.

Not long after Gail got dressed, Mike returned with Colson.

Gail let Colson enfold her in his arms. "Mike told me about your gruesome find." She stayed in his embrace while he confirmed that the second sample from the rubble was Keri. "Did they find more than one body part?" Gail asked.

"No, just the one leg, or what was left of it, after the blast." Colson said.

"Someone went through a whole lot of trouble to prevent anyone from finding her," Gail said and moved away from him. "Dismembering her, and then dumping her body parts in different places. Because I didn't see anything else but her head, so it means the rest of her was probably dumped someplace else."

"Or maybe several different places," Mike said.

"What kind of a monster would do such a thing?" Gail asked.

"I don't know. But whoever it is probably knows where Brian is," Colson said.

Gail could not bear the thought that Brian may have suffered the same fate as Keri, and she would never find him. She shivered and waved off Colson. "Did you find anything else in the apartment that could point us in the right direction?" Colson asked.

"There was a letterhead design on her computer for the security company Protector

Max," Gail told them. "Daniel and the guy who attacked me at the inn had phones registered to the same company."

"Do you think she was part of this scheme?" Mike asked.

"I don't know, but if she was, they took her out of the game before Brian was kidnapped."

"How do you know that?" Colson asked.

"Just a guess," Gail said. "An educated guess." She saw that Colson and Mike needed more information to be convinced. "When you turn on your computer, tablet, or even your smart phone, what is it you do every day, several times a day?"

Colson and Mike looked at each other.

"Given the nature of the question I probably should have only asked Mike. So what is it you do almost every day?"

"Check e-mail," he said.

"Right," Gail said. "Keri had unread e-mail messages from the day she quit, but there were files created and deleted after that date. There were files deleted two days ago. There's no way she would be spending that amount of time on her computer and not click on a single e-mail. Someone was using that computer, but it wasn't Keri."

"You're probably right," Colson said. "They needed to get rid of her to make a way for

Jeanine. But it seems that once Jeanine completed her part, they got rid of her too."

"She was seeing someone named Nathan Clare. I don't know anything about him yet but I'm curious as to his whereabouts," Gail said.

"I'll have one of the guys check it out," Colson said.

Gail said nothing, she simply stared at him, or more precisely, through him. She was deep in thought, trying to put all the pieces together in a way that made sense.

"We're going to find him. I won't stop until we do. Please don't run off by yourself again," he said as he kissed her head. Colson walked to the door, then stopped right in front of Mike. "Stay with her for me. Will you?"

"Sure," Mike said.

"Colson," Gail called. He turned around and looked at her. "They knew we were going to be at that cabin before we got there."

"What are you saying?"

"We need to figure out how they came by that information, and you need to be very careful. Until then, keep this information between the three of us."

"All right," Colson said. "Let me know if you need anything."

Mike and Gail looked at each other. She deliberately had not told Colson about her husband's intimate involvement with Keri because she did not think it would help them find Brian any sooner. It would probably make him resent Brian. Colson seemed genuinely concerned about her and she didn't want him to have second thoughts about finding her husband.

She felt Mike's eyes on her. "Thanks for not saying anything."

"Anything about what?"

"About Brian and Keri. He doesn't need to know."

Mike sat on the bed and opened a file he'd gotten from Colson. "Knowing him, it's only a matter of time before he finds out."

"I'll deal with it then."

"It's your call."

Gail opened the laptop. She wanted to find out more about Protector Max and their employees. Learning about Brian's relationship with Keri affected Gail more than she let on. The pounding headache was the only telltale sign that she was hurt by his actions. Trying to find some form of relief, she went to the bathroom and washed her face with some almost hot water.

"Are you feeling nauseous again?" Mike asked.

"No, I have a headache."

"When did that start?"

She looked at him, and without saying a word, saw that he figured it out.

"It's tension. You should try to relax, and being on that laptop will only make it worse."

"I know."

"Let me try something."

"No, don't touch my feet," Gail told him. "Although that might work."

"There's something else I want to try. Something I learned from you."

"Me?"

"There's something you did when I was all stressed out and it totally relaxed me. I don't think you even realized what you were doing, but it worked every time. He stood up and faced her. "Close your eyes."

She reluctantly closed them.

"Okay, now just go with the flow, don't fight it." Mike positioned her head so that it rested on his chest and the back of her neck was slightly stretched. He moved her hair away and then gently massaged the back of her neck with his fingers. Before long, Gail could feel the tension melting away.

"How's that?" he asked.

"Better, thank you." Headache diminished and back in focus, she was ready to start. Gail found out that Protector Max provided personal bodyguards for hire. Among their very short list of clients were several companies, including Zsulrick Inc.

"I think the company your mother worked for had some connection to Zsulrick Inc.," Mike said as he flipped through some papers.

"Yes, I remember that. So Protector Max is working for Zsulrick."

"It's not uncommon for executives to have personal protection, especially if they're attending certain events," Mike said. "But if Zsulrick is behind the kidnapping, then this would be a way for the company to explain payment to Protector Max for services rendered. Although lately there could be a legitimate reason for a number of their executives to feel less than safe in public."

"Why?"

"They had a drug on the market that was causing some unusual bleeding. It has since been recalled. I think there were some casualties. I really don't know all the details but my point is, the executives of Zsulrick may have good reason to seek the services of professional bodyguards."

"I'll see if I can find the names of the executives who were assigned Protector Max bodyguards."

"That could be helpful if one or more of

them hired those guys to come after you. Or it could send you running after the wrong person, if the real mastermind's name is not on the client list at all."

"So what do you suggest?"

"Well it's safe to say that one or more persons at Zsulrick want you dead. We need to figure out why they feel so threatened by you. What is it they think you know that's worth killing so many people over? It probably has to do with your mother's work."

"I only know what Colson told me," Gail said. "But it's not like you can take down a multi-billion dollar company by saying they did all these terrible things without solid proof. I'm sure they know that. There has to be something else."

"Can you find out if there any class action suits against Zsulrick?" Mike asked.

"That's a good idea. I'll check." She paused for a moment.

"What is it?"

"I'm wondering if Brian is alive. These people are killing their own people, so why would they keep him alive?"

"We can't know for sure until we find him, but my guess is that they will probably keep him alive as bait. They will use him to draw you out."

As bad as that sounded, Gail took comfort in the thought.

Zsulrick Inc. Headquarters in New York

It was almost the end of the workday. Alvin walked up to the front desk where a receptionist was seated. "Hello, I'm here to see Wade Mohler."

She tapped away at her computer, then asked, "And you are?"

"Alvin Craig."

"One moment, Mr. Craig." She dialed a number. "Yes, there is an Alvin Craig here to see Mr. Mohler. Will do." She hung up. "Mr. Mohler is at the tail end of another meeting. Please have a seat. I'll let you know when he's available."

"Thank you." Alvin's law firm had offices that operated in New York, California and, very soon, Washington. Zsulrick Inc. wanted desperately to settle some lawsuits brought against them for a medication they'd since pulled from the market. Mohler made Alvin an offer that was difficult to turn down. Mohler told him, for his part, he would be rewarded in three ways. First, he would receive one million dollars wired to an offshore account. Second, his New York office would be retained for legal consultation by Zsulrick Inc., and last but not by any means least, Mohler would hand over the information they'd collected about his law firm regarding overbilling their clients which dated back to when his father was alive.

For his part, Alvin needed to find out if the ability of the boy in the video was real, and if he was related to the one person who could potentially destroy the corporation. The plan, as Alvin understood it, was to have Gail's husband kidnapped. According to Mohler, he wanted her to be kept busy chasing her prime suspect, Colson. She would not have time to watch the news, let alone be a threat to them.

Once they'd settled the cases brought against them. They would release her husband unharmed. However, Alvin was getting the sense he hadn't been told the full story. Nevertheless, he hoped he could walk away with at least one of the three promises made to him.

"Mr. Craig?"

"Yes."

"Mr. Mohler will see you now. Follow me."

Alvin was escorted to a small conference room where he waited for Mohler to arrive. Alvin felt a bit uneasy. The gentleman who escorted him looked like he was part of the security team for the building, and the conference room he was in wasn't even on the same floor as Mohler's office. The room was long and narrow, with most of the space occupied by a very long modular table and chairs. Alvin was instructed to sit closer to the far end of the room. The gentleman who escorted him sat close to the door.

The wait was long and arduous. Alvin shifted positions in his chair several times. He looked at his watch a number of times, quite often within the same minute. Alvin looked around the room for anything that could hold his attention, even for a little bit.

Nothing. The blinds were closed so there was no view. His eyes landed on the man sitting at the other end of the table who hadn't moved an inch since he sat down. That view did not help. If anything, it made Alvin more nervous.

Mohler finally strolled in. "Alvin, I don't recall us having a scheduled meeting. What's so pressing that it couldn't wait?"

"I was at our New York office and thought I'd drop by." He paused for a moment to steady himself. "Mr. Mohler, I'm just going to cut to the chase. We had an agreement. I've lived up to my end of the agreement and I'm expecting you to do the same."

"Of course, but we're not at the finish line yet. There are still a number of people who've not accepted our offer. The team has done a great job to keep it out of the press so far, but we can't afford to get comfortable. Not when there's a threat to this corporation running around."

"So what are you suggesting?"

"I'm not suggesting anything. The corporation is on the brink of releasing a new innovative drug, and the threat is more extensive that I'd originally communicated. However, this is not something for you to concern yourself with. We have qualified personnel to take care of that."

"I thought that was what you wanted. As a matter of fact that's what you told me. You wanted her to be busy running around looking for her husband. When she finds him she'd be thankful and count her lucky stars. When did things get so far? No, you can't do this," Alvin said.

"Look, we don't know how much she knows. Our approach is to take whatever steps necessary to neutralize the situation. The wheels are already in motion, my friend. You might as well sit back and enjoy the ride."

"You made a lot of promises to me. None of which you've kept. You promised me a million dollars and I've yet to receive a penny."

Mohler laughed. "A million dollars? You're worried about a million dollars? Alvin, if you stick with us you'll be making several millions."

"What about those files? The agreement was

you'd give me everything you have. I think I've earned at least that."

"All in good time, Alvin," Mohler said as he beckoned to the guy in the suit to come and escort Alvin out.

Chapter 20

There was a knock at the door. Gail and Mike looked at each other.

"It's open," Mike yelled.

"Hi, I hope I'm not interrupting," Tolido said. "Can I talk to you for a second?" he asked Gail.

"Now?" Gail asked.

"Yes, now would be good."

"It's not a good time, Tolido, I'm right in the middle of something here. Whatever it is, I'm sure it can wait."

"Actually, it can't."

Gail sighed. "Okay, make it quick."

Tolido looked at Mike and then at Gail, and back at Mike again.

"I can leave if you want me to," Mike said.

"That's not necessary," Gail said. "All right, Tolido, let's here what's so important."

Tolido cleared his throat. "I'll start with the good news. Colson is indeed your biological father."

"That's the good news? What's the bad

news?" Gail asked.

"Your white blood cell count is extremely high. This means your body is fighting an infection. I may have to put you on some antibiotics if necessary."

"That's not so bad, because I feel fine," Gail said.

"I'm not finished," Tolido said. "You have a genetic marking that I am unable to identify."

"What does that mean?" Mike asked.

"Just what I said. I don't know where it came from."

"Maybe the sample was contaminated. Why don't you take some more blood and run it again," Gail said hoping that would get rid of Tolido.

"That's what I thought. But then I compared your genetic markings to the one that was done when you were a teenager. There was an unidentified marking on that result as well, except it has changed."

"What has changed?" Mike asked.

"The unidentified marking has changed, it's not the same as it was years ago," Tolido explained.

Gail recalled some of her mother's recordings mentioned something about her test had changed, but her notes did not say what. She sat in silence as Mike kept throwing questions at Tolido.

"What is this marking?" Mike asked.

"I don't know," Tolido replied.

"What does it mean?"

"How the hell should I know?" Tolido shouted. "I'm sorry for the outburst."

"Don't worry about it," Mike said.

"At the risk of being booted out of the room, I'm going to ask you to let me run another scan on you," Tolido said to Gail.

"You've got to be kidding. I've more pressing matters to deal with, body scans can wait," Gail said.

"I'll make it quick. I want to see where those pellets are. The ones that were still inside you."

"Tolido, do you know why I'm here?" Gail asked.

"Here, meaning the center?"

"No, this room. Of course the center."

"You need Colson's help to find your husband?"

"Bingo," Gail said. "And that is my priority. With all due respect, I know you're fascinated with science, but I'm not here to be your personal lab rat."

"Let me help you," Tolido said.

"I think you're already helping, Tolido," Gail said. "And I really appreciate it."

"No, I mean help the both of you."

Gail and Mike looked at each other.

"Help us to do what, exactly?" Mike asked.

Tolido pulled the chair next to the bed and sat on it. "I know a lot about drugs and if you're researching Zsulrick, which I know you *are*, you'll find my wealth of knowledge quite invaluable."

"Okay, what do you know about Zsulrick's latest drug recall?" Gail asked.

"Not so fast," Tolido said. "We need to first come to some agreement before I actually help you."

"What do you want from me?"

"I'll help you, if you agree to let me run some more tests on you."

Gail thought about Tolido's proposal.

"Are you seriously considering this?" Mike asked.

She knew it was a risk to let one more person in, but she didn't believe Tolido was a threat. With his trained eyes and extensive knowledge, if there was a link between her mother's research and drug Zsulrick was manufacturing, then he could find it faster than she could. If she'd any chance of finding Brian alive, they'd need to move fast. "Absolutely, give him my mother's research and anything else you think he needs," Gail said.

Tolido's eyes lit up as he went through the

documents. Talk about a major geek.

"What do you do for fun?" Tolido asked.

Gail and Mike looked at each other because they weren't sure who he was talking to. Either way, Gail was not the least bit interested in small talk. They both resumed what they were doing without responding.

"Gail, that question was meant for you," Tolido said.

Talking about herself made Gail uncomfortable, and she always avoided any such situation, as much as she could. "I'm not interested in this 'get to know me' segment. Besides, you're supposed to be working, not talking."

"I work better when I talk, so humor me. What do you do for fun?"

"I paint," she said trying to keep the conversation to a minimum.

"On canvas?"

"Yes."

"So, I take it you're not married," Tolido said, looking up at Mike.

Mike did not respond, he kept flipping through the file. Gail was beginning to wonder if she'd made a mistake.

"How did you two meet?" Tolido continued.

"None of your business, "Mike said. "Just focus on what you're doing."

"That kind of hostility is really uncalled for," Tolido said. "Besides, I'll have you know that despite my flapping lips I'm making great progress." He spent a short moment being quiet then he was at it again. It was Gail's turn again. "Does your husband know that you are...hmmm...how should I put this?"

"A freak?" Gail asked. "No, he doesn't."

"I didn't say you're a freak, but I wonder how he would take the news if he didn't already know."

Gail wondered the same thing, but at this point it no longer mattered because he didn't need to know. But the question she was asking herself was what kind of life would she have? At some point this madness will come to an end, and she would want a normal life. Normal, she thought. How could she expect to have a normal life, when she was anything but normal?

"I'm sorry. I didn't mean to snap at you," Gail said to Tolido. It was a valid question but one that led to too many other questions for which she had no answer.

The minutes with Tolido finally paid off.

"I found a drug Zsulrick had on the market. It was targeted for people who were at risk for myocardial infarction. It worked by keeping the blood free of clots," Tolido said.

"We know about that drug. The marketing

push was that it did not cause upset stomach, and doctors could prescribe a loading dose for people who actually have blood clots. However, some patients suffered unusual bleeding, and there've been a few deaths that may be linked to the drug," Mike said.

"Yes, but there are some similarities in the symptoms caused by the Zenoprit and the drug your mother worked on years ago."

"How long was Zenoprit on the market?" Gail asked.

"Gail, what I'm telling you is not definitive," Tolido said.

"I know. How long?"

"Not sure," Tolido said.

"More than a year?"

"I think so, yes."

"Zenoprit was cheap and on the market for a while before it was recalled, therefore I'm quite sure a *lot* of people had taken it. And even those who had no bleeding issues may develop some severe complications later. If this information got out, Zsulrick Inc. would be looking at a whole lot more civil suits. Tolido, I could kiss you," Gail said jokingly.

"Really?" Tolido asked with a grin.

"That's not going to happen," Mike said.

"Do I detect a hint of jealousy?" Tolido asked.

Both men laughed.

"You are not as bad as I thought, Tolido. Inappropriate questions aside, you did an awesome job. Thank you," Mike said as he shook Tolido's hand.

"Thanks, Tolido," Gail said as she reached to shake his hand too.

"How about a hug?" Tolido asked.

"Sure. Why not," Gail said as she hugged him.

Tolido wasted no time in asking for what he wanted. "Now how about that scan?"

"Yeah, sure. Why don't you give me a few minutes? I'll come by, as long as you make it quick."

"Consider it a date," Tolido said as he left the room.

Mike closed the door and stood there looking at her.

"What?" she asked.

"You want to talk about it?" Mike asked.

"Talk about what?"

"What Tolido said about how Brian would feel if he knew what we know?"

"Doesn't matter," she said.

"Good. Then what's bothering you?" he asked. "I mean, other than the obvious?"

"Nothing, I'm good."

"You see, whenever you say you're good it

usually means you have something on your mind. What is it?"

"Give it a rest, Mike."

"Do you think this is going to change the way I feel about you?"

"Let's continue this discussion another time." Gail packed up the papers Tolido was working on.

"No, I want to hear it."

"It's not important," she said.

"It's important to me. If it makes you doubt me then it's extremely important to me."

She sat on the bed with the files in her lap.

He knelt in front of her. "You're still the same Gail I've known all these years."

"Are you telling me you don't see me in a different way since you learned all that strange stuff about me?" she asked.

"No. Well, yes. Sort of," he said.

"I don't blame you."

"It's not what you think. I see there's a chance that I might finally have what I've always wanted but was too foolish to make happen, and yes, I think you could kick my ass if you wanted to, but none of that other stuff matters," Mike said.

"So what, you think that you and I'll be a couple and live happily ever after?" Gail asked.

"Why not?"

She got up and walked to the door. "I'm going to check with Colson to see if he has any new leads."

Mike dashed to the door before she could leave. "I'm sorry. I was being selfish again."

"How's your head?" she asked.

Mike looked confused.

"We should wait until you've fully recovered. Besides, I can't make any decisions right now. I'm sure you understand."

"No pressure," he said. "I'll wait."

"Good to know." Gail eased the door open. "I'll be back after I talk to Colson."

"What about the scan?"

"Right. I'll swing by Tolido after I'm done with Colson."

"I'd like to see the scan, if you don't mind," Mike said.

"Not a problem. I'll meet you by Tolido's lab then."

"Gail, I hope what I told you doesn't change our relationship. I don't want you to feel awkward around me. I want us to be able to still embrace each other without you worrying about where it may lead. It's not going anywhere until you make a decision that this is what you want. Okay?" In keeping with his speech, he hugged her.

Gail headed down the corridor and listened

as he closed the door. She grabbed a drink from the dining area and made a quick call to Celia and Alex as she headed to the basement. She decided to stop by Tolido first to let him know he needed to wait a few more minutes. Suddenly, she wasn't feeling like she wanted to avoid the tests. Mike was willing to accept her despite her abnormalities. She couldn't help but let her mind drift off to think about Brian and how things would've turned out if they'd taken the trip. Would she have had the guts to tell him what she knew then about herself? Maybe this was an easy way out for her. No need to open up who she was, or even what she was, to Brian. On the other hand, she wondered if it was possible for Brian to accept her, the way Mike did. No point in playing "what if" games now.

Gail was almost finished with her drink by the time she reached Tolido's lab.

"Gail, I was wondering whether or not you were going to show up. I see you're a woman of your word," Tolido said.

Gail stopped at the door. She heard someone whispering. She tried to zero in on where the sound was coming from.

"I—"

"Shh." Gail put her index finger to her lips. She left Tolido in his lab and slowly followed the sound further down the hall and around the corner. Some of the rooms in that area had medical equipment but that was it. A man said something about New York. She stopped right in front of the door where the whisper came from. Then she heard, "Colson knows he's in New York."

"We can't have him talking to Colson," said the man at the other end of the line.

Tolido came around the corner. "What are you doing? Those rooms are empty."

The whispering stopped and Gail heard the click of a gun.

Chapter 21

She kicked the door open and threw her bottle of water at the man with the gun. Gail ran up the side of the wall and dove down fist first in his right jaw as he tried to deflect the bottle. She grabbed the hand with the gun, drove her elbow into his ribs and hit his arm so hard against her knee. As his straightened elbow hit her knee, he screamed. The gun fell to the floor. Gail dove after the gun, picked it up and pointed it at him.

"Don't move," she said. "Who are you?" She noticed his cell phone was on the floor in pieces. "Who were you talking to?"

"I can't," he said.

"You can't what?" Gail asked.

"They'll kill me."

"I hate to break it to you buddy, but *they* are the least of your problems right now. Your primary concern is me with a gun pointed at you."

"Go ahead and kill me. At least they'll not hurt my family, and my little girl will get treated, like they promised," he said.

"Who promised to treat your little girl?"

The man didn't respond.

"Talk to me, damn it. What's wrong with your daughter?"

The man was shaking.

"So you're doing this for your daughter?"

He nodded.

"Did you tell them about this place?"

He continued shaking. His right arm appeared broken at the elbow.

"I need to know if this location was compromised. Was it?"

"No."

"Do you know where my husband is?"

"Who?"

"My husband. Your people kidnapped my husband."

"No, no, I don't know anything about it. I had nothing to do with that."

"What do you know about the man you were talking to on the phone? What's his name?" Gail asked.

"I can't tell you. If I talk they'll kill me and then they'll kill my family. They don't wait for you to talk. If they suspect you will, they'll kill you before you have a chance."

"Who's in New York?"

The man did not respond.

"Please, I'm not going to hurt you, but I really need your help. Who is in New York?"

"Alvin."

"Alvin Craig?'

"Yes."

"Do they think Alvin might talk? Are they going after him?"

"They will eliminate anyone they consider a threat. If they even think I'm alive after today, my family will not be safe."

"Who're *they*? Give me a name."

"And then what? You're' just going to let me waltz out of here and we pretend this never happened?"

"Well, for starters, I won't kill you, but the rest we'll have to figure out along the way. If you help me find my husband, I swear I'll do everything I can to help your family. I'll pay for whatever treatment she needs."

The man began to weep. "You don't get it. I'm already dead. It's my family I'm worried about."

"How old is your daughter?"

"Ten," he said through the sniffles.

"What's wrong with her?"

"She has cancer." He broke down even more. "She'd been receiving treatment but she's not getting any better. They promised they'll have a new treatment that will wipe the cancer out of her system."

"Who told you that?"

"I talked to a man on the phone and he said they could cure her."

"Zsulrick? Did a man from Zsulrick promise you treatment for your daughter?"

He nodded. "They said she'd be a part of the trial group if I did what they asked me to. I didn't mean for anyone to get hurt but I didn't want her to lose that opportunity."

"The man you were talking to on the phone just now, was he from Zsulrick?"

"No."

"Who was he?" she asked.

The sound of footsteps approaching grew louder and louder. With the gun still aimed at the man, Gail glanced in the direction of the door, then back at the man. He had a gun pointed at her, then, he quickly put the gun to his temple.

"Don't, plea —"

The man shot himself as Mike got to the door.

"God!" Gail kicked the wall several times.

"What the hell happened here?" Mike asked as he entered the room.

She had so wanted this man to live. Not only for the sake of milking him for information, but for his family.

Mike wrapped both his arms around her and moved her away from the wall. He held her for a while. "Can I let you go?"

"I'm okay now," she said and pulled away.

"Who's he?" Mike asked.

"I don't know, but I think he was feeding them information." She crouched by the body to search his pockets and took out his wallet. He had photographs of his wife and daughter in it. She looked over at the dead man lying on the floor, and it occurred to her that this might be the man who almost caused her to lose Mike. Don't feel sorry for him, she told herself. He deserved to be punished. Then Gail looked at the photographs in her hand. What about his family? What had they done wrong?

"Did he tell you who he was in contact with?" Mike asked.

"No. I guess he'd rather die than talk."

"His phone is in pieces, but one of the tech guys could probably still get something off it."

"I think that'd be a waste of time. These guys are using disposable phones. I'm sure whoever he was talking to dump that phone the moment he realized this guy's cover was busted," Gail said as she continued to look at the photographs again in her hand.

"What are you thinking?"

"I need to get his family somewhere safe."

"How are you going to do that and search for your husband at the same time? You have to pick your battles, Gail. You can't fight them all. I don't understand. Why do you care? He was working with the people who are trying to kill you. The same people who blew up the cabin."

"I know."

"But?"

"It's not that simple."

"Why?"

She gave him the photograph of the little girl. "What if this was your little girl and someone promised you they can make her well again. Would you be tempted?"

Mike stared at the photograph. Gail could see the change in his face. He finally understood.

"You see, it's not as simple as it seemed. He made a terrible choice and he paid for it with his life. His little girl did nothing wrong. I don't think she should pay for his misdeeds."

Life had thrown this man one hell of a curveball and he'd made the best decision he could. She hated that he was a part of something that had brought a lot of hurt to her family and the other people involved, but she forgave him mainly because his motivation was not selfish. He hadn't done it for the promise of a house on the beach or money in an offshore account. He was trying to secure what he thought was the best treatment for his little girl. What parent could honestly say he wouldn't be tempted to do the same?

The question that bugged her was how could anyone promise to cure this little girl? She had already been through a series of chemotherapy. How is it possible for them to say definitively their drug can wipe away the cancer from her body? Gail was no oncologist, but the last time she checked, not even the greatest specialist in the world made those guarantees. What did Zsulrick know that no one else did? Or maybe they were feeding him a story? Evidently he believed it or he wouldn't be lying there today.

Tolido stood at the door as Colson came in the room with Burdock and a few others behind him. Gail explained what happened with the dead man on the floor. Burdock bent down over the man, looking quite sorrowful.

"How well did you know him?" Gail asked Burdock.

"I served with him. You could say I owe him my life," Burdock replied.

"How did he end up here? Did you bring him on this 'team,' as Colson calls it?"

"He had a number of odd jobs. It's not always easy for people like us to find work. The corporate world don't want to deal with employees like us. They quite often assume you are likely to be suffering from Post-Traumatic Stress Disorder. Once you put it on your resume, you eliminate yourself from the pool," Burdock explained.

Gail wasn't sure if what Burdock said had any merit, but it certainly fit. The closest person to her who'd served was Mike, but his situation was vastly different. Mike was a medical doctor. Finding work was not a problem for him. If Burdock was right, then it painted a picture of a really desperate man and someone who took advantage of him.

"Is there anyone else on this team that served with you?" Gail asked.

"No. just him."

"How do I know you're not lying?"

"Why would I lie?"

"I don't know. Maybe you worked out a sweet little deal for yourself. Money seems to have magical powers. It makes otherwise good people do terrible things. Now, empty your pockets," Gail said to Burdock.

"What?" Burdock asked, looking quite shocked.

Gail aimed the gun at Burdock. "You heard me. Use the thumb and index finger of your left hand to remove your weapons. If I see any more finger touching the weapon, I will shoot you."

"That's enough," Colson said. "Gail, lower your gun."

"Not a chance," Gail said as she fixed her eyes on Burdock. "Put the gun on the floor and kick it over to me."

Burdock complied.

"Mike, pick up that weapon."

"Will you stop this nonsense?" Colson yelled.

"Of course. As soon as I'm satisfied that he's not one of them."

"He's not one of them. He'll never be one of them, because he hates everything about them," Colson said.

"Is that what he told you when he signed up for this gig?" Gail asked.

"He didn't come to me. I reached out to him," Colson said. "Your husband may still be alive. But his mother died a few years after receiving fertility treatment at the clinic your mother worked. She died of cancer and he holds them responsible for her death."

Gail lowered her gun. "So was he conceived through the clinic?"

"No, he was conceived naturally. The babies from the in vitro fertilization never made it," Colson explained.

"I'm sorry," Gail said, as Mike handed Burdock his gun. "What about the other guys on the team?"

"Most of them have been touched by this in some way or another. They're not here because of money. They're working for a cause they believe in. This fellow on the ground might have been the only one who was not harmed by their unethical practice."

"Don't be too sure about that." Gail showed him the photographs of a beautiful little girl who'd lost all her hair.

The conversation continued as Colson requested the area to be cleaned up and they moved to the basement.

"I'm going to New York tonight," Colson told Gail.

"I don't think so," she said.

"Alvin is in New York. He might know where Brian is," Colson said.

"I know, but you're not going."

"The hell I'm not," Colson said.

"They'll be expecting you. They'd kill you before you got to Alvin. No, you're staying here. Make arrangements for me to go."

"I don't take orders from you. In case you haven't noticed, I'm in charge here," Colson said as he packed up his briefcase.

Gail pushed him into the chair he was standing in front of. "Now you listen to me, you stubborn little bastard. You're not going. I'll shoot your pilot if I have to. You're the one who started this crap about being my father. Now you want to run off and get yourself killed?"

"I'm trying to do what I can to keep you safe."

"I know. But it's *my* turn to keep *you* safe."

Mike came and stood next to Gail. "You know, you could have saved yourself a lot of trouble if you'd just told him you loved him and…"

Gail gave him a look. He got the message and stopped talking.

Gail turned her attention back to Colson. "So, what do you say? Can you sit this one out for me?"

"I'll have to rework the plans," he said. "What size are you? You are going to need clothes."

Gail decided to pretend she hadn't heard that as she walked over to one of the desks, but she couldn't ignore what came next.

"Mike is going with you," Colson said.

Gail did not want him going with her. She couldn't put him in any more danger than she already had. "I don't think Mike is well enough to travel." She looked at Tolido for some re-enforcement.

"I feel fine," Mike said.

Tolido remained mummed. Gail did not like

where this was heading.

"Dr. Tolido, is Mike well enough to go on this trip?" Colson asked.

Gail glared at Tolido as he took his time before he attempted to answer. "Well, I would have liked —"

"Yes or no will suffice," Colson said.

"Yes."

"Why Mike? Why not send someone else?" Gail asked.

"He's trained, I trust him, I know he'll protect you with his life, and you two will need to pose as husband and wife at an event Alvin will be attending. So, if there is someone else here you think you can pull that off with and look convincing, I'm all ears," Colson said.

Gail knew there was no one else she could pose with and look believable. "Why don't I attend the function alone?"

"Because the both of you will be replacing a couple at a fundraising event. You will raise less suspicion if the husband and wife attend the event instead of the wife alone."

"And how exactly are we going to get their tickets?" Gail asked.

"I'll take care of that," Colson said.

After reluctantly agreeing to take Mike along with her to New York, Gail requested some help for the family of the man who shot himself.

Colson agreed, and he and the others left.

Finding a mole in Colson's camp opened a lot of questions. Were there more of them? How had they missed that? Gail sat at the desk as she went through the cards in the dead man's wallet.

Mike sat next to her. "What's going on?"

"There's a lot going on. You have to be a little bit more specific."

"I felt like Colson had to twist your arm for me to go on this mission with you. Why is that?"

"I'm trying to keep you out of danger, especially after what happened to you."

"And this has nothing to do with the fact that you may be scared of crossing that friendship line while we're pretending to be a couple?"

"Nope," Gail said, still flipping through the cards. One caught her attention. It was a rather plain business card that said Personal Bodyguard and had a number.

Chapter 22

What are the odds that this number is connected to Protector Max?" Gail said as she showed Mike the card.

"I guess he did some odd jobs with them."

"What do we know about this company?"

"Other than they provide personal bodyguard services and Zsulrick is one of their clients, not much. I can do some more digging if you want," Mike said.

"I'd appreciate that."

"I'll be right back."

"If you see Tolido, tell him I want to see him. By the way, where're you going?"

"I'm going to get the laptop from the room."

"Use one of those," she said pointing to the available workstations with computers.

"Are you going to have the scan done now?" Mike asked.

"No. No time for that."

"Then what do you want Tolido for?"

Gail spotted Tolido at the far end of the basement. "Tolido!" she called. He looked in her direction and she waved her hand. Tolido came over.

"You rang!" He pulled up a chair next to her.

"Nice to see you're in good spirits."

"I'm not. But I don't want to seem like a wuss, since I maybe the only one here who is completely useless in defending himself."

"Tolido, if that makes you a wuss that means everyone has been a wuss at some point in his life."

He chuckled.

"You're not a wuss. You may not be the 'shoot 'em up' type, but you have skills those guys don't, and I need your skills to help me. What do you say?"

"I'd say you are now my second favorite person," Tolido said.

"Second? Who has the number one spot?"

"Colson."

"Right." Gail could see that was not said lightly. There was clearly a deep connection but she wanted to stay away from it for now. If he wanted to talk she would listen but she would not be the initiator.

"So, how can I help?"

"I want to find out what drugs Zsulrick have in the pipeline. What they have in testing. Specifically, cancer drugs. Can you do that?"

"Well, that kind of information is not lying

around for everyone to see it. It is going to take some time."

"Then get started."

"What about the scan?"

"I think we have more pressing matters to attend to. Wouldn't you agree?"

"Tell that to Colson. He insisted that I run a scan before you leave for New York."

"You can run the scan as soon as I get back. Deal?"

Tolido shook his head. "I can't make you take the scan, but Colson will not let you leave if you don't get it done."

Gail frowned at him.

"I'm just telling you like it is. I like you, I really do, but I don't want to get caught between the two of you. Strange as this might sound, I see a lot of him in you."

"Fine, let's get it over with," Gail said.

She submitted herself to another scan. By the time she was laying on the table, Mike showed up.

"What are you doing here?" she asked.

"He was asked to be here," Tolido said.

"Who asked for him to be here?" Gail asked.

"I did," Colson said as he entered the lab. "He's a doctor and a second pair of eyes is always welcome."

After the scan was completed, Tolido asked

Gail, "Did you have another bout of vomiting?"

"No, no vomiting. Why?"

"I don't see the pellets anymore. There were a few of them there but they seem to have disappeared."

"Good. Then I won't need to have yet another scan," Gail said. She moved next to Mike while Colson quizzed Tolido about her results.

"Did you find out anything useful about Protector Max?"

"Most of the information is what we already know, except the name of the man at the top, Johnathan Clarke."

She had a theory that Johnathan and Jeanine had studied Keri's pattern. "Learned what they could about her and about Brian. Once they were ready for their plan to move to the next phase, one or both of them got rid of Keri. Then Jeanine applied for Keri's old job, knowing the agency would be desperate to find a replacement."

"A plausible theory," Colson said. "I wondered if that husband of yours was not so deceitful, maybe, just maybe, things would have played out in a different way."

Gail looked at Mike, wide-eyed, wondering if Mike had told Colson about Brian and Keri. Mike shrugged his shoulder. "Don't blame

Mike. He didn't tell me anything if that's what you're wondering," Colson said. "To be quite frank, I don't much like this husband of yours. I'll do what I can to help you find him, but I'm doing it for you and Alex. Otherwise I'd let him rot wherever he is for what he's put you through."

His cell phone rang. "Hello? Put them in Gail's room." He ended the call. "You two meet me downstairs in a few minutes so we can run through the plan to retrieve Alvin."

"Retrieve Alvin?" Gail asked.

"Yes. Get him out of there and bring him to me," Colson said.

"I thought we agreed that you would stay here."

"Slight change in plans. I don't think he'll tell you anything. Whatever he knows, I can get him to talk," Colson said.

"If that's your reason, then don't worry, I know I can get him to talk," Gail said.

"Yes, I am aware of your abilities to get people to talk, but that's a last resort. After you get the information from him, then what? You leave him there? You and Mike can get him out of there faster if he's not sedated," Colson said.

"How do we know Alvin will be attending this event?" Gail asked.

"The event is being hosted by one of his

potential clients. This is part of his attempt to seal the deal, so to speak. He's still checked in. Therefore, if he's not at the event, then you should still be able to find him in that hotel. According to my source, Alvin dropped by Zsulrick earlier in the evening. After that, he went straight to his hotel and he hasn't left the building."

"If I'm going to leave that place with Alvin, I might as well put a bulls-eye on my forehead. Why should I risk my life and Mike's to save Alvin?"

"I don't want them to harm him, and I am willing to go in there and get him myself if I have to," Colson said.

He obviously had a soft spot for Alvin and Gail thought she understood. Alvin had been Leon's best friend. This wasn't just about saving Alvin. It was about preserving a memory, a memory of when Colson's son was alive.

"Okay," Gail said. "Whatever you're planning, do it fast because we don't have a lot of time."

"The guys will attempt to access the hotel's security cameras. That'll give us an opportunity to see who's coming and going."

"Did you have a camera placed in Alvin's room?" Gail asked.

"Not yet. They're working on that as we

speak," Colson said.

"When is the event?" Mike asked.

"Tonight," Colson said. "I suggest you both get changed and be ready to leave. We'll talk specifics on the way."

"Change into what?" Mike asked.

"Clothes. I called in a favor from a very dear friend. They are in Gail's room. If there's nothing else, I'll see you both downstairs in a couple of minutes."

"Ha, ha. Hair and makeup might take a little longer than a couple of minutes," Mike said jokingly as he look over at Gail.

"Not tonight," Colson said as he left the room.

Gail and Mike headed up the stairs. She was not clear what the plan was, but she was not about to sacrifice Mike to save Alvin. "I don't want you trying to be a hero tonight. We'll do what we can to save Alvin, but don't you put yourself between him and anyone with a gun," Gail said.

"You don't seem as sympathetic towards Alvin as I thought you would be, considering you knew him. You wanted to save the other guy who shot himself even though you knew he was a part of this. What's so different about Alvin?" Mike asked.

"I don't want anything to happen to Alvin

and I'll do everything I can to keep him safe, but there's a different level of involvement. Alvin was part of the planning team that plotted to kidnap Brian. The dead guy became part of their team after the kidnapping. I see him as a victim of circumstance. Then there is the motivating factor. I tend not to feel sorry for people who are motivated by greed. Alvin has no wife or child, so he can't tell me he's doing this for his son, daughter, or wife. He's doing this for himself. He chose to destroy my life to make his better. Do you really expect me to feel sympathy for him?"

"No. Not when you put it like that. But I don't buy that act for a second. You want me to believe you don't care about Alvin…that's not you. You're only saying that because you don't want me to risk my life to save him."

It was scary how well this man knew her. "I don't know what you're talking about."

"Well, I can understand where Colson is coming from."

"Really? How so?"

"I can understand his connection to Alvin, and why he'd want to protect him. Alex is not my son, but God forbid that he got in some kind of trouble when he gets older, I'd certainly want to protect him. Colson is doing what any father would do. You can't fault him for that."

"I don't, but I don't want his fatherly love for Alvin to get anyone else killed."

"I won't let anything happen to you."

"It's not me I'm worried about. Don't worry about protecting me, worry about protecting you."

"What does that mean?"

Gail sighed. "Promise you won't pull off any macho stunt trying to protect me. I can heal. Remember?"

"I can tell you what you want to hear, but the truth is, my instinct is to protect you. I can't control that and I really don't care that you can heal. My mind doesn't work like that."

"Try to resist it, Mike, or it may get you killed." Her phone rang. "Hello?"

"Is that Colson?" Mike asked.

Gail covered the phone with her hand. "No. It's Celia. I gave her this number in case she needed to reach me."

"Hi, Celia. How's Alex?"

"He doesn't want to stay here anymore."

"Where is he? Let me talk to him."

"He's sleeping now, but he was quite restless earlier. Do you want me to wake him?"

"No, let him rest. I'll talk with him tomorrow and hopefully that'll help."

"It's not just him. I have some personal issues to deal with so I can't stay here for the entire two weeks."

"I understand, but if you could give me some more time. Brian is still missing, and it'd be a lot easier to focus on trying to find him if I knew Alex is safe."

"So, do the police have any leads?"

Gail had not reported it to the police at Colson's request. He believed she could be putting herself in danger since they knew they were dealing with people who had a lot of money, more than enough to corrupt a few officers. She couldn't tell Celia the whole story. That would simply freak her out. "We're following up on some leads. I know this is a lot to ask, but I really need you to keep him there. I don't think it's safe for him here. I'll talk to him tomorrow."

"I don't understand how he could just disappear. Wasn't he on his way to the airport?"

"I'm not sure. I think he was kidnapped and that is why I do not want Alex here."

"Oh, God! We need to put out a reward for his return."

"No. Celia, please, I really need you to keep Alex there."

There was no response.

"I have to go. I'll talk to you tomorrow. Don't worry, we're going to find him."

Gail tapped the phone on her palm,

frustrated and praying Celia wouldn't go off half-cocked as usual and spread the news her brother had been kidnapped. Mike respected her silence on the way to her room.

Their outfits were laid out, including a wig and a pair of glasses for Gail.

Mike picked up the glasses and peered through them. "I guess this is a part of your disguise."

Gail was still going over the conversation with Celia in her head. The mere thought of Alex coming back had her on edge. She had no idea what kind of danger he would be in and she did not wish to find out.

"You seem kinda out of it. Is Alex all right?"

"He wants to come home."

"Yeah, it must be tough for him. He's never spent a night away from you. I know he loves Celia but she's not you."

"I know. I don't want him here until I know he'll be safe."

"When'll that be?"

"I wish I knew. I'm trying to figure it out as I go. The truth is, if I find Brian tonight, it still wouldn't be safe for Alex to return. Not with those trained killers running around doing the bidding of Zsulrick Inc."

"You really think they'd go after a seven-year-old?"

"I don't know. Maybe I'm just paranoid."

"I know this is going to be tough for you, because I'm here and I know the situation but...try to set aside more time to talk to him on the phone. Maybe that'll help. I'll talk to him too if you want. Maybe I could help cheer him up a bit."

"That's not a bad idea, although I get the sense that Celia is not telling me something."

"About Alex?"

"I'm not sure. I don't know how else to explain it. I know she and Brian are close and this whole ordeal has taken a toll on her, but I get the feeling that something else is wrong. Not sure what, though. If everything goes well tonight, Alvin should be able to tell us where Brian is."

"What if he doesn't know?" Mike asked.

"He can at least point us in the right direction."

"You should start getting dressed. I'll give you a head start, since you'll need a lot more time to get ready."

"Lucky for me, my hair is already done. That saved me a lot of time. I just need to put it on. I'll be ready in a flash."

Gail got dressed, wig and glasses included. She wore a black body-hugging gown with a plunging back.

"Wow!" Mike spun her around. "You look amazing, like a completely different person."

Her blond wig had bangs that covered her forehead, and the glasses added a nice touch. Gail was more focused on what lay ahead than about feeling glamorous.

They went to meet Colson in the basement. As they entered the area, there was a deafening silence. The team appeared almost frozen. No one was tapping away at their keyboard as expected. Gail fixed her eyes on Colson. He slumped in a chair with his eyes glued to the computer screen in front of him. His face was as pale as if he had been a three-course meal for Dracula.

She glanced at the screen were Colson's eyes were focused. There was an image on the screen. Her heart began to race as she moved closer and the image became clearer.

"No!"

Chapter 23

The plans were already in place for them to leave for New York, but the image of a man lying on the floor in a pool of blood changed everything.

The man appeared to have been shot several times in the chest. The image on the screen was a frozen frame from a hotel room. Alvin appeared to be dead on the floor.

Just as Gail thought she was getting close, she was finally going to see the man who very likely knew where her husband was, her hopes were splattered much like Alvin's blood in that room.

Like Colson, Mike lost his tongue. In fact no one said anything for a while. Although she felt like a rug was pulled from under her, she knew she had to forge ahead, and she was not only running out of time, she was running out of options.

"Could someone replay that so I can see what happened?" she asked.

Rick Mosley, a short stocky tech guru,

beckoned to her to come over to his desk. He replayed the feed from the hotel room. Alvin went to the door and let a man in. As soon as Alvin closed the door, the man reached inside his jacket and pulled out a gun fitted with a silencer.

"Freeze it here," Gail said. She wanted to get a good look at the man's face. "Who're you working for?" Gail asked as she sized up the man on the screen.

She went over to Colson, he was still slumped in the chair. Gail held his hands and stooped in front of him. "I'm sorry about Alvin. I know how much he meant to you and I promise you I'll make that son of a bitch pay for what he did."

Colson was not the type of man to show his emotions. He was from that "boys don't cry" era. He kissed her hand and touched her face. "You look so much like your mother," Colson said.

She touched her hair. "It must be the blond wig."

"Walk with me," he said, as he got up slowly and made his way to the end of the room that had the beverages. He poured himself some vodka. "The man on the screen is not your problem. Focus on finding another link that can bring this mess to a close. They took a huge risk in killing Alvin, a prominent attorney, in his hotel room. That tells me the stakes are high, higher than we originally thought. Find out what they're trying to hide and you can bring them to their knees."

"I already have Tolido looking into something for me. I'll stop by his room after I get out of these clothes."

"You can go ahead. I'll be here for a while."

Gail turned and walked away.

"Gail!"

She looked back at him.

"You're all I have now. Please, don't let me mourn you."

He'd only just started drinking, but that vodka sure looked like it was kicking in. "Not just me. You have a grandson too, and don't worry, I don't plan on dying any time soon."

"I have grown quite fond of Mike too. Could you ask him to come over for a minute?"

"Sure." Gail passed Colson's message to Mike on her way out. She went looking for Tolido in his lab but he was not there. She went upstairs to change but decided to check Tolido's room since it was on the way. She knocked on the door. "Tolido!" No answer. She knocked several times. "Tolido!"

"Just a sec." Tolido answered the door dressed in a robe. "Good God, you're gorgeous!"

Gail gave him a stern look.

"Sorry."

"I want us to continue that research we started on Zsulrick."

"Absolutely. What time tomorrow do you want to start?"

"Tonight."

"Tonight? No. I'm about to take some 'me time.' Wait, I thought you were leaving tonight for the Big Apple."

"Alvin is dead. He was murdered not too long ago...I really need your help tonight, Tolido."

"Of course. I'm sorry. I didn't know. I'll go put some clothes on."

She walked away in the direction of her room.

"Where do you want us to meet?" Tolido asked.

"Anywhere you want. As long as we're getting the work done."

"I'll come by your room in a few minutes."

Tolido had no clue how to hack into anything, but he knew where to look. Gail believed with him pointing her in the right direction she may be able to find something on Zsulrick that she could use as leverage. So far she had no luck chasing the people she believed were a part of the kidnapping. Every time she thought she was close, the person she was chasing became a corpse before she got to them. Colson was right, she needed to work things from a different angle.

Before Gail was finished changing, there was a knock at the door. "Give me a minute!"

When she opened the door, Tolido came in armed with his laptop and ready to work. He took a seat in the reclining chair. "Where do we start?"

"Well, we already know that Zsulrick is trying desperately to settle the cases against them from the drug that caused unusual bleeding. Plus, someone from Zsulrick allegedly promised to cure a little girl of cancer."

"What does one thing have to do with the other?"

"I'm still trying to figure that one out. One drug has been recalled. The other one is not on the market yet. I think we should start by looking at all the drugs that Zsulrick Inc. has in testing right now."

He handed Gail his laptop. "Get me through the door and I'll start looking."

Once Gail had access to the database Tolido wanted to search, she handed the laptop back to him. Then, true to form, he started with the questions. "So what's with you and Mike?"

"What do you want to know?"

"I don't know. Tell me anything. I work better while I talk."

"All right. He's my best friend. Actually, he's my only friend, and we've known each other since what seems like forever."

"How did Brian feel about your friendship with him?"

"Brian had nothing to worry about. Mike was the one who introduced us to each other."

"Why did he do that?"

"Do what?"

"Introduce you to another man. Given the way he looks at you I would have thought that he would…"

Mike walked in the room. "I'm going to change out of these clothes," he said to Gail as he headed off to his room.

"I think I might have something," Tolido said. "Zsulrick has several drugs in clinical trials. One of them is a cancer treatment drug."

"Anything special about their drug?"

"I don't know yet. If you can find the clinical data, we can see the claims and if the claims have any merit."

Mike came in and sat beside Gail on the bed. "How is Colson doing?" she asked him.

"It's going to take some time, but he'll be all right."

"What'd he want to see you about?"

"He wanted me to have a drink with him, keep him company a little."

She knew he wasn't telling her everything, but she chose not to press him for more information with Tolido there. "Is he still drinking?"

"No. I walked him to his room after the guys left. What're you two working on?"

"Honestly, Mike, I'm not sure. I have a feeling that Zsulrick is hiding something and it either has to do with the drug they recalled or a cancer treatment drug they now have in testing. I need to find something that I can use as a bargaining chip for Brian."

"Johnathan is the only one from the trio who is still alive and would know where Brian is," Mike said. "We need to focus our energy on finding him. I think if we find him, we'll find Brian."

"Assuming Brian is still alive," Tolido said.

Mike tried to shush him but it had already resonated with Gail. "I'll give up only if I see his body. Until then, I'm going to keep looking," Gail said. "I agree that we need to find Johnathan. Colson and his team can help me track him down, but I need to find a way to level the playing field somewhat."

"Meaning what?" Mike asked.

"They have something I want, I need to get my hands on something they want, or maybe something they want to be kept a secret. We're not abandoning one search for another. We're simply working from two different angles. The guys downstairs are good at finding people and Tolido knows drugs like the back of his hand," Gail said.

"So what have you guys found so far?"

"Right now I'm looking at some data from the clinical trials," Tolido said.

"You can sit here so all three of us can see the information," Gail said to Tolido as she patted the space between herself and Mike.

"This is the information the FDA will use to determine if the drug is safe for approval," Tolido said. "Speaking of cancer drug, according to a news report, by the year 2030 the number of new cancer cases will increase by nearly forty-five percent. If this drug is approved, it will be one of many cancer treatments available, but with that kind of market, they will still make a lot of money."

"What if they can make their treatment stand out from the others? Wouldn't they corner a larger percentage of the market, irrespective of the number of competing drugs?" Gail asked.

"They would, but how would they do that?" Mike asked.

"That's what we need to find out. Other than making wild promises to a desperate man, there must be something they can use to get the FDA's approval to spin it as a wonder drug," Gail said.

As she combed through the clinical data, she found a significant number of the participants in the study went into complete remission. The cancer was nowhere to be found after three months of being on the drug. The people who participated in the study did not receive chemo or radiation therapy. Twenty-five percent of the participants did not respond to the treatment at all. That was impressive, and if these results were authentic then the public would really benefit from this drug. But were they authentic? She could not find anything to indicate that Zsulrick tweaked the results. She'd hit another dead end.

Tolido said he was tired and decided to call it a night. She encouraged Mike to do the same but he refused to leave.

"I'm sorry things didn't turn out the way you expected them to," Mike said.

"Me too," Gail replied, as she paced the floor and replayed the screen shot of the clinical data in her mind. The people who responded favorably to the treatment had different types of cancer, and in varying stages. But something told her there was more to the study than met the eye. She grabbed the laptop. "I'm going downstairs."

"Downstairs, as in the basement?"

"I need access to more screens. I want to check something."

"You know, it wouldn't be a bad idea to get some rest and pick this back up in the morning."

"Actually, I prefer to do it now while the place is quiet."

Mike got up to follow her.

"You don't need to come."

"I know, but I want to."

Once they got to the basement, Gail wasted no time getting the computer up and running. She connected the laptop to a large monitor and brought up a graph of the clinical trial. She leaned back in her chair and looked at it. "Why is it that some people were wiped clean of cancerous cells and yet others, albeit a few, didn't respond at all?"

"Nothing works for everyone. You know that. Everyone knows that."

"Yes. Of course." She found the name of the participants in the study.

"What're you thinking?"

"I want to know if these people really had cancer or if this clinical trial was filled with participants pretending to be cancer patients." She selected a name at random and searched for that person's medical history. She could see when the person had been first diagnosed, all the drugs that were prescribed, even over-the-counter medications. She moved on to another name. By the time she got to the third name, Mike sat in front of the screen and read the name to her. As she went through she memorized each name, the date of diagnosis and the medication he or she had been taking.

They checked the names of ten participants. Of the ten, eight responded well to the treatment, the other two did not respond at all. But they were all cancer patients. The names of the physicians for all ten persons checked out.

"You have your answer. I think we can safely let this one go. If there was something amiss, you'd have found it."

Gail agreed that everything seemed in order, but her gut told her something was wrong. She leaned back in her chair again and replayed each participant's information in her head. Then she noticed a repeating occurrence between some of the participants. Coincidence?

She created two separate list of names. One with the patients who responded favorably to the treatment and another with the participants who did not respond to the treatment. She checked the medical history for several of the participants who did not respond to the treatment. Then she did the same for the participants who had improvement. What she found was not only mind-boggling; if her theory was correct, Zsulrick wasn't just worried about losing money. Their executives would face criminal charges for what appeared to be one of the most atrocious acts committed on the American population by any organization.

Chapter 24

"I think I got something," Gail said.

"What is it?"

"Look at this. Every person who had a positive response to the cancer drug in the trial all had one thing in common. They all took Zenoprit. The drug Zsulrick recalled."

"Are you sure?"

"Well, I haven't checked every name, but it certainly seems like a pattern."

They checked a few names and the results were the same.

"Look, Mike. If the patients were taking Zenoprit prior to being diagnosed with cancer, their cancer was either gone or going away. Either way, they were improving. The others didn't get better or worse on the treatment."

"So, what, you think a history of taking Zenoprit has something to do with the drug working for these people?" Mike asked.

"I believed that the Zenoprit is what caused these people to get cancer in the first place. Even worse, I think this was a deliberate act by

Zsulrick to facilitate a way to make a lot of money. Zenoprit is causing people to get cancer much like the drug that my mother worked on many years ago, but not as aggressive. I think they found a way to reverse the effects of the drug. So they put small amounts of it in Zenoprit, this very inexpensive drug that would be used by millions of people, to create a market for their new cancer drug."

"That is some serious theory you have there, but you'll need proof. The question is, how do we go about finding it?"

"We'll need a sample of Zenoprit as well as a sample of their cancer treatment drug. Then we can test them in the lab."

"Zenoprit has been recalled and the cancer drug is not on the market yet. How do you propose we get samples?" Mike asked.

"Beg, borrow, steal...whatever it takes."

"All right, we'll think a lot better after we get some rest."

Gail was not ready to sign off but agreed to call it a night for Mike's sake. It didn't take Mike long to fall asleep. She plugged in his cell phone to charge and noticed that he had a picture of Alex as his wallpaper. That picture had been taken when he lost his first tooth and it brought a smile to her face. She took the phone to her room and focused on the picture of her son as a way to center herself. Gail's mind was racing at the speed of light and if she was going to get some needed rest, she needed to shut her mind off.

Gail was awakened by the sound of a bell. She had fallen asleep and the low battery signal on Mike's phone served as an unintentional alarm shortly before six AM. She promptly returned the phone to the charger in Mike's room. As expected, he was still sleeping, and she suspected Tolido would be sleeping as well. But Mike opened his eyes and saw her.

"Hey, what time is it?"

"It's still early. You should try to rest for at least another hour."

"Did you get any sleep?"

"Yes."

"Did you sleep in here?"

"No. Go back to sleep."

Gail wanted so badly to get things moving but thought it would be a good time to talk to Alex since they were three hours ahead over there. As she was leaving Mike's room she noticed he was up.

"Do you want some coffee?" he asked.

"Sure. I'm going to call Celia."

"I want to talk to Alex if you don't mind."

"You know I don't."

"I'll get the coffee," he said, as he left for the

dining area.

She dialed the number. Celia answered. "Hello?"

"Hi, Celia. I hope I'm not calling too early."

"Gail. Hi, I'm kind of in the middle of something right now. Can I call you back?"

"Is everything all right?" Gail asked.

"Yes, I'm on another call."

"Where's Alex?"

"He's watching TV. He's fine, Gail. I'll call you back. Okay?"

"Okay, sure," Gail said, then Celia ended the call.

Mike returned and handed her a cup of coffee. "What happened?"

"Celia is on another call. She said she'd call me back."

"Okay, so why do you have that look on your face?"

"What look?"

"The look of worry. Alex will be okay. He's in good hands."

"I know. Was there any sign of Tolido or Colson?"

"This early?"

"You're right. It's too early."

They waited for Celia to call back but she never did. Gail decided to call her again. The phone rang without an answer. "Why isn't she answering the phone?"

"It could be any of a million reasons. Give her some more time and then try again. In the meantime I think I know how we can get some Zenoprit."

"How and where?"

"Quite often after a drug has been recalled. People still have them in their medicine cabinet. All we need to do is find someone who purchased the drug just before the recall. Chances are they'd still have it."

"That shouldn't be hard." Gail booted up her laptop. She found the closest pharmacy to their location.

"You need to write down the address."

"I don't."

"Actually, you do, because you are not going. I am."

"I can't have you breaking and entering people's property especially in a state where you live and work. What if someone recognized you? No, it's not a good idea for you to go," Gail said.

"I couldn't agree with you more," Colson said as he walked into the room.

"You agree with Gail?"

"I agree with both of you."

"Right! By the way, why were you eavesdropping on my conversation?" Gail asked.

"If I were you, I would not be accusing anyone of eavesdropping considering you do it every day, maybe even several times a day."

"Whoa! What's going on between the two of you?" Mike asked.

"It's a harmless jibe," Colson said. As I was saying, I don't think either of you should go. This matter can be easily taken care of by someone else."

Gail saw right through Colson. He had an empty place in his heart from losing Alvin. Mike seemed to be perfect and she had no problem with it. As long as he did not expect that she and Mike were going to be anything more than they were now. On the plus side, he would want to protect Mike as much as possible and that served her well, as Mike would be more inclined to back down from a mission if Colson asked him to. Gail chuckled as she thought of how much she was going to enjoy that.

"That's better," Mike said.

Mike and Gail spent the next few minutes bringing Colson up to speed on what they uncovered about Zsulrick. She then wrote down the information he needed to get her the Zenoprit.

"I don't need the address, just the name of the drug," Colson said. "We'll save the breaking and entering for another time. And while you're at it, give me the name of the cancer treatment drug Zsulrick is testing. I'll see what I can do to get you what you need without either of you putting yourself in danger."

"We appreciate that," Gail said.

"Forgive me if I get a little overprotective at times," Colson said.

"You didn't get that way. You were always overprotective. I didn't understand it then. Now I do," Gail said.

"I'll let you know when I have something," Colson said as he left the room.

There had been no response from Celia so Gail decided to call again. "Still no answer. I don't like this. Where's she?"

"You said the house was near the beach. Maybe she and Alex are having fun at the beach. She left her cell phone inside because the house is so close. Sounds plausible?"

"Plausible, yes, but I want to know definitively," Gail said. She wasn't sure what was happening with Celia and could not wait to speak to her son. Until then, she needed to forge ahead. We need to give Tolido all the information we have," she said to Mike.

"Yes, we do. We also need to let him have his breakfast before we start picking his brain. So, do mind telling me what's going on with you and Colson?" Mike asked.

"Nothing. Why don't you tell me what's going on with the both of you?"

"What do you mean?"

"What did you guys talk about last night?"

"Gail, please don't ask me to go into details, because the last thing I want is to cause a problem between the two of you."

"Don't worry, you won't. I have a pretty good idea what the discussion was about."

"If you know, then why are you asking me? Better yet, why didn't you ask Colson?"

"Because you are my best friend and I know I can count on you to tell me the truth. I want to know if he was talking about Brian. Was he?"

"Yes."

"And? Come on. What? What did he say?"

"Gail, you have to swear to me that you will not breathe a word of this to him."

"I won't. I promise."

"Nor will you act different around him."

"Yeah, yeah. What did he say?"

"My memory is not as good as yours so I'm going to paraphrase. He's worried that you may blame yourself for what is happening with Brian and you may feel sorry for him and give him another chance. He said you deserve better and doesn't want you get caught in that never ending cycle thinking he's going to do better, only to find he did the opposite."

"I don't see what was so bad about telling me that. I appreciate him looking out for me. Or was there more? Come on, spit it out."

"No, I can't tell you," Mike said.

"Why not? You've been doing great so far."

"He wants you to set your sight somewhere else, so to speak, so when you do find Brian, it'll be less likely the marriage will survive. He doesn't like Brian at all, at least, not as your husband."

Gail scoffed and shook her head. "So in other words, he wants me to cheat?"

"Well, he didn't say that and I don't know if that would technically be cheating if you've already decided that your marriage is over."

"He doesn't know that. Did you tell him I said that?"

"No, of course not."

"I appreciate everything he's done and continues to do for me, but that doesn't give him any right to meddle in my personal life," Gail said. "I get the feeling you're conveniently leaving something out. He wants to fix me up with someone right at a time when I'm stressed and very vulnerable. And that someone is you. He wants you to help steer me away from Brian. How am I doing so far?"

"Gail, it's not like that."

"Really? Is that why you've been feeding me all this crap about you and me being more than friends?" She sighed. "I should've known."

"Gail, you know me. Would I do that to you?"

"I don't know, Mike. Would you?" Gail didn't wait around to hear his response. She walked out the door.

"Gail!" Mike called.

She just kept walking.

She called Celia several times as she headed to the basement... still no answer. Her worry meter was now off the charts.

Mike followed her, like he'd been doing for the last three days since this fiasco started.

"What's the matter?" Colson asked.

"I've not been able to get through to Celia. This isn't like her. She said she'd call me back but it's been hours."

"What do you want me to do?"

"Can you get me on a flight to the Virgin Islands?"

"I can do better. I can have a private plane take you there."

"Great. Thank you."

"I think you should take someone with you."

"I think I'll go solo on this one. In the meantime you can make sure Tolido and Mike run those tests and gather all the proof we need."

Then Gail's phone rang. The call was from an unknown number. "Hello?"

"Gail, sorry I didn't call you back," Celia said.

Gail felt a sense of relief. "Celia, where's Alex?"

"He's with me. He's fine."

"Where're you calling from?"

"Well, that's what I was going to tell you. Nathan and I decided it was best I came home."

"Why didn't you call me?"

"Alex and I left early this morning and I haven't been able to find my phone."

"Where're you now?"

"We're…wait a second, Nathan wants to talk to you."

"Hello, Gail. This is Nathan Clare. I've heard quite a bit about you."

She knew that name. More importantly, she knew that voice. She had spoken to him before. Nathan Clare was Johnathan Clarke.

Suddenly Gail's worst nightmare was now a reality. Now they had something she valued more than her own life. They had her son.

Chapter 25

Gail felt like all the blood drained from her body as Johnathan continued to speak.

"Celia and I will call you later and let you know where to pick up Alex. Celia, why don't you take Alex and get him a drink while I assure Gail that everything is fine with the both of you."

Gail was surprisingly calm and spoke slowly in a low voice. "Johnathan, I want you to listen to me very carefully. I want you to let Celia and Alex go. I can meet you anywhere you want, after you release them. You don't want to do this."

"How do you know what I want? The way I see it, I'm holding a very valuable card and therefore I'm in control."

"Are you? In control?" Gail asked.

"What is that supposed to mean?"

"What do you think it means? A man running off to another country to kidnap a seven-year-old boy at the request of his superior. Does that sound like someone who is in control? I don't know. You tell me."

Johnathan did not respond.

"I think the real person in charge is the one who's pulling your strings. You can't make a move until he tells you to."

"You think I can't make a move? How about I put a bullet in this boy of yours?"

"Interesting play. I'm wondering how your 'client' at Zsulrick would feel about that? As a matter of fact, maybe your client would be willing to negotiate with me."

"My client and I see eye to eye on everything."

"Everything? Does that include killing everyone else who knew about the scheme?"

"Like I said, we see eye to eye on everything."

"I hope you feel the same way when they send someone to eliminate you. Don't tell me it hasn't crossed your mind that at some point you'll become a liability. Maybe we can help each other. You release my son unarmed and —"

"If you're going to tell me that you have something of monumental value to my client," Johnathan said, "don't bother. I already know. Hence the change of strategy. We needed to acquire something of equal value to you. It wasn't hard, since I already had Celia in the palm of my hand. I have been a source of comfort since her brother Brian has gone missing. Now, we can talk about returning what you stole."

"Stole? That's a rather strong term. What exactly do you and your client think I stole?" Gail was still calm but noted with satisfaction his voiced sounded increasingly flustered.

"Don't play coy with me," he said. "They know the server was hacked, and guess where the cyber-criminal was looking? On drug information, clinical data and such files. That doesn't sound like any hacker I've heard about. Does that strike you as anyone you know? You couldn't keep your meddling little fingers and eyes quiet. You had to go snooping into my client's data. When you decided to crank up the temperature, you should have prepared yourself for the heat."

"What does your client want? Tell me what you want in exchange for the safe return of my family, including Brian," Gail said.

Johnathan laughed. "That's a rather tall request, wouldn't you say? I mean, anything can happen to anyone at any time, intentionally or unintentionally. It kind of makes it hard to make those types of guarantees, even with the best of intensions, and I'm not one of those people who have good intensions."

"If you hurt my son, I promise you, I will rip your balls off and stuff them down your throat."

"Save it. Your threats don't scare me, little girl. You are way out of your league. I've been doing this so long it's like second nature."

"If you have anyone anywhere in this world that you care about, even just a little bit, I will find that person, and I will kill him or her, very slowly."

"You can't find your own husband, how are you going to find someone you're not sure even exists? Come on, who are you kidding? You don't know anything about me. Heck, you didn't even know I spent time at Celia's house while your son was there. I'm way ahead of you, Gail. As far as this game is concerned, I'm the professor and you're still in kindergarten."

He was right. Gail knew nothing about him or if he had anyone he would want to protect. But his question told her that he did. "Are you willing to take that chance? Me, finding that one person you care about, especially if I have nothing left to lose? Because I will make what you did to Keri look like child's play. That person will die a very slow and painful death, and he will know who's to blame for the hell that will be unleashed."

Gail had no intention of following through on that threat, but she wanted him to believe that she would. A threat of sending him to meet his maker in a gruesome manner may not hinder him from harming Alex, but the thought that Gail would harm someone he cared about would cause him a world of hurt. He would want to be sure that Gail was dead before he lifted a finger towards her son and that was the most she could hope for at the moment.

His silence told Gail that she'd hit a nerve. Something she'd said gave him pause, and that pause might just have been enough for her to get to Alex in time.

"I have to hand it to you, Gail. You have guts, lots of guts. You've seen my work, so you know what I'm capable of. Why are you so calm?"

"That's when I'm at by best, or worst, depending on which side of the fence you're standing. Yes, I know what you're capable of. The problem for you is that you don't know what I'm capable of and you better pray that you never get to find out."

She heard Alex's voice in the background. "Let me talk to my son."

"I don't think so. Keep your phone close. I'll call you."

The call ended.

Mike and Colson were staring at her. She had never seen Mike look so scared in all the

years she'd known him. He and Colson knew
the man responsible for a lot of people being
killed now had Alex.

"How did he find him?" Mike asked.

"He was dating Celia."

"What? Johnathan was dating Celia?"

"He was using the name Nathan Clare."

"Nathan Clare? Isn't that the guy dating the
receptionist from Brian's office, Keri?" Mike
asked.

"How did I miss this? I didn't get a last name
from Celia but if I had put the pieces together
before...I should've seen it."

"What do you mean?" Colson asked. "You
should have seen what?"

"His alias was taken from his original name,
just like Jeanine's," Gail said.

"You lost me," Mike said.

"Make that two of us," Colson said.

Gail grabbed a pen and a piece of paper and
she wrote **Jean**ine **Grays**on: Jean Gray, J**eanine**
Grayson: Nina Ray. Joh**nathan Clarke**: Nathan
Clare. "Do you see what I'm saying now?"

The look on their faces told her they saw it,
but it was far too late for them to do anything
about it.

"Are they still on the island?" Colson asked.

"No, I think they're in the US, but I need to
get your guys to verify that Alex came back into

the country. Most likely through Los Angeles airport."

"I'll have them get right on it."

"One more thing. Johnathan has at least one person he holds dear. Find out who and get me a photograph," Gail said to Colson.

"Could you really follow through with that threat?" Mike asked.

Gail turned and looked at him. "Let's hope we never have to find out. In the meantime I need you to hold on to this for me," she said as she handed him a jump drive.

"What's on it?"

"Leverage."

"You downloaded the information we were looking at?" Mike asked.

"How else am I supposed to use it as leverage if I don't have a copy?"

"Is this the only copy?"

"I think it's best if you don't know the answer to that question."

"Have they located Alex?" she asked Colson, who was hovering.

"Alex, Celia, and Nathan are on a flight from LA to Seattle. The flight will arrive in another hour and a half. That gives us enough time to get to the airport."

"Why come to Washington State if the child you kidnap is from here?" Mike asked.

"Other than the fact that Johnathan's number one target is here? He may also have a base, connections with local authorities, all the support he needs to accomplish his goal while staying under the radar," Colson said.

"Maybe his base is where he's holding Brian. We need to find all the possible places he could be using," Gail said as she checked the time. "I'll meet you back right here."

"Where are you going?" Colson asked.

"I need to see Tolido about something."

"Can't it wait?" Mike asked.

"Not really. I'll be ready whenever you guys are." She left for Tolido's lab. When this first started, Gail's aim was simply to get Brian back alive. Now things had taken a different turn. Getting her family back was only part of the equation and it was the part she should focus on first. Secondly, she was dedicated to taking down Zsulrick Inc.

Tolido was in his lab working on the Zenoprit Colson got for him. "How're things coming along?" she asked.

"Okay, I guess, although it's really hard to say, considering I just started. I still have some blood tests that I need to run for you."

"Forget everything else for now. This is your number one priority."

"Have you cleared that with Colson?"

"I don't need to. Colson will tell you the same thing I told you."

"Maybe if you told me what I should be looking for I could get you what you need a little faster."

"We've discussed this before, but I want to know for sure if that drug my mother created years ago is part of the formulation of Zenoprit."

"You mean the drug they got rid of years ago because it was causing cancer?"

"Yes."

"The same drug that is a part of, no offense, your DNA?"

"Yes. None taken."

"Well, if that's the case, we may have them by the balls, figuratively speaking. I know you won't be a ray of sunshine until you actually find your husband and hopefully alive, but you are really looking cloudy today."

"Johnathan has my son."

"Oh, God! I'm sorry."

She handed Tolido a jump drive. "I downloaded the formulation for the new cancer drug."

"What do you want me to do with it?"

"Once you have what we need, I want you to try to recreate it."

"Why? Is this part of that leverage you talk about?"

"No, but after my family is safe I still have to think about the millions of people who will need that treatment, many of whom may be unable to afford it."

Gail left Tolido's lab and headed to the area where her team was being assembled.

Colson had selected two guys to accompany Gail to the airport. Mike was not included.

"This boat is not sailing without me," Mike said. He was ready to go, and he argued every point Colson made about staying.

Although Gail didn't want one more person to worry about, she thought it might be good to have him there. "Let him come."

She moved closer to Colson to prevent Mike from hearing what she was about to say. "Look, if I could have it my way he would not be going, but there's no stopping him. Alex means a lot to him, there is no way he's going to sit this one out, and I think it would be very useful to have him come along."

"I can send another guy if you need more people."

"It's not about having more people. Alex knows him, which would make it easier for him to grab Alex and run if he had to. Any of these two guys try to touch him and he would most likely scream."

Colson nodded in acknowledgment. "The

only reason I say yes to you going," Colson said, "is because I have no choice and that's tough enough as it is. With Alex being out there with that madman, I didn't want both of you gone right now... All right, keep your eyes open at all times."

"Rick, let me know when the flight arrives," Gail said as she waved her phone. There were several technical guys on the team, but Rick Miller was her "go to."

They had a little over an hour to get to the airport, which was enough time before the flight arrived. They took one of the seven-seater SUVs with the hope that two more of those seats would be occupied on their return.

"Does Celia know what this Johnathan guy is up to?" Mike asked.

"Unfortunately, no. To her he's her knight in shining armor and he doesn't want to be without her."

"So, Johnathan, aka Nathan, got involved with Keri as a way to learn more about Brian and have his partner in crime to replace her. When the time was right, he swept Celia off her feet so he could have easy access to Alex. He's one twisted fellow," Mike said. "Maybe you could send her a text. Give her a heads-up who this guy is. Hopefully she checks her messages before she gets off the flight."

"That won't help. She doesn't have her phone. That's why her phone kept ringing without an answer. I can't call her and she won't be able to call me, not without him knowing."

"Well, if Celia doesn't know, I guess it'd be fair to say that Alex doesn't know he's in danger."

"Yeah. Maybe it's better that way for now."

"Did Johnathan say anything about Brian?"

"No, but for him to go after Alex...makes me wonder what became of Brian. Johnathan has no idea what he's done, going after my son." Gail had been haunted by the thought that Brian may have met his demise. She would not stop until she found him, but now her pain and anger had increased tenfold with the kidnapping of her son.

Mike took out his phone to look at the picture of Alex. He kept his eyes fixed on the picture for a good thirty seconds or more. "If he hurts Alex, I'll rip him apart limb by limb."

"You'll have to get in line."

They got to the airport before the flight landed. Gail opened the door and was ready to go.

"I have no doubt Johnathan is expecting you to be here, so he must have a few guys lurking around somewhere. I say we wait here until the flight arrives. That way you'll be less exposed,"

Mike said.

Gail kept checking her phone for the flight information. Finally the flight landed. "All right, let's move," Gail said. "Mike, if you get a chance to take Alex, grab him and run. Don't wait for me. Do you understand?"

"You'd want me to leave you in danger?"

"I'd want you to make Alex your priority."

Her phone rang with an unknown number. She pressed the answer button and lifted the phone to her ear.

"I know you're here, "Johnathan said. "If you come anywhere near them, Celia will know something is wrong and I'll have to kill her. Which is no big deal because I really don't have much further use for her anyway. So, it's your choice. Get out of my way and everybody lives, or you can attempt to take your son which I guarantee will fail, and for that you can say bye-bye to your sister-in-law. Just for kicks, I'll let your son watch me kill her."

The call ended.

Chapter 26

Gail halted in her tracks. She felt pressure building inside her, like she was about to explode. Alex was close, she could feel it. Could she do this? Could she come this close and then walk away from what might be her only chance of getting her son back alive?

If she went ahead with her plan, she may get to Alex or she may not, but one thing was for sure, Celia would not leave there alive. Was that something Gail could live with? Protecting her own and forsaking all others. Could she adapt that mantra just for today? Was she prepared to live with the consequences?

"What is it?" Mike asked.

"We have to abort."

"Why? What happened?"

"Johnathan knows we're here. I can't let them see me or he'll kill Celia."

"I'll go," Mike said. "He doesn't know what I look like."

Gail looked at him while she considered the

possibility. Was there any way at all Johnathan could know about Mike? She couldn't think of any way their paths had connected. "Okay, but don't try anything and don't let Celia or Alex see you. Celia's in the dark where Johnathan is concerned, and that's the only thing keeping her alive."

"How much longer before she figures out something is off?"

"I don't know, but it's not going to be now. We've to find another way. They're going to be coming out any time now. I've to get out of sight."

"What do you want me to do?" Mike asked.

"Tell those two guys to see if they can get visual confirmation that Alex and Celia are okay. Then meet me by the van. Don't linger. I can't afford for them to see you or all hell will break loose."

"Got it," Mike said.

Gail made her way back to the parked vehicle and sat in the back. Had she made the wrong decision sending Alex away with Celia? Should she have taken Alex and disappeared? She couldn't leave, knowing in her heart that Brian was in danger. Would it have made a difference if she'd known about his relationship with Keri?

Her mind kept throwing questions at her

and the more questions popped up in her head, the worse she felt. So far she still had not found Brian. Now Alex and Celia had fallen prey to Johnathan Clarke. What she was doing was not good enough. She needed to step it up if she had any hopes of getting them back alive. She called Colson.

"Please tell me you have Alex," he said.

"I wish I could," she said as she closed her eyes and reached deep down emotionally to strengthen herself. Then she told Colson about the phone call she received from Johnathan.

Colson shouted a curse word into the phone. "I'm sorry," he said. He never swore in front of her, but that didn't mean she hadn't heard him swear before.

As for Gail, there were not enough curse words to express how she felt. "Find me something I can use against Johnathan. Have them check his accounts, see if he's been sending money to anyone. If he has a child, a sister, even a third cousin that he's sending something to, then I want everything they can find on that person and I want eyes on them at all times," Gail said.

"The guys are already working on it," Colson said.

"They have to work faster. It won't be long before both Alex and Celia realize something is wrong. He needs Alex alive, but if I'm still empty-handed by then, he'll have no reason to let Celia live."

"Let's hope they find something and fast. Where's Mike?" Colson asked.

"He's..."

Mike opened the door and sat beside her.

"He's right here," she said.

"Who is that?" Mike asked.

"Colson."

"All right, you guys get back here as soon as possible...Gail, did you hear me?"

"Yes, of course."

"I know this is not easy for you but you have to step back a little or there will be too many casualties."

"I know," she said.

"So abolish any thought you had of following them. Just get back here. Let me talk to Mike," Colson said.

"He wants to talk to you," Gail said as she handed Mike the phone. Any other time, she would have been actively listening to the conversation between Mike and Colson. Not this time. She completely zoned out. The driver and the other guy with him returned to the vehicle.

"We'll be there soon," Mike said as he ended the call with Colson.

"Did you see them?" Gail asked.

The driver handed her his phone. He'd taken a few shots of them as they left the airport. She looked at the pictures and could no longer hold back the tears she'd been fighting since she found out Johnathan had her son.

Mike put his arms around her. "Head back to the center," he told the driver. "We'll get him back," Mike told her. "One way or another. If it's the last thing I do."

The ride back to the center seemed like it took forever even though they actually took less time to return from the airport. Colson met her at the door and hugged her. "I have dispatched a man to every state. If there is someone, we will find them and we will keep an eye on them. I will not rest until my grandson is safe."

Gail nodded. "I need to keep busy." She went to sit with Rick. "Any leads?"

"Not yet. So far we can't find where he has sent money from any of his accounts. I'm checking accounts in both names, but so far nothing."

"Was he ever married? Any record of a wife or ex-wife?"

"None that we know of."

"Parents. Are any of them alive?" Gail asked.

"Both deceased."

"How?"

"How what?"

"How did they die?"

"I don't know. Is that information really relevant?" Rick asked.

"I need to know everything I can about the monster who has my child. So yes, every bit of information you can find out about him and anyone related to him is relevant."

"Everything all right over there?" Mike asked.

"Yeah, we're okay," Rick said.

"Gail?"

"I'm fine."

"I'm sorry. It didn't occur to me to research all that information," Rick said.

"I should be the one apologizing. So for what it's worth, I'm sorry," Gail said.

"Don't worry about it," Rick said as he put his fingers to work on the keyboard.

"Let me know when you have something." Gail wandered to Colson and Mike who were looking at an aerial map on a large computer screen. They were focusing on Celia's address.

"You guys read my mind. I was just thinking that I should swing by Celia's home quietly. It is very likely they'll go there first."

"I already have eyes on the house," Colson said. "As soon as—" His cell phone rang. "Yes?"

He ended his call. "They're at Celia's house."

Gail's heart rate increased. "I'm going over

there," she said.

"Johnathan has some of his men strategically placed around the perimeter of the property. He will know you are coming before you get to the house. I strongly advise against that move, for the same reason you retreated earlier," Colson said.

Gail knew he was right. Still she struggled with the decision. She looked at Mike, trying to read his thoughts on the matter.

"He's right. You know that and I know that. But if you decide to go, I'll go with you," Mike said.

"I'm not going to risk getting Celia killed. I won't go now if I don't have to." She looked at Colson. "You better tell your 'eyes' to keep *his* eyes open."

Gail's cell phone rang. Another unknown number. "I think it's Johnathan."

"Put it on speaker," Mike said.

Gail pressed the answer button on the phone and then put it on speaker so Mike and Colson could hear.

"Hello, Gail. You made a wise choice today. Celia owes you her life. I'm particularly impressed that you chose not to follow me. That must have been hard for you but it was the right decision," Johnathan said.

"What do you want, Johnathan?"

"I have one simple request for tonight."

"Let me talk to my son first."

"Well, as it turns out, that's kind of why I'm calling. You see, Celia is going to call you. You will be on speaker phone so don't try to slip her any subtle message. I need you to tell her that the police are following up on a lead regarding Brian's kidnapping. You are going to be very busy and you want her to keep Alex for a few days because you are going to be out of state."

"Are you out of your mind?" Gail asked.

"Gail, this offer expires in fifteen minutes, because in fifteen minutes Celia *is* going to call you. What happens after that depends on you."

"Interesting proposition. I thought you said you had no further use for her."

"I don't. But the kid does. I have no patience for that kind of thing. I never did."

"Is that your way of telling me you don't have a child out there somewhere? Or maybe you do, but you weren't man enough to be a father."

"You're fishing. Let me throw you a bone for free. I have no children. I never have and I never will."

"Is that why you killed Keri, because she wanted the baby and you didn't?"

"Funny you should bring that up, since that unborn child was either fathered by your husband, or any other of the many guys Keri was seeing. But definitely not me."

"How could you be so sure? Is something wrong with you in that department?"

He ended the call.

"Are you deliberately trying to aggravate that man?" Colson asked Gail.

She knew it was risky but she wanted to throw him off his game. "I'm just trying to rattle his cage." As crazy as Johnathan's offer was, Gail knew there was no other way and she needed to buy herself sometime. However, she had no intension of appearing weak and defeated.

"Well, you certainly did that. Let's hope you didn't push him too far," Colson said.

"I don't want him to think he's completely in control." She walked over to Rick's desk. "You got any medical history for Johnathan?"

"Yeah, but I haven't gone through it yet. What exactly are you looking for?"

"I want to know if he had a vasectomy or some kind of testicular trauma that rendered him incapable of producing sperm."

"Why do you want to know that?" Rick asked as he brought of the records on the screen.

"I'm fighting a war here, Rick. I need all the types of ammunition I can get, even the psychological ones."

Mike came over. "Did you find something?"

"Not really, but we're still looking," Gail said.

"Is that his medical records? What do you expect to find in there that can be of help?" Mike asked.

"Wait, scroll up," Gail told Rick. "There," she said, pointing to the information on the screen. "He went to a fertility clinic. Which means he, or someone he was with, wanted a child."

"Is he married?" Mike asked.

"Was," Rick said. "Based on the dates he was married at the time but his wife is now deceased. Wait, there's more. He couldn't have children. He was thirty-one at the time. What a bummer," Rick said.

If he couldn't have children, it would also mean that Keri was not pregnant with his child. Which meant Brian may be the father. This was not where she needed her head space to be. There was too much at stake.

Focus. Was there a way to reach the man who wanted to have a child many years ago, or was that man long gone, replaced by the man who viciously murdered a pregnant woman, chopped her into pieces and then stuffed her head in a refrigerator.

Gail was grasping at straws, looking for a way to use emotional tactics, psychological mind games, anything she could do to make him stop and think before hurting Alex or Celia. Was it too late for Brian? She took a deep breath.

"I guess there will be no kid to find," Rick said.

"Not necessarily," Mike said. "He may not have created a child, but that's different from not having one. The child does not have to be biologically his, but could still mean the world to him."

Mike's words brought momentary silence, as it was no secret how he felt about Alex.

"I know," Gail said. It was a possibility worth exploring but it would take time. What Gail wanted to know was how does that influenced the way Johnathan viewed Alex since he was not averse to killing children, even the unborn.

Rick had found quite a bit of information on Johnathan. Gail tried to scan through as much of it as she could before Celia called. She needed something, anything that could give her even a little bit of edge. If there was something in there, she hadn't found it, but there was still more information. She worked her way through the information at her speed, one that Mike and Rick could not keep up with, until she was distracted by her phone. Celia's home number. She turned her eyes back to the screen and continued scrolling through the pages. The phone kept ringing.

"Gail, are you going to answer that?" Mike asked.

"Just a second," she said. She did not take her eyes off the screen, but she could tell Mike was nervous. She heard it in his voice. Once again the phone rang, but she kept looking.

Mike was growing restless, pacing the floor. "Gail, for heaven's sake, will you please answer the phone."

She still did not take her eyes of the screen. There was something here. There had to be. She needed to know he had something to lose. Just then, her eyes caught sight of a report on the screen. A glimmer of hope emerged from the dregs of his pathetic life. Johnathan had a sister.

Chapter 27

Gail pressed the answer button on the phone, then placed it on speaker. "Hello?"

"Hi Gail, it's me. I wanted you to know we're home," Celia said.

"Great. Where's Alex?"

"He's sleeping."

"Already?"

"He was tired and said he wanted to lie down. I think the flights wore him out. Maybe you could let him stay here tonight and pick him up tomorrow."

Gail took a deep breath and held it.

"Gail, did you hear what I said?" Celia asked.

Gail slowly exhaled. "I heard you. I may have to ask you to keep him for a few days."

"Is that because of Brian?"

"Yes. I need some time to sort through a few things."

Celia started to sob. "Who would want to hurt Brian? I don't understand. What do they want? Money?"

"I will do everything I can to find him, but I need you to keep Alex safe for me. Can you do that?"

"Of course. I told Nathan about what happened to Brian and he said he would stay here with me because he doesn't think it's safe for me to be here by myself."

"How generous of him," Gail said.

"Well, he's into security so I feel safer with him here. He has some of his employees patrolling the yard so Alex will definitely be protected. You don't have to worry, Gail, Alex is safe here with me. You know I love him as if he were my own son and I promise that Nathan and I won't let anything happen to him."

"Hmm, I see. I'm assuming Nathan is standing next to you."

"Yes, how'd you know? Say hi, Nathan."

"Hello, Gail, so nice to speak to you again."

"Hello, Nathan, Celia is the sister I never had. I trust you will ensure that no harm come to her or my son?"

Silence.

Had he gotten her subtle message? At that point, Gail wasn't sure the woman was alive or where to find her, but it was better than nothing. "If you are unable to guard them, then maybe it would better if I —"

"They will be safe," Johnathan said hastily. He got the message and he answered one other question she had. His sister was definitely alive.

"That's good to hear. Celia, we'll talk again tomorrow. You can call me at this number anytime, okay?"

"Okay," Celia said.

"I'll be in touch," Gail said, then she ended the call. She looked at Rick. "Johnathan has a weak spot. Find her!"

"You got it," Rick said.

According to Johnathan, his goals were currently aligned with those of Zsulrick's. There was no doubt they wanted her to disappear for good, but first they needed to secure any damning information she had on them. At some point Alex would be part of their power move. She toyed with the idea of trying to rescue them that night but it would have been too risky. Celia was under the impression that her boyfriend Nathan was actually protecting her. By the time Gail got past his goons outside, he could put a bullet between Celia's eyes before Gail got to him. No, not tonight.

Gail took small comfort in the fact that Johnathan was caught on the back foot when she said Celia was like a sister to her. Her sister-in-law and son would be okay for tonight, but Johnathan was a smart man. She couldn't harm his sister if she couldn't find her. Gail needed him to feel that his sister's life was in danger. It would make him angry. He would desperately want to eliminate that threat, that threat being Gail. That might force him to conjure up his own plan of action instead of waiting on directives from Zsulrick.

"You think they'll be okay for tonight?" Mike asked.

"I do, but it doesn't make it any easier."

"I'm sorry if I raised my voice at you. This whole thing just have me on pins and needles," Mike said.

If he raised his voice, she hadn't noticed, but then she could understand if he had. "Don't worry about it. We are all on pins and needles."

She touched Rick on his shoulder. "What do we know so far?"

Rick spun his chair around to face Gail, Mike, and Colson, who walked over to join in. "She had a car accident in early 2000 and that's the last record we have of her."

"Maybe she died in the accident," Mike said.

"No. She's alive. I'm sure of it," Gail told them.

"What makes you so sure?" Colson asked.

"I made Johnathan nervous. No way could I have done that if she were dead. That woman is alive." She thought for a minute. "Tell me about her accident," she said to Rick.

"All right. Give me a minute." Rick brought the information up on the screen. "Okay, here we go. These are some shots from the scene of the accident."

As they studied the mangled remains of what was Johnathan sister's car, Mike said, "There is no way that she walked away from that accident."

"That we agree on," Gail said. In his line of work, Johnathan must've angered a lot of people. His own strategy of going after other people's family members would inform his decision to not leave her exposed. "I think he changed her name. He probably used letters from her original name. Rick, start looking for names that can be created from the letters of her original name. Let me know the minute you find something."

"What's the latest on Zsulrick?" Gail asked Colson.

"They've managed to keep things relatively low profile. The clinical trials of the cancer drug are still in progress. We don't have any new data on those results."

"What about the Zenoprit case?" Gail asked.

"They have another hearing in two days. I think it's fair to assume they'll want to keep things as quiet as possible, and hope that they can reach a settlement then," Colson said.

"In other words, they may ask Johnathan to sit on his hands until they're ready. No demands, no exchange, nothing until after the plaintiffs have signed on the dotted line," Mike said.

Two days. Gail should have her son back by then. As for Brian, she wasn't sure if she was trying to save him or recover his body.

"Tolido is working non-stop on the Zenoprit. Hopefully he'll have something for you soon," Colson said.

"That's where I was going next," Gail said.

"No need. You had a really rough day coupled with the fact that you didn't sleep last night. You might want to take it easy on yourself a little. Things will get done. That's why we're here and I'm drinking coffee instead of vodka. I know you won't sleep but you should try to get some rest. You are going up against a rather ruthless man and his band of killers and you can't afford to be sleep-deprived," Colson said.

"I'll just sit here," Gail said as she pulled up a chair.

"You're as stubborn as they come," Colson said.

"She is her father's daughter," Mike mumbled under his breath.

"What's that, Mike?" Colson asked.

"Oh, I said, don't worry, I can get her to relax."

"I wish you luck with that. I have some phone calls to make, let me know if you guys need anything," Colson said as he walked towards the office on the far left of the basement.

"Take your boots off and put your feet up," Mike said as he positioned himself to receive her feet in his lap. Rick looked around at Mike then quickly turned back to his computer screen. Gail could not believe he was offering to do that here, right now with so many people around. She thought maybe if she ignored him he would get the message.

"Come on. We both know you're not leaving here any time soon. You could relax and still be in the midst of all the activities," Mike said.

"Not going to happen," Gail said.

"Why? What are you afraid of?" He moved his chair closer to her. Gail got up and walked away. "Where're you going?" Mike asked.

"I'm going to see how things are going with Tolido."

"I'll come with you."

As soon as they were on the stairs and away from prying eyes, Gail shoved him. "Are you crazy?"

"What? What did I do?"

Gail frowned.

"You're mad at me because I offered to rub your feet?" Mike asked.

"In the middle of the office in front of everybody!"

"Technically, it's not an office, it's a basement and these guys are like family. It's not like we're talking about strangers and, for the record, I think only Rick heard what I said."

"That's not the point."

"What's the point?"

"It would give people the wrong impression," Gail said.

"And what impression would that be, if you don't mind my asking?"

"I don't have time for this." Gail stormed up the stairs.

Mike ran past her and blocked the door to the hallway that led to Tolido's office. "Okay. I get it. I'm sorry. I didn't see it as a big deal especially since they all know that your marriage at the moment is nothing but a piece of paper."

"How could they know that?" Gail asked.

"They spent the last few days digging into Brian's life and he had quite a record. I don't think anyone would blame you if you chose to pursue some kind of comfort."

"Right." She pushed him out of the way and

headed for Tolido's lab.

"Gail!" Tolido said.

Mike came in behind her.

"...And Mike. Just the two people I wanted to see. I was able to reverse engineer Zenoprit and confirm your suspicions," he told Gail.

"Do you mean that Zsulrick deliberately laced the drug with something they knew would cause cancer?" Mike asked.

"That's correct, but the amount is very small so the effects are not immediate. It takes time depending on how much of the drug you take," Tolido explained.

"I guess that means anyone who's ever taken even one Zenoprit is at risk of developing cancer despite having a clean bill of health today," Gail said.

"Unfortunately, yes, those effects will probably not show up until months later. The good news is the cancer drug they have in testing works. It puts the cancer in remission and keeps it there if the patient continues to take it."

"What happens if they stop taking it?" Mike asked.

"That, I don't know. We would need a lot more time to test that," Tolido said.

"No wonder Zsulrick is trying so hard to keep this quiet," Gail said.

"If this information got out, it'd be bad for them at any time but I think they are on high alert with the hearing in only two days. Gail, whatever we do, we need to get Alex out of there before the trial," Mike said.

"We agree on that, but if we don't do this right, we won't get Celia out of there alive. I want to get them out without killing Johnathan and that's not going to be easy," Gail said.

"Which part?" Tolido asked. "Getting them out, or the not killing part?"

"Why are you so worried about Johnathan?" Mike asked.

"Because he might be the only one who knows where Brian is. I want him alive."

"I see what you're saying but knowing who we're dealing with, I know he'll try to kill you the first chance he gets. I'm not going to let that happen."

"Maybe you should," Tolido said.

"What? Let him kill her? Are you kidding?" Mike asked.

"Yes and no," Tolido said. "She can heal, but he doesn't know that. Does he?"

Mike held up his hand to Tolido indicating that he was not interested.

"Let's hear him out," Gail said.

"Are you seriously listening to Tolido?"

Gail raised her eyebrows.

"You can't be," Mike said. "You hurt and bleed like everyone else. We don't know how much your body can take and I guarantee that Johnathan will not be satisfied putting just one bullet in you. No, absolutely not. I can't let you do that." Mike's face turned red. "Why would you even suggest that?" he asked Tolido.

Cowering away from Mike, Tolido said, "Please, hear me out."

"If it involves her deliberately putting herself at risk to be killed. I don't want to hear it," Mike said.

"Mike, let's hear him out. All right, Tolido, the floor is yours," Gail said.

Tolido took a deep breath. "I have been analyzing your samples. I realize your body reacts to an injury pretty much the same way a normal person would react to a virus. For the record, I'm not saying you're not normal," Tolido said as he glanced at Mike even though he was speaking to Gail. "So basically the same way we can fight off or prevent disease because our bodies were exposed to them before, your body repairs itself faster each time you experience physical trauma, like a gunshot. It's like it changes to a better, stronger version of itself."

"Am I hearing you right? The more time she gets hurt the faster she heals?" Mike asked.

"Theoretically, yes," Tolido said.

"Theoretically? So you don't know this for sure?" Mike looked quite annoyed, standing there feet shoulder-width apart and arms folded.

"Well, there is only so much I can do with samples," Tolido said.

"Then how do you know that this would work?" Mike asked.

"My answer to that question brings me back to the new cancer treatment drug. I could not recreate the formula and then I decided to take a break from it and work on something else. Gail's samples were the something else. Anyway, I think I may have contaminated some of my samples with Gail's blood. I was about to throw them out, but I decided to check the slide under the microscope."

"And?" Mike asked.

"See for yourself. This is a sample that shows the long-term effects of taking Zenoprit."

Mike looked at the sample under the microscope and Gail did the same.

"Now, this slide was just like that one, except it was contaminated with Gail's blood."

Mike looked at the slide. He looked at Gail.

The look of shock was all over his face. Mike knew pretty much everything about her. What could be on that slide that made him look so stunned?

Chapter 28

It was Gail's turn to look at the contaminated samples. The sample that had her blood in it showed normal cells. The cancer was completely eradicated.

"Are you sure this sample was not treated with Zsulrick's new drug?" Gail asked Tolido.

"I'm positive. I can show you the samples that were treated with that drug. There was no observable change after several treatments," Tolido said.

"That's to be expected," Mike said. "The treatments work over months."

"True," Tolido said. "But something in Gail's blood attacks the cancer immediately. Now this may sound strange but I could not reproduce the new drug because I was unable to identify a component in the formula. I believe that missing component is what makes the drug works and I also believe it came from your blood," Tolido told Gail. "The cure is in your blood."

"How would Zsulrick get my blood?"

"According to your mother's records, she

was taking blood samples from you every month. I think someone there found the connection, maybe by accident, and they found a way to isolate the component that works. Once they have that, they replicate it in a lab and *voila,* they have a never ending supply," Tolido said.

"Can you prove that?" Gail asked.

"Not really," Tolido said. "But it makes sense. This drug was introduced to your system as an embryo. It didn't harm you, and instead your system seems to have found a way to counteract the negative effects other people experience. Which it seems to do for anything that can damage it."

"Like a gunshot wound?" Gail asked.

"Yes," Tolido said.

Mike sighed. "So we're back to that discussion again."

"It is a theory I would like to explore, if Gail would allow it."

"What do you need from me to make it happen?" Gail asked.

"Your time. I will need to run a few tests."

"How much time are we talking about?"

"Hard to say at this point since I've never done anything like this before."

"You got an hour," Gail said.

"I'm going to need some time to prepare," Tolido said.

"How long is that going to take?"

"I'll be ready before you know it." Tolido was off, leaving Gail and Mike in the lab.

He was looking at her. He clearly had something on his mind but he didn't say anything.

"You don't approve?" Gail asked.

"Does it matter?"

"I wouldn't ask if it didn't. You don't want me to conduct the tests?"

"I don't have a problem with the test. I think it's good for us to understand more about how your body works, but Tolido has planted an idea in your head and I don't like it one bit. I know that's not what you want to hear, and I'm trying to support you as best as I can, but offering yourself like a lamb to a slaughter is not an idea I can support," Mike said.

"I didn't say I was going to do it, but I want to know what's possible."

"Are you sure? Or are you telling me what I want to hear?"

"Why don't we see how things work out with these tests, and then we can have this conversation again."

"So it's not off the table, then. You'd consider it a viable option. Despite what Tolido tells you, no one will know for sure what will tip the scale for you. One extra bullet may take your body past the point where it could repair itself fast enough before you bleed out."

"I know that, and I appreciate your concern, but a madman has my son. If I have to offer my life for his, I'd do it in a heartbeat. Unfortunately, we're not just talking about Alex. If that were the case, I could go in and get him and we would not be having this conversation."

Tolido returned to the lab, wheeling a cart.

"What's this for?" Gail asked.

"Nothing, I needed the space in the other room that we will be using."

"We're not doing the tests in here?" Gail asked.

"No. I need to use the Electroencephalography to monitor your brain activity and that's in the other room, plus I don't want to risk contaminating any of the other samples I'm working on. Are you ready?"

"Lead the way," Gail said. She noticed that Mike had not moved. "Mike, are you coming?"

"I think I'm going to wait here."

"I want you to be there."

"Actually, I *need* you to be there," Tolido interjected. "We're going to have to shoot her and I...I can't do that part. So I definitely need you and a gun with the thing on the end, silencer."

Gail blinked when she heard Tolido say

"shoot her," but she wasn't surprised. How else would he hurt her so he could monitor the effects of her healing properties?

Mike blanched and then scoffed at Tolido. "Seriously? You want me to shoot her?"

"Well, I can't do it." Tolido looked at him earnestly, as if his proposal was perfectly natural. "I have never held a gun in my life."

Gail smothered an urge to laugh. "Would you do it if I asked you to?" Gail asked to get Mike's attention.

"Are you asking me to?"

"I am. Will you do it, for me?" Gail asked.

He gazed at her for about five seconds, then nodded. "Okay," he said in a low voice.

Once they got to the room that Tolido had set up he solicited Mike's help to attach the probes to Gail's head.

"Is there a particular reason you choose to monitor her brain activity?" Mike asked.

"I want to see what's happening when she's healing," Tolido said.

"Like what?" Gail asked.

"I'm not really sure, but your mother's notes made reference to a mind-body connection. In other words, you can control if and when your body heals."

"I thought her healing was automatic," Mike said.

"It is, but according to what her mother documented, Gail could block it, sort of like how she can block what she hears. If she uses the same technique, then she could theoretically prevent her body from actively heal itself, and her healing would be much slower."

"Her mother's notes said that?" Mike asked.

"Well, not those exact words, but that is what I gleaned from it," Tolido said.

"You probably made the whole thing up, so you could get her to agree to this little experiment which you seem overly eager to conduct."

"Mike," Gail whispered.

"I'm sorry," Mike said.

The probes were in place and the machine was ready. They were ready to begin. Gail gave Mike her gun.

"Okay, pick a spot and shoot. I'll say when," Tolido told Mike.

"What? Oh, yeah, sure," Mike seem nervous as he prepared to shoot her. "Why don't you pick the spot?" he asked Tolido.

Tolido touched her lower right abdomen. "How about here?" he asked.

"No, not there," Mike said.

"Why?"

"I don't want to put a bullet through her ovary."

"Okay, back to my original suggestion. You pick a spot," Tolido said.

Gail watched as Mike struggled to find a place on her body to point the gun.

"One more thing," Tolido said. "Gail, could you try to delay healing, if you can? I want to see if my interpretation was correct."

"Okay," Gail said, unsure what exactly she could do to rearrange the mind-body connection he had mumbled about. But since they were all raving lunatics trying the most ridiculous experiment on the planet, delaying a healing reaction seemed like something she should know how to do about as well as speeding up the process. After all, hadn't she vomited bullets she hadn't even known were inside of her? "Are you ready?" she asked Mike.

"We'll see," he said.

"You need to step back, Mike. If you shoot her at that close range, the bullet will go right through her. I want it inside, so I can see what her body does with it."

Mike backed up. He took aim.

"Now!" Tolido yelled.

"Squeeze the trigger, Mike," Gail said when he hesitated.

Mike kept the gun aimed at Gail for a while, then he finally lowered it. "I can't do it, I'm sorry. I can't bring myself to hurt you. Do you understand?"

"It's okak. Give me the gun," Gail said as she stretched her hand out to him.

"I can't do that either."

"Oh, for the love of God. Will you just hand over the darn thing since you are too afraid to use it?" Tolido asked.

Mike pointed the gun at him. "I'm not afraid to shoot *you*."

"I'm sorry. That's not me, it's just my frustration talking," Tolido said hurriedly.

"All right, that's ..." before Gail could finish her sentence, the door to the room swung open.

"What the hell is going on in here?" Colson asked. "Planning on shooting somebody, Mike?"

Mike gently placed the gun on a cart next to him.

Gail quickly yanked the probes that were attached to her head.

"Tolido wanted to ..." Gail noticed Tolido making a sign with his hand. It was obvious Colson had absolutely no idea what they were doing.

She wanted to tell him the truth but opted to spare Tolido from any backlash, because she knew, like Mike, Colson would not agree with this.

"...run some more test to see if everything

was all right," Gail explained.

"And you agreed to it?" Colson asked Gail.

"I did."

"Uh huh. What are you not telling me? I know you, Gail. There is no way Tolido could convince you to agree to running follow up test, not at such a crucial time." He faced Tolido. "Why don't you explain to me what this thing was doing connected to her and what tests you were running? And please, do furnish me with the results of your tests." He kept staring at Tolido while he waited for him to respond.

Tolido buckled and told Colson everything. Colson's stare changed from one of intimidation to that of sheer disappointment. He was quiet for a while; the whole room was. All eyes were on Colson as he seem to slowly let the information sink in. "Mike, are you in agreement with this?" he asked.

"No," Mike said.

"Good, me neither. We'll find another way. Tolido, the next time you have any bright ideas like putting a bullet through my daughter, be sure to run it by me first," Colson said as he left the room.

"Yes, sir. But if I could just explain…" Tolido exited the room behind Colson leaving Gail and Mike alone.

"I'm sorry," Mike said.

"For what?"

"That I didn't do what you and Tolido wanted me to."

"Don't be. As much as I wanted to follow through with this test, it actually felt good watching you not being able to squeeze that trigger."

"Really? So you're not upset?"

"On the contrary. I appreciate the fact that you didn't want to hurt me, although I probably wouldn't feel it. I'm already in so much pain just thinking about what Brian did. I know it's selfish to be thinking of myself and what I'm feeling when he might be going through hell right now."

"Hey, anyone who's been on the receiving end of infidelity knows how painful it is. You can't put off the hurt or postpone it until the time is right. It's going to happen with our without your permission so you can't blame yourself for hurting."

"Maybe you're right but I still feel responsible for what happened to Brian and it adds to the confusion that's going on inside my head."

"It'll get better," Mike said, stroking her cheek. "But it's going to take time. Seeing you hurt like this made me realize why my ex hated me. I can't imagine what she was going through."

"I thought you said you didn't cheat on her."

"I said *technically*, I didn't cheat, but for all intents and purposes I guess you could say I did."

"Oh, that's surprising. I really thought you'd changed."

"I have."

"Then how do you explain what you did to Erica?" Gail sighed. "I'm not trying to grill you. In a way, I'm hoping it will give me some perspective."

"It won't. Brian and I are two different people. My situation was different. My cheating took place in my head. There was no physical contact."

"So you two talked about it but did not actually..."

"Not even that. We talked, but she didn't really know how I felt."

"Oh. That's certainly different from Brian's situation indeed."

"It was, but the more I think about it the more I realize that it doesn't make the pain any less. Erica has moved on and I'm very happy for her. I wonder if she still hates me."

"Are you really happy for her?"

"I am. I know I couldn't love her the way she wanted me to. I tried but it wasn't happening. I was willing to live with it though because she's a wonderful woman, but I messed up."

"You still haven't told me who she is."

"No, I haven't."

"That's it. You're still being tight lipped about this. Well, you're a free man now. You should go after her, whoever she is."

"You really mean that?"

"Of course."

"It doesn't bother you, even a little bit?"

"Not at all."

Lies. All lies. She was sorry she'd brought up the subject, but she knew there must be a reason why all these years they were never anything but just friends. What was she thinking? Did she actually believe all the things he was feeding her? It was a ploy, concocted by Colson to get her to see a life beyond Brian. She felt kind of stupid for allowing herself to think that there was something there, more than the love of a friend.

"You sure?" Mike asked.

"Why wouldn't I be?"

"Okay, from a woman's perspective. What's the best way for me to approach this? Should I try to find out how she feels about me? Because although I'm crazy about her I'm not really sure how she feels about me."

"Mike, I know I started this but my head is

someplace else right now. I'm sure you understand. I'm still trying to work out how to rescue Alex and Celia."

"I know. I was hoping this discussion would take your mind off that even for a few minutes," Mike said. "So please, humor me."

"Just tell her how you feel. I think that should be a good start."

"So, be bold?"

"Yeah, sure. Do whatever feels right. Don't worry too much about how you do it, just make sure you do. Otherwise she'll never know and she may start going out with someone else while you're twiddling your thumbs trying to figure out how to tell her how you feel. So yeah, be bold and just do it."

"Great, thanks for the advice. I think I'm going to head downstairs to see how things are going with Rick." He opened the door. "Are you coming?"

"You go ahead, I'll catch up with you in a few minutes." She needed time to lick her wounds. She wasn't sure if she should kick herself, or pat herself on the back for being a good friend. Yeah, a really good friend. She had done the right thing. But enough with the distractions. There was a monumental task ahead of her and she needed to keep a clear head. She heard foots steps coming towards the room. The door pushed open and Mike stuck his head inside.

"Gail."

"Yes?"

"That girl, she likes when I massage her feet."

"You, you called Erica my—"

"Hmm."

Gail froze as Mike's words caught her by surprise.

"Come on," he said, as he reach out and took her by the hand. They walked towards the stairs. Mike was still holding her hand. The moment she saw Tolido exit the lab she removed her hand from his grasp. They watched Tolido until he disappeared into another room.

"What? I shouldn't hold your hand, either?"

"It's complicated."

"I know that, but I thought we were past a certain point. I promise I'll give you all the time you need. Just tell me what you want."

"I can't focus on my wants right now. My head is completely messed up and in all honesty I don't think I'd be good for you. Even if I find Brian tomorrow and we get divorced, do you really think you could have a normal life with me?"

"Why not?"

"I'm as screwed up as they come. Other than the complexity of my biological makeup, I've psychological issues to work through. You ever wonder why you're the only friend I have? I'm socially inept. At least that's what I was told as a teenager. Ask Colson how many boys he had to chase away from me when I was growing up. None. The only boy who spent time with me was Leon, who I now know was my half-brother."

"Is that why you kept hanging on to Brian? You think he's the only man who could love you?"

"I'm not hanging on to him."

"Good. Then tell me I'm not alone in this. Tell me you want it too and I'll wait as long as it takes."

Chapter 29

Gail's phone rang. It couldn't have happened at a better time. "Hello? We're on our way down." She shoved the phone back in her pocket. "Rick found something. Can we continue this conversation another time?"

"Of course. I probably shouldn't have brought it up now anyway." He held out his hand for her. "I promise I'll let go before we get downstairs."

They got to the basement where Rick was waiting for them. "Hey, Rick. Where's Colson?" Gail asked.

"He went to make a phone call."

"So what have you got for me?"

"As you suggested, since we were unable to locate Johnathan's sister, we searched for names that could be created from her original name. We found more than one person, but one of them is in a home for people with special needs."

"That would probably be her. She might

have had extensive injuries from that car accident," Mike said.

"Do you know what's wrong with her?" Gail asked Rick.

"No, not yet."

"Pull up her medical record," Gail said. "Mike and I will look through it."

"I don't have it. I'm not sure if this is the person we're looking for. I think it is but I didn't want to go digging in this woman's life before I get your feedback."

"Fair enough. Do we have anything that links Johnathan to this woman?"

"So far, no."

"What about the home she's staying in? Check if Johnathan is making payments to the place. Remember to check all his accounts."

She glanced over at Colson who had just finished a call. "I'll be right back," she said and crossed the room.

"I have someone en route to each location," Colson told her. "Either one of these women turns out to be Johnathan's sister and they'll already be in place. Ready to take action."

"I have no plans to hurt this woman. You understand?"

"I understand, but I hope you understand that I have no plans on letting that maniac hurt Alex or you. I have no plans to hurt her either, but if anything happens to that little boy, all bets are off."

"You can't hurt an innocent woman, not in my name or Alex's. Otherwise you would be no different from the monster you're trying to protect us from. This was supposed to be a scare tactic, nothing more."

"I know, but I'm an angry old man and sometimes I let my emotions get the better of me."

"I need you to promise me that no harm will come to this woman."

"I think I need a drink first. It usually helps to clear my head."

"Colson, I swear if you harm this woman I will have nothing to do with you, and you can forget about having a relationship with Alex."

He seemed shaken by her threat.

"Give me your word."

He nodded.

"I want to hear you say it."

"You have my word. No harm will come to her by my hands."

Gail breathed a sigh of relief because, truth be told, she wanted him in her and Alex's life as much as he wanted them. "I need you to do something else for me." She tore a page from a notepad and wrote on it. "Can you have this taken care of for me?"

"Are you sure?"

"Positive."

"How soon do want it done?"

"Yesterday."

"Understood. Consider it done."

"One more thing. Keep this between us."

"Of course," Colson said. "I'll get on it right now." He opened his phone, searched for a number and then placed the call. Mike was walking towards them. "I better take this call somewhere else," Colson said, as he headed to the office.

"Everything all right?" Mike asked.

"Sure."

"Rick is still trying to find a link. Let's say he does, then what?" Mike asked.

"I don't have all the answers yet. The court hearing is in two days. They want everything to stay quiet until after that date. I want Alex out of there by tomorrow. How am I going to do it? I'm still trying to work that out."

"We'll figure it out. I wish we knew where Brian was. That bit of unknown can throw a monkey wrench into any plan we have."

"I know. I've rolled it over and over again in my head." But that was not her only gripe. She didn't want Mike going with her. Watching him slip in and out of consciousness after the explosion at the cabin was tough for her. Maybe more than she wanted to admit. She was already blaming herself for Brian's misfortune and prayed she had the opportunity to make amends. She can't have anything happen to Mike. She needed his help, but she also wanted to keep him out of harm's way.

"Maybe Brian is dead. Since he disappeared, we've not seen nor heard anything that would indicate he's alive. All of the main conspirators in the kidnapping have been murdered, except for one. It would not be a stretch to think they killed him as well, either deliberately or by accident. Either way, I would not suggest you get your hopes up," Mike said.

"You may be right, but there's nothing to indicate that he's dead, either. Until I see his body with my own eyes, I'll continue to believe he's alive and I will not rest until I find him."

Rick finally found the connection that linked Johnathan to the woman they believed to be his sister. Colson wasted no time in dispatching one of his guys to find her. It was night time, so Gail might not get a picture of her until the next day. The guys called it a night and shortly after, so did Colson. Gail kept checking her phone although she knew full well that it was highly unlikely they would get that picture tonight.

"You've done all you can. At this point the best thing you can do is rest so you can be ready for what lies ahead tomorrow," Mike said.

"Easier said than done." Rest was the furthest thing from her mind and, as Tolido would put it, there was a mind and body connection, because she did not feel the least bit tired. Her thoughts were filled with Alex as she wrestled with the decision she'd made the day Brian had not shown up at the airport, and how that decision was ultimately what placed Alex in danger. She started looking through a pile of information that Colson had left on one of the desks. There was data on all the persons they knew were involved. It was nothing she had not seen before but it was something to do, something to keep her mind occupied.

"What's that?" Mike asked.

"Colson has a comprehensive file of all the people involved and what looks like some background information on each of them. You should go ahead. I'm going to look through here for a bit and then I'll come up."

"Okay. I guess I'll see you in a few minutes."

"Yeah, but don't wait up for me. Get some sleep." She buried her head in the papers until Mike left. Now she was more tormented than ever. She went into Colson's office and looked around aimlessly, pulling out desk drawers, hoping to find more information for her to read through. Her leg brushed against something under the desk. She reached under and pulled out a bin that had what looked like items Colson wanted to dispose of.

She riffled through the bin and then realized why Colson was able to produce the Zenoprit so quickly. He was taking it. Why hadn't he said anything?

It must have taken her about thirty seconds to sprint up the stairs and started banging on Tolido's door.

"Tolido!" After banging persistently for more than a minute, Tolido finally opened the door. "Gail?"

"What's Colson's blood type?" she asked.

"What?" Tolido appeared as if he was still half asleep.

"Blood type. What is Colson's blood type?"

"Same as yours. AB negative. Is that it?"

"Yes, thank you."

"Good." Tolido closed the door.

Gail knocked on the door again.

"What now?"

"Hypothetically speaking, what would happen if you gave someone who was on Zenoprit my blood?"

"Assuming your blood is compatible, it would potentially reverse any damage the drug created."

"How much blood would we need to

accomplish that?"

"Are we still speaking hypothetically?"

"Yes. How much?"

"I don't know. Your blood is way more potent than the drug Zsulrick has and I guess it would depend on how much damage has been done. Hmm, really hard to say."

"You don't have to be exact. Give me an educated guess."

"I guess five milliliters would probably be good, but..."

"But what?"

"Your blood is not exactly what I would call normal, so I am not sure how someone else my react to it."

"Okay. Have a good night."

Mike stood outside his door. "How long have you been standing there?" she asked.

"Long enough to figure out that you think Colson was on Zenoprit."

Gail headed to the direction of the stairs. Mike caught up with her. "Did he tell you he was taking it?"

"No. I found his leftovers he threw out. How could he not tell me something like this?"

"I guess because he didn't want you worrying about him."

"I guess everybody has a good reason for either lying to me or withholding information from me. What else is new?"

"You have a lot to worry about as it is. I'm sure he thought he was doing the right thing by keeping this from you."

"Maybe you're right, but why keep it to himself? It's obvious Tolido didn't know he was taking it." They got to the lab and Gail took what she needed and laid it on the table. She gave her arm to Mike. "I need five milliliters of my blood in this syringe."

"Don't you think you should ask Colson first before you move ahead with this?"

"He's sleeping."

"Good point. Why don't you wait until morning and talk to him about it then."

"I could do that. I still want you to take the blood now. Tomorrow will be a really tense day for me. I might as well get this done now."

Mike took the blood from her and handed her the syringe. "Put it in the refrigerator," he said.

Gail removed the used needle, then attached a new one to the syringe. She studied the syringe of blood in her hand.

"It's a good thing the both of you have the same blood type, but there is still no guarantee that this will work."

"Right. Nothing is guaranteed, is it?"

"Uh, no. Are we still talking about Colson, or

something else?"

"Let me ask you something. You love Alex. Right?"

"Of course, like he's my own. I'm surprised you had to ask."

"Given the current situation with Brian being missing, if I asked you to keep Alex out of the country because he may be in danger, would you return a day after I tell you that?"

"Not unless you told me everything was resolved, no. Where're you going with this?"

"It just occurred to me that I know very little about Celia other than she's Brian's sister. How could Celia guarantee that Alex would be safe? What does she know that made her sure nothing will happen to Alex? Her love for Alex is real, that much I know."

Gail looked at the syringe of blood in her hand. "Give this to Colson," she said as she handed Mike the syringe. "You may need to watch him for a while after."

"Now? You want me to wake him up and give this to him now? How am I supposed to explain this to him?"

She was done waiting around to figure out whether she was doing the right thing. "Fine. I'll give it to him myself." She snatched the syringe from Mike's hand.

Colson was snoring up a storm when they

got to his room. Gail thought they could be in and out in no time, but as she got close enough to touch him, he switched the light on and pointed a gun at her.

"Don't shoot, it's just me," Gail said.

"What the hell?"

"I don't have time to explain this to you but I want you to trust me. Do you trust me?" she asked Colson.

"Why wouldn't I?"

"Okay. Give me your arm." She cleaned his hand and injected the blood into his vein. "Mike is going to stay with you for a while."

"Why? Are you expecting something to go wrong?"

"No, but I want to be sure that in the event you get ill, he's right here. How do you feel?" Gail asked.

"The same way I felt before you stuck me with the needle, minus the needle prick."

Mike laughed. "I think he's going to be fine."

Her cell phone rang. The call was coming from Celia's house.

"Who is it?" Mike asked. As he leaned over to look at the name on the phone display. "Celia? Why would she be calling now?"

"Put it on speaker phone," Colson said.

Gail answered. "Hello?"

"Gail!" Celia sounded as if she was crying.

"What is it?" Gail asked.

Celia kept crying.

"Talk to me, Celia."

"It's Alex."

Gail felt a sharp pain at the bottom of her stomach. "What happened to Alex?"

"He-he's roasting with fever. I gave him some medication but he threw it up. I can't seem to get the fever down. You have to come and help him."

"Fever? Take him to the emergency room. I'll meet you there."

"I can't. Nathan won't let me."

"I'm on my way," Gail said.

"Wait, Nathan wants to talk to you."

"I'm going to make this real simple," Johnathan said when he came on the line. "You, in exchange for Celia and the boy. Come alone or the deal is off."

As soon as the call ended. Gail called Rick. He picked up on the second ring. "I take it you weren't sleeping."

"Not yet," Rick said.

"I need a favor. Find out everything you can about Celia Wilson."

"Celia Wilson, your sister-in-law?"

"Yes. Call me on this number with anything you think I need to know."

"You want to tell me what's going on? Why

are you checking into Celia's past?" Mike asked.

"Something doesn't feel right," Gail said. "She called with an emergency. Then Johnathan told me to come alone."

"Well, it's obvious you're being set up. That explains it."

"I know that, but something about Celia has started to perplex me. I want to know if she was coerced or a willing participant."

"That's your pain talking. There's no way Celia would hurt Alex. She loves that kid," Mike said.

"I know she loves him, that's the reason I trusted her with him, but answer this. How many times have I told you Alex has a fever?"

"I don't recall you ever telling me he had a fever. The boy is as tough as nails. Holy crap!" Mike said.

"Exactly," Gail said.

She put her hand to Colson's forehead. "I'm fine. You two go ahead."

Chapter 30

The call from Rick came as Mike parked the van at the end of the road to Celia's house.

"Talk to me, Rick," Gail said, clicking on the speaker.

"You're not going to believe this. Celia is a major shareholder in Zsulrick, courtesy of her deceased husband."

"So Celia was part of this all along? But why would she agree to let them kidnap her own brother?" Mike asked.

"They're not related by blood," Rick said.

"Say what?" Gail asked.

"Celia was adopted. Then years later, her parents had a child. Brian," Rick said.

"Thanks, Rick," she said and ended the call. Celia was a wild card Gail had not anticipated. "I'll try to get Celia to take Alex to you. Let me know as soon as you have him."

"I can't let you go in there alone," Mike said.

She cupped his face with both hands. "I need you to stay here. I need you to make sure my son is okay. Can you do that for me?"

He nodded slowly. Fear was written all over his face. Gail knew she was walking into a trap. She may never see him again. "Mike, I—"

He covered her lips with his fingers. "Tell me when we see each other again." He hugged her.

It was time for her to go. "Stay alert!" Gail said as she took off towards Celia's house.

The lights were on and the front door open. Two men stood alert on either side of the door, each with a gun. "Put your weapon on the ground," one of the men shouted.

Gail gently stooped and placed the gun in her hand on the ground while keeping her eyes on the two guys in front of her.

"Where's my son?"

One of them beckoned for her to step forward. She slowly walked to the door and stepped inside. Celia stood on the stairs holding Alex. He appeared to be sleeping with his head resting on her shoulder.

"How's he doing?" Gail asked.

"Still burning up," Celia replied.

Gail reached out her hands. "Let me see."

Johnathan appeared at the top of the stairs. "I don't think so."

Celia moved hurriedly as she exited.

Gail's sense of smell had gotten better. She could smell the medicine Alex got as Celia passed her. "Mike is at the end of the road waiting for you. Let him help Alex."

"Thank you," Celia said, as she went out into the night with Alex in her arms.

"Hand over the information you stole," Johnathan said.

Gail had already made an assessment of how many men were in the room and how she was going to kill them, if she got the chance. There were five of them that she could see, plus Johnathan. They all had their guns pointed at her. She needed to make sure Mike had Alex before she made a move.

"Where's my husband?" Gail asked.

"You're still looking for him?" Johnathan laughed. "What makes you think he's alive?"

She heard a beep on her phone. At this point she had both hands in the air. "I need to make sure Celia and my son are safe first." Gail slowly lowered her left hand. "I'm just getting my phone." She removed the phone from her pocket and held it up. A text message came in with a picture of Johnathan's sister. The woman was in a wheelchair. Gail noticed a painting on the wall behind her. It was one of her own, a gift she had given to Celia. "I'm going to make a call."

Johnathan waved his gun and laughed. "For all the good it will do. One attempt at calling for help and they're dead."

She called Mike. "Celia is on her way to you with Alex."

"Okay. What do you want me to do?"

"Take a whiff of his breath and you'll know how to make him better. Make sure you don't catch anything from Celia." The coded message to Mike was to tell him to watch his back.

"I understand," Mike said.

Gail hung up and pulled out the jump drive that she had taken from Mike earlier.

"How do I know this is the only copy?" Johnathan asked.

"You don't."

"At this point, it doesn't matter," Johnathan said, as he fired two shots at her. A burning pain tore through Gail's chest as she fell to the floor. Her eyes were still open when Johnathan came and stood over her. He fired two more shots into her. She felt nothing, except the blood leaving her body.

Johnathan reached in his pocket for his phone. She lay motionless with her eyes closed, and listened to the clicks from the camera. Gail opened her eyes ever so slightly as he walked towards the stairs and made a call. "It's over," he said. "Finally. I'm sending you confirmation now."

Gail was getting weaker, her body felt cold. She thought it was fate, that maybe she deserved it for the horror she caused for Brian. Gail closed her eyes. Her heart was racing as it desperately tried to circulate what little blood she had left. Johnathan was still talking on the phone. She was going to die. At least she knew her son was safe. She could hear her own heart beating like a drum in her ear.

Then the sound and pain stopped.

Yes, she would die, but not tonight.

Gail released the daggers from her sleeves so they slid into her hands. She reached over and stabbed the guy standing closest to her in his foot. As he hunched over in pain she wrapped her legs around his neck and brought him down on her other knife. She took his gun and used him as shield as she killed the others.

She checked each body, but Johnathan was not among them. He must have slipped out of the room while the shots were blaring. She was sure he had not gotten past her. He must be in the house.

She closed the door and quietly made her way up to the top of the stairs. Gail checked the guest room to the right. She had a gun in her hand ready to shoot but had no intension of killing him yet. She checked every room on that floor including the newly decorated bedroom with Alex's name on the wall.

The only room left was the master bedroom.

Johnathan was not there, either. She headed back downstairs.

There was a clanking noise, followed by shuffling sounds coming from the finished basement. She moved stealthily towards the direction the sound came from, and crept down the carpeted steps. She tried the handle to the bedroom door to the left. Locked.

Gail kicked the door open.

"Don't move!" Johnathan yelled. He stood behind Brian, holding a gun to his head.

"It's over, Johnathan, just let him go."

"What the hell are you? I killed you."

Gail noticed that Brian's hand was cuffed to the metal bedhead.

"Last chance, Johnathan."

"Unless your cheating husband can come back from the dead like you, I would suggest that you get back, or I swear I'll —"

Gail fired a shot through his right eye, splattering Brian with crimson drops. Johnathan fell to the ground with a thud.

She kicked the body before she removed the tape from Brian's mouth.

"Oh, God!" Brian bellowed.

Gail ignored him to take the keys from Johnathan's pocket and unlock the cuff on his hand. Brian was still wearing the same clothes he had on the day he disappeared.

"What did he mean when he said he killed you?" Brian asked, eyeing her front. She looked down at her shirt, covered in warm, wet blood. Tolido should see her now.

"Do I look dead to you?"

"No. I'm sorry. I'm so happy to see you." Brian tried to hug her despite the mess.

Saying she was happy to see him would be an understatement, but she backed away from him. "Do you know why you were kidnapped?" Gail asked as she went through Johnathan's pockets.

"I'm...I'm not really sure," he said as he wiped Johnathan's blood off his face with his hand.

"I thought Celia was hurt, until..." He shook his head. "I overheard *that* guy on the phone with her," Brian said, as he glanced at Johnathan's body on the floor. "I couldn't believe she would be a part of something so...so *evil.*"

He was shaking and his wrist had been bruised from the restraint he'd once worn. Gail wanted to hug him, but instead, she closed her eyes, took a deep breath and held it for two seconds, then slowly exhaled.

"Gail, I'm sorry, for everything. I really am."

"It's okay. You're safe now. That's all that matters."

"Can you ever forgive me?"

She couldn't hate him while she thought his life was in danger, but she thought for sure once that was over the abhorrence would kick in, but it hadn't.

Was it because she felt sorry for him for all that he went through, or was it because there was no space in her heart for hate because it was filled with something that was at the opposite end of the spectrum? Yes, love. It was filled with love. "I already have," she said. "But there is something I need to tell you."

She heard footsteps entering the basement. With her finger on the trigger, Gail signaled Brian to crouch on the other side of the bed and moved to the door to wait for the oncoming visitor.

The footfalls stopped outside the door. Slowly a hand appeared, pushing the door inward.

"Mike!" She lowered her gun the moment she saw him.

He did the same as she stepped outside the room to meet him.

"Hey, are you all right? I couldn't reach you on your phone and I got worried." His gaze moved away from her face, eyes wide when he noticed her shirt. "Are you hurt?"

She checked her pocket and held up her

phone. "No wonder." Her phone had a bullet hole in it. "I'm fine."

"Let me see," he said, as he checked the area of her chest where she'd been shot. "You healed." He hugged her, sticky wet blood and all. "I was so worried."

"Don't worry, I'm fine. Where's Alex?"

"He's okay. Colson has him."

"Celia?"

"She shot herself when she saw me trying to flush Alex's stomach. I think she gave him an overdose of cough medicine so he could sleep. By the look on her face, I think she realized that she may have hurt him. But he's fine now. Still a little groggy, but awake."

"Did he see any of it?"

"Not a thing. He was completely out."

"Hey, Mike," Brian said.

"You're okay!" Mike said, finally realizing he and Gail weren't alone. "Uh, that's good, man. We were really worried."

There was an awkward pause.

"I think I should give you two some privacy," Mike said.

As he turned to leave, Gail held on to his hand. She laced her fingers between his. A look of surprise and joy washed over his face. "Could you wait for me upstairs?"

"I don't think that will be necessary," Brian

said. "I think I already know what you're going to tell me, Gail. It's all over your face. I knew Mike was in love with you so that's nothing new. But you, your eyes lit up when you saw him."

"Brian—"

"Save it, Mike. I guess you finally got what you've always wanted, but I only have myself to blame for that."

Brian started up the stairs, then he stopped and turned around. "Gail, I don't understand any of this, especially what Mike meant when he said you healed. I've always known you were special, and I don't want to lose you." He paused. "I know I've caused you enough pain to last you two lifetimes and I wish I could undo it all. It doesn't mean I stopped loving you. I didn't. You know that, but if you're happy with Mike, I won't stand in the way." His eyes glossed over with tears.

That was the first time she recalled seeing him cry. There were so many things she could've said that would have driven the nail a little deeper and inflicted a little more pain, but she couldn't.

She watched as Brian disappeared upstairs. Mike held her face with both hands and placed his face so close to her that their lips barely touched.

"I'm so in love with you, Gail," he said, then he kissed her.

Colson wasted no time in serving the divorce papers to Brian, prepared by his new attorney, per Gail's request. They parted ways amicably and agreed to share custody of Alex.

"I'll be ready in ten minutes, Grandpa," Alex bellowed to Colson.

Colson was staying with Gail for the time being, and Alex seemed to enjoy having one more art student to make a mess with.

"I'm glad you're here," Gail said to Colson as she watched Alex race in the direction of the studio.

"He's going to be fine. The kid is more resilient than you think." Her eyes met his. "I'm happy to be here," he said as he sat next to her on the sofa. So, Mike is off to work?"

She nodded.

He cleared his throat and started tapping his knee with his fingers.

"What?"

"Nothing. I'm just curious about you and Mike."

"We're taking things slow."

"That means *you* want to take things slow, and poor Mike agreed."

"Something like that."

"I like him."

"I know that."

Colson gazed around the family room. "He's crazy about you."

"I know that too."

"I think it's great he's moved so close so he could be here for the both of you, and Alex adores him."

She held his hand. "You're not telling me anything I don't already know."

"Are you going to tell that snake of a —"

"I have to tell him. Maybe not everything, but he is Alex's father."

"I don't like him."

Gail released his hand and changed the subject.

What are you going to do about the information I downloaded from Zsulrick Inc.?"

"I don't know yet. They think you're dead and I would like to keep it that way. I was thinking of sending the information to some major news networks anonymously."

"Don't send it to a random inbox. Send it to a few investigative journalist." She leaned back and folded her arms across her chest. "You do realize once this information hits the airwaves, they'll try to find the person responsible for the leak."

"I know," Colson said with a smirk. "We'll make sure everything leads to Johnathan Clarke."

"He's dead."

"They don't know that. I provided Johnathan with a fiery grave, and the scene at the house was staged to make it appear he'd gone rogue and killed the others."

"Grandpa, I'm ready," Alex called.

"Coming," Colson hollered and hurried off.

"Try not to make too much mess this time, will you?"

Gail picked up the cell phone she'd taken from Johnathan's pocket and looked at the last number he called. It was the same number that he'd sent a text of what looked like a picture of her dead body. Whoever was giving Johnathan his to-do list was still out there and he wanted her dead. She needed to know who *he* was.

Gail was about to hit the redial button, but stopped herself. "Colson is right. It's better if they think I'm dead."

About the Author

Sandra spent a number of years working in the IT industry before studying nursing and formerly taught in both areas. She currently lives in Washington State with her family, and homeschools one of her two children.

Visit www.ssroswell.com